Praise for *Queen Camilla*:

'Wickedly satirical, mad, ferociously farcical, subversive. Great stuff' *Daily Mail*

Praise for *The Queen and I*:

'Absorbing, entertaining . . . the funniest thing in print since Adrian Mole'
Ruth Rendell, *Daily Telegraph*

Praise for *Number Ten*:

'A delight. Genuinely funny . . . compassion shines through the unashamedly
ironic social commentary' *Guardian*

Praise for *Public Confessions of a Middle-aged Woman Aged 55¾*:

'Proof, once more, that Townsend is one of the funniest writers around' *The Times*

Praise for *The Ghost Children*:

'Bleak, tender and deeply affecting. Seldom have I rooted so hard for a set of
fictional individuals' *Mail on Sunday*

Prai... ...Adrian...

'Adrian Mole really is a brilliant comic creation' *The Times*

'Every sentence is witty and well thought out, and the whole has reverberations beyond itself' *The Times*

'The publishers could offer a money back guarantee if you don't laugh and be sure they wouldn't have to write a single cheque' Jeremy Paxman

'A classic. The Adrian Mole diaries are thoroughly subversive. A true hero for our time' Richard Ingrams

'The real greatness of Townsend's creation comes from the gap between aspiration and reality. Adrian Mole is one of literature's great underachievers; his tragedy is that he knows it and the sadness of this undercuts the humour and makes us laugh not until, but while, it hurts' *Daily Mail*

'Adrian Mole is one of the great comic characters of our time . . . [Townsend] never writes a sentence which doesn't ring true; she never gets Adrian's voice wrong or attributes a thought or feeling to him which strikes one as false. Whatever happens, we may be sure that new troubles will assail Adrian, that new disasters will threaten, but that he will survive them all. Like Evelyn Waugh's Captain Grimes, Adrian is "one of the immortals" and the series of his diaries the comic masterpiece of our time' *Scotsman*

Adrian Mole
The Wilderness Years

Sue Townsend

PENGUIN BOOKS

PENGUIN BOOKS

Published by the Penguin Group
Penguin Books Ltd, 80 Strand, London WC2R ORL, England
Penguin Group (USA), Inc., 375 Hudson Street, New York, New York 10014, USA
Penguin Group (Canada), 90 Eglinton Avenue East, Suite 700, Toronto, Ontario, Canada M4P 2Y3
(a division of Pearson Penguin Canada Inc.)
Penguin Ireland, 25 St Stephen's Green, Dublin 2, Ireland
(a division of Penguin Books Ltd)
Penguin Group (Australia), 250 Camberwell Road, Camberwell, Victoria 3124, Australia
(a division of Pearson Australia Group Pty Ltd)
Penguin Books India Pvt Ltd, 11 Community Centre, Panchsheel Park, New Delhi – 110 017, India
Penguin Group (NZ), 67 Apollo Drive, Rosedale, Auckland 0632, New Zealand
(a division of Pearson New Zealand Ltd)
Penguin Books (South Africa) (Pty) Ltd, 24 Sturdee Avenue, Rosebank, Johannesburg 2196, South Africa

Penguin Books Ltd, Registered Offices: 80 Strand, London WC2R ORL, England

www.penguin.com

First published in Great Britain by Methuen 1993
Published in Mandarin Paperbacks 1994
Reprinted in Arrow Books 1998
Published in Penguin Books 2003
Reissued in this edition 2012
004

Printed in Great Britain by Clays Ltd, St Ives plc

A CIP catalogue record for this book is available from the British Library

ISBN: 978-0-141-04645-7

www.greenpenguin.co.uk

To my sisters, Barbara and Kate

'What's gone and what's past help
Should be past grief.'

William Shakespeare
The Winter's Tale

Winter

Winter

Tuesday January 1st 1991

I start the year with a throbbing head and shaking
limbs, owing to the excessive amounts of alcohol I was
forced to drink at my mother's party last night.

I was quite happy sitting on a dining chair, watching
the dancing and sipping on a low-calorie soft drink,
but my mother kept shouting at me: 'Join in, fishface,'
and wouldn't rest until I'd consumed a glass and a half
of Lambrusco.

As she slopped the wine into a plastic glass for me,
I had a close look at her. Her lips were surrounded by
short lines, like numerous river beds running into a
scarlet lake; her hair was red and glossy almost until
it reached her scalp and then a grey layer revealed the
truth: her neck was saggy, her cleavage wrinkled and
her belly protruded from the little black dress (*very*
little) she wore. The poor woman is forty-seven,
twenty-three years older than her second husband. I
know for a fact that he, Martin Muffet, has *never* seen
her without make-up. Her pillow slips are a disgrace;
they are covered in pan-stick and mascara.

It wasn't long before I found myself on the impro-
vised dance floor in my mother's lounge, dancing to

'The Birdie Song', in a line with Pandora, the love of my life; Pandora's new lover, Professor Jack Cavendish; Martin Muffet, my boyish stepfather; Ivan and Tania, Pandora's bohemian parents; and other inebriated friends and relations of my mother's. As the song reared to its climax, I caught sight of myself in the mirror above the fireplace. I was flapping my arms and grinning like a lunatic. I stopped immediately and went back to the dining chair. Bert Baxter, who was a hundred last year, was doing some clumsy wheelchair dancing, which caused a few casualties; my left ankle is still bruised and swollen, thanks to his carelessness. Also I have a large beetroot stain on the front of my new white shirt, caused by him flinging one of his beetroot sandwiches across the room under the misapprehension that it was a party popper. But the poor old git is almost certain to die this year – he's had his telegram from the Queen – so I won't charge him for the specialist dry cleaning that my shirt is almost certain to require.

I have been looking after Bert Baxter for over ten years now, going back from Oxford to visit him, buying his vile cigarettes, cutting his horrible toenails, etc. When will it end?

My father gate-crashed the party at 11.30. His excuse was that he wanted to speak urgently to my grandma. She is very deaf now, so he was forced to shout above the music. 'Mum, I can't find the spirit level.'

What a pathetic excuse! Who would be using a spirit level on New Year's Eve, apart from an emergency plumber? It was a pitiful request from a lonely, forty-nine-year-old divorcee, whose navy blue mid-eighties suit needed cleaning and whose brown moccasins needed throwing away. He'd done the best he could with his remaining hair, but it wasn't enough.

'Any idea where the spirit level is?' insisted my father, looking towards the drinks table. Then he added, 'I'm laying some paving slabs.'

I laughed out loud at this obvious lie.

My grandma looked bewildered and went back into the kitchen to microwave the sausage rolls and my mother graciously invited her ex-husband to join the party. In no time at all, he had whipped his jacket off and was frugging on the dance floor with my eight-year-old sister Rosie. I found my father's style of dancing acutely embarrassing to watch (his role model is still Mick Jagger); so I went upstairs to change my shirt. On the way, I passed Pandora and Bluebeard Cavendish in a passionate embrace half inside the airing cupboard. He's old enough to be her father.

Pandora has been mine since I was thirteen years old and I fell in love with her treacle-coloured hair. She is simply playing hard to get. She only married Julian Twyselton-Fife to make me jealous. There can be no other possible reason. Julian is a bisexual semi-aristocrat who occasionally wears a monocle. He strains after eccentricity but it continues to elude him. He is a deeply ordinary man with an upper-class accent. He's not even good-looking. He looks like a horse on two legs. And as for her affair with Cavendish, a man who dresses like a tramp, the mind boggles.

Pandora was looking particularly beautiful in a red off-the-shoulder dress, from which her breasts kept threatening to escape. Nobody would have guessed from looking at her that she was now Dr Pandora Braithwaite, fluent in Russian, Serbo-Croat and various other little-used languages. She looked more like one of those supermodels that prowl the catwalks than a Doctor of Philosophy. She certainly added glamour to the party: unlike her parents, who were dressed as usual in their fifties beatnik style – polo necks and corduroy. No wonder they were both sweating heavily as they danced to Chuck Berry.

Pandora smiled at me as she tucked her left breast back inside her dress, and I was pierced to the heart. I truly love her. I am prepared to wait until she comes to her senses and realizes that there is only one man in the world for her, and that is *me*. That is the reason I followed her to Oxford and took up temporary residence in her box room. I have now been there for a year and a half. The more she is exposed to my presence, the sooner she will appreciate my qualities. I have suffered daily humiliations, watching her with her husband and her lovers, but I will reap the benefits later when she is the proud mother of our six children and I am a famous author.

As the clock struck twelve, everyone joined hands and sang 'Auld Lang Syne'. I looked around, at Pandora; at Cavendish; at my mother; at my father; at my stepfather; at my grandma; at Pandora's parents,

Ivan and Tania Braithwaite; and at the dog. Tears filled my eyes. I am nearly twenty-four years of age, I thought, and what have I done with my life? And, as the singing died away, I answered myself – nothing, Mole, nothing.

Pandora wanted to spend the first night of the New Year in Leicester at her parents' house with Cavendish, but at 12.30 a.m. I reminded her that she and her aged lover had promised to give me a lift back to Oxford. I said, 'I am on duty in eight hours' time at the Department of the Environment. At 8.30 sharp.'

She said, 'For Christ's sake, can't you have one poxy day off without permission? Do you have to kow-tow to that little commissar Brown?'

I replied, with dignity, I hope, 'Pandora, some of us keep our word, unlike you, who on Thursday the second of June 1983 promised that you would marry me as soon as you had finished your "A" levels.'

Pandora laughed, spilling the neat whisky in her glass. 'I was sixteen years old,' she said. 'You're living in a bloody time warp.'

I ignored the insult. 'Will you drive me to Oxford as you promised?' I snapped, dabbing at the whisky droplets on her dress with a paper serviette covered in reindeer.

Pandora shouted across the room to Cavendish, who was engaged in conversation with Grandma about the dog's lack of appetite: 'Jack! Adrian's insisting on that lift back to Oxford!'

Bluebeard rolled his eyes and looked at his watch.

'Have I got time for one more drink, Adrian?' he asked.

'Yes, but only mineral water. You're driving, aren't you?' I said.

He rolled his eyes again and picked up a bottle of Perrier. My father came across and he and Cavendish reminisced about the Good Old Days, when they could drink ten pints in the pub and get in the car and drive off 'without having the law on your back'.

It was 2 a.m. when we finally left my mother's house. Then we had to call at the Braithwaites' house to collect Pandora's overnight bag. I sat in the back of Cavendish's Volvo and listened to their banal conversation. Pandora calls him 'Hunky' and Cavendish calls her 'Monkey'.

I woke up on the outskirts of Oxford to hear her whisper: 'So, what did you think of the festivities at Maison Mole, Hunky?'

And to hear him reply: 'As you promised, Monkey, delightfully vulgar. I enjoyed myself enormously.' They both turned to look at me, so I feigned sleep.

I began to think about my sister Rosie, who is, in my view, totally spoilt. The *Girls' World* model hairdressing head she had demanded for Christmas had stood neglected on the lounge window sill since Boxing Day, looking out onto the equally neglected garden. Its retractable blonde hair was hopelessly tangled and its face was smeared with garish cosmetics. Rosie was dancing earlier with Ivan Braithwaite in a manner totally unsuited to an eight-year-old. They looked like Lolita and Humbert Humbert.

Nabokov, fellow author, you should have been alive on that day. It would have shocked even you to see Rosie Mole pouting in her black miniskirt, pink tights and purple cropped top!

I have decided to keep a full journal, in the hope that my life will perhaps seem more interesting when it is written down. It is certainly not interesting to actually live my life. It is tedious beyond belief.

Wednesday January 2nd

I was ten minutes late for work this morning. The exhaust pipe fell off the bus. Mr Brown was entirely unsympathetic. He said, 'You should get yourself a bicycle, Mole.' I pointed out that I have had three bicycles stolen in eighteen months. I can no longer afford to supply the criminals of Oxford with ecologically sound transport.

Brown snapped, 'Then *walk*, Mole. Get up earlier and *walk*.'

I went into my cubicle and shut the door. There was a message on my desk informing me that a colony of newts had been discovered in Newport Pagnell. Their habitat is in the middle of the projected new ring road. I rang the Environmental Office at the Department of Transport and warned a certain Peter Peterson that work on the ring road could be subject to delay.

'But that's bloody ludicrous,' said Peterson. 'It would cost us hundreds of thousands of pounds to re-route that road, and all to save a few slimy reptiles.'

That is also my own private point of view of newts. I'm sick of them. But I am paid to champion their right to survive (in public at least), so I gave Peterson my standard newt conservation lecture (and pointed out that newts are amphibians, not reptiles). I spent the rest of the morning writing up the Newport Pagnell case.

At lunchtime I left the Department of the Environment and went to collect my blazer from the dry cleaner's. I had forgotten to take my ticket. (It was at home, being used as a bookmark inside Colin Wilson's *The Outsider*. Mr Wilson is Leicester-born, like me.)

The woman at the cleaner's refused to hand over my blazer, even though I pointed to it hanging on the rack! She said, 'That blazer has got a British Legion badge on it. You're too young to be in the British Legion.'

An undergraduate behind me sniggered.

Enraged, I said to the woman, 'You are obviously proud of your powers of detection. Perhaps you should write an *Inspector Morse* episode for the television.' But my wit was lost on the pedant.

The undergraduate pushed forward and handed her a stinking duvet, requesting the four-hour service.

I had no choice but to go home and collect the ticket, go back to the cleaner's, and then run with the blazer, encased in plastic, slung over my shoulder, all the way back to the office. I have got a blind date tonight and the blazer is all I've got to wear.

My last blind date ended prematurely when Ms Sandra Snape (non-smoking, twenty-five-year-old, vegetarian: dark hair, brown eyes, five foot six, not unattractive) left Burger King in a hurry, claiming she'd left the kettle on the stove. I am now convinced, however, that the kettle was an excuse. When I returned home that night, I discovered that the hem was down at the back on my army greatcoat. Women don't like a scruff.

I was twenty-five minutes late getting back to work. Brown was waiting for me in my cubicle. He was brandishing my Newport Pagnell newt figures. Apparently I had made a mistake in my projection of live newt births for 1992. Instead of 1,200, I had put down 120,000. An easy mistake to make.

'A hundred and twenty thousand newts in 1992, eh, Mole?' sneered Brown. 'The good citizens of Newport Pagnell will be positively inundated with amphibia.'

He gave me an official warning about my time-keeping and ordered me to water my cactus. He then went to his own office, taking my paperwork with him. If I lose my job, I am done for.

11.30 p.m. My blind date did not turn up. I waited two hours, ten minutes in the Burger King in the town centre. Thank you, Ms Tracy Winkler (quiet blonde, twenty-seven, non-smoker, cats and country walks)!

That is the last time I write to a box number in the *Oxford Mail*. From now on, I will only use the personal column of the *London Review of Books*.

Thursday January 3rd

I have the most terrible problems with my sex life. It all boils down to the fact that I *have* no sex life. At least not with another person.

I lay awake last night, asking myself why? Why? Why? Am I grotesque, dirty, repellent? No, I am none of these things. Am I normal-looking, clean, pleasant? Yes, I am all of these things. So what am I doing wrong? Why can't I get an average-looking young woman into my bed?

Do I exude an obnoxious odour smelled by everyone else but me? If so, I hope to God somebody will tell me and I can seek medical help from a gland specialist.

At 3 a.m. this morning my sleep was disturbed by the sound of a violent altercation. This in itself is not unusual, because this house provides a home for many people, most of them noisy, drunken undergraduates, who sit up all night debating the qualities of various brands of beer. I went downstairs in my pyjamas and was just in time to see Tariq, the Iraqi student who lives in the basement, being led away by a gang of criminal-looking men.

Tariq shouted, 'Adrian, save me!' I said to one of the men, 'Let him go or I will call the police.'

A man with a broken nose said, 'We *are* the police, sir. Your friend is being expelled from the country, orders of the Home Office.'

Pandora came to the top of the basement stairs. She was wearing very little, having just left her bed. She said in her most imperious manner: 'Why is Mr Aziz being expelled?'

'Because,' said the thuggish one, 'Mr Aziz's presence is not conducive to the public good, for reasons of national security. Ain't you 'eard there's a war on?' he added, ogling Pandora's satin nightshirt, through which the outline of her nipples was clearly visible.

Tariq shouted, 'I am a student at Brasenose College and a member of the Young Conservatives: I am not interested in politics!'

There was nothing we could do to help him, so Pandora and I went back to bed. Not the same bed though, worse luck.

At nine o'clock the next morning, I rang the landlord, Eric Hardwell, on his car phone and asked if I could move into the now vacant basement flat. I am sick of living in Pandora's box room. Hardwell was in a bad mood because he was stuck in traffic, but he agreed, providing I can give him a £1,000 deposit, three months' rent in advance (£1,200), a banker's reference and a solicitor's letter stating that I will not burn candles, use a chip pan, or breed bull terrier dogs in the basement.

I shall have to stay here in the box room. I need to use my chip pan on a daily basis.

Lenin was right: all landlords *are* bastards.

Somebody who looked like Tariq was on *Newts At Ten*; he was waving from the steps of an aeroplane which was bound for the Gulf. I waved back in case it was him.

Correction: I meant, of course, to write *News At Ten*.

Friday January 4th

Woke up at 5 a.m. and was unable to get back to sleep. My brain insisted on recalling all my past humiliations. One by one they passed in front of me: the bullying I endured from Barry Kent until my grandma put a stop to it; the day at Skegness when my father broke the news to me and my mother that his illegitimate son, Brett, had been born to his lover, Stick Insect; the black day when my mother ran away to Sheffield for a short-lived affair with Mr Lucas, our smarmy neighbour; the day I learned that I had failed 'A' level Biology for the third time; the day Pandora married a bisexual man.

Then, after the humiliations came the *faux pas*, a relentless march: the time I sniffed glue and got a model aeroplane stuck to my nose; the day my sister, Rosie, was born and I couldn't remove my hand from the spaghetti jar where the five pound note for the taxi fare to the maternity hospital was kept; the time I wrote to Mr John Tydeman at the BBC and addressed him as 'Johnny'.

The procession of *faux pas* was followed by a parade of bouts of moral cowardice: the time I crossed the road to avoid my father because he was wearing a red pom-pom hat; my craven behaviour when my mother was stricken with a menopausal temper tantrum in the Leicester market place – I should not have walked away and hidden behind that flower stall; the day I had a jealous fit, destroyed the complimentary tickets for Barry Kent's first professional gig on the poetry circuit and blamed the dog; my desertion of Sharon Bott when she announced she was pregnant.

I despise myself. I deserve my unhappiness. I am truly a loathsome person.

I was relieved when my travelling alarm clock roused me from my gloomy reverie and told me that it was 6.30 a.m. and time to get up.

> *Nipples by A. Mole*
> Like raspberries
> taken from the freezer
> Inviting tongue and lips
> but warning not to bite
> Not yet
> soon
> But not yet

I am on flexitime and had agreed to start work at 7.30 a.m., but somehow, although I left my box room at 7 a.m., I didn't arrive at work until 8 a.m. A journey of half a mile took me an hour. Where did I go? What did I do? Did I have a blackout on the way? Was I mugged and left unconscious? Am I, even as I write, suffering from memory loss?

Pandora is constantly telling me that I am in urgent need of psychiatric help. Perhaps she is right. I feel as though I am going mad; that my life is a film and that I am a mere spectator.

Saturday January 5th

Julian, Pandora's upper-crust husband, has returned from his Christmas sojourn in the country with his parents. He shuddered when he walked through the front door of the flat.

'God!' he said. 'The pantry of Twyselton Manor is bigger than this bloody hole.'

'Then why come back, sweetie?' said Pandora, his so-called wife.

'Because, *ma femme*, my parents, poor, deluded creatures, are paying mucho spondulicks to keep me here at Oxford, studying Chinese.' He laughed his neighing horse's laugh. (And he's certainly got the teeth for it.)

'But you haven't been to a lecture for over a year,'

said Dr Braithwaite (12 'O's, 5 'A's, BA Hons. and D. Phil.).

'But my lecturers are all such boring little men.'

'It's such a waste, husband,' said Pandora. 'You're the cleverest man in Oxford *and* the laziest. If you're not careful, you'll end up in Parliament.'

After Julian had thrown his battered pigskin luggage into his room, he returned to the kitchen, where Pandora was chopping leeks and I was exercising my new sink plunger. 'So, darlings, what's new?' he said, lighting one of his vile Russian cigarettes.

Pandora said, 'I'm in love with Jack Cavendish, and he's in love with me. Isn't it absolutely marvellous?' She grinned ecstatically and chopped at the leeks with renewed fervour.

'Cavendish?' puzzled Julian. 'Isn't he that grey-haired old linguistics fart who can't keep his plonker in his pants?'

Pandora's eyes flashed dangerously. 'He's sworn to me that from now on his lifestyle will be strictly non-polygynous,' she said.

She stretched up to replace the knife on its magnetic rack and her cropped T-shirt rode up, revealing her delicate midriff. I thrust the plunger viciously into the greasy contents of the sink, imagining that Cavendish's head was on the end of the wooden stick, instead of the black rubber suction pad.

Julian neighed knowingly. 'Cavendish doesn't know

the meaning of the word "non-polygynous". He's a notorious womanizer.'

'*Was*,' insisted Pandora, adding, 'and *of course* he knows the meaning of the word "non-polygynous": he is a professor of Linguistics.'

I left the plunger floating in the sink and went to my box room, took my *Condensed Oxford Dictionary* from its shelf and, with the aid of the magnifying glass, looked up the word 'non-polygynous'. I then uttered a loud, cynical laugh. Loud enough, I hoped, to be heard in the kitchen.

Sunday January 6th

Woke at 3 a.m. and lay awake remembering the time when Pandora and I nearly went All the Way. I love her still. I intend to be her second husband. And what's more, she will take my name. She will be known as 'Mrs Adrian Albert Mole' in private.

On Seeing Pandora's Midriff
The glorious shoreline from ribcage
To pelvis
Like an inlet
A bay
A safe haven
I want to navigate
To explore
To take readings from the stars

To carefully trace my fingers
Along the shoreline
And eventually to guide my ship, my destroyer,
   my pleasure craft
Into and beyond your harbour

6.00 p.m. Sink still blocked. Worked for three hours in the kitchen, adding vowels to the first half of my experimental novel *Lo! The Flat Hills of My Homeland*, which was originally written with consonants only. It is eighteen months since I sent it to Sir Gordon Giles, Prince Charles's agent, and he sent it back, suggesting I put in the vowels.

Lo! The Flat Hills of My Homeland explores late twentieth-century man and his dilemma, focusing on a 'New Man' living in a provincial city in England.

The treatment is broadly Lawrentian, with a touch of Dostoevskian darkness and a tinge of Hardyesque lyricism.

I predict that one day it will be a GCSE set book.

I was driven out of the kitchen by the arrival of that wrinkled-up ashtray on legs, Cavendish, who had been invited to Sunday lunch. He hadn't been in the flat two minutes before he was pulling a cork out of a bottle and helping himself to glasses out of the cupboard. He then sat on *my* recently vacated chair at the kitchen table and began to talk absolute gibberish about the Gulf War, predicting that it would be over within months. I predict that it will be America's second Vietnam.

Julian came into the kitchen, wearing his silk pyjamas and carrying a copy of *Hello!*

'Julian,' said Pandora, 'meet my lover, Jack Cavendish.' She turned to Cavendish and said, 'Jack, this is Julian Twyselton-Fife, my husband.' Pandora's husband and Pandora's lover shook hands.

I turned away in disgust. I'm as liberal and civilized as the next person. In fact, in some circles I'm regarded as quite an advanced thinker, but even I shuddered at the utter depravity that this introduction signified.

I left the flat to get some air. When I returned from my walk around the Outer Ring Road two hours later, Cavendish was still there, telling tedious anecdotes about his numerous children and his three ex-wives. I microwaved my Sunday lunch and took it into my box room. I spent the rest of the evening listening to laughter in the next room. Woke at 2 a.m. and was unable to get back to sleep. Filled two pages of A4 devising tortures for Cavendish. Not the actions of a rational man.

Tortures for Cavendish
1) Chain him to the wall with a glass of water *just* beyond his grasp.
2) Chain him naked to a wall while a bevy of beautiful girls walk by, cruelly mocking his flaccid *and* aroused penis.
3) Force him to sit in a room with Ivan Braithwaite, while Ivan talks about the finer details of the Labour Party's

Constitution, with particular reference to Clause Four.
(This is true torture, as I can bear witness.)
4) Show him a video of Pandora getting married to me.
    She radiant in white, me in top hat and tails, putting
    two gloved fingers up at Cavendish.

Let the punishment fit the crime.

Monday January 7th

Started my beard today.

Some of the Newport Pagnell newts have crossed
the road. I telephoned Peterson at the Department of
Transport, to inform him. There has obviously been
a split in the community. I expect a female newt is at
the bottom of it: *cherchez la femme*.

Wednesday January 9th

For the first time in my entire life I haven't got a single
spot, pustule or pimple. I pointed out to Pandora over
breakfast that my complexion was flawless, but she
paused in applying her mascara, looked at me coldly,
and said, 'You need a shave.'

Spent ten minutes at the sink with the plunger
before going to work, but to no avail. Pandora said,
'We'll have to get a proper man in.'

Does Pandora realize the impact the above words,

so apparently casually uttered, have had on me? She has disenfranchised me from my gender! She has cut my poor, useless balls off!

Thursday January 10th

Brown has advised me to shave. I refused. I may have to seek the advice of the Civil and Public Service Union.

Friday January 11th

Applied to join the CPSU.

Pandora found Cavendish's A4 torture list. She has made an appointment for me to see her friend Leonora De Witt, who is a psychotherapist. I agreed reluctantly. On the one hand, I am terrified of my unconscious and what it will reveal about me. On the other, I am looking forward to talking about myself non-stop for an hour without interruption, hesitation or repetition.

Saturday January 12th

Pandora's most recent ex-lover, Rocky (Big Boy) Livingstone, came round to the flat today, asking for the return of his mini sound-system. At six foot three and fifteen stone of finely honed muscle, Rocky is a 'proper' man, if ever I saw one. Pandora was out, meeting some of Cavendish's children at the Randolph Hotel. So, in her absence, I gave the sound-system to him. Since he and Pandora split up, Rocky has opened new gyms in Kettering, Newmarket and Ashby de la Zouch. He and his new girlfriend, Carly Pick, are still happy.

Rocky said, 'Carly's a real star, Aidy. I respect the lady, y'know.' I told Rocky about Professor Cavendish. He was disgusted.

He said, 'That Pandora is a *user*. Just 'cos she's clever, she finks she's . . .' He flailed about for the right word and finished, 'clever'.

Before he went he unblocked the sink. I was very grateful. I was getting sick of washing the pots in the bathroom hand basin. None of the saucepans would fit under the taps.

I went to the window and watched him drive away. Carly Pick had both her arms around his neck.

Sunday January 13th

The Gulf War deadline expires on the 15th, at midnight. What will I do if I am called up to fight for my country? Will I cover myself with honour, or will I wet myself with fear on hearing the sound of enemy gunfire?

Monday January 14th

Went to Sainsbury's and stocked up with tins of beans, candles, Jaffa cakes, household matches, torch batteries, paracetamol, multivitamins, Ry-King and tins of corned beef and put them in the cupboard in my box room. Should the war spread over here, I will be well prepared. The others in the flat will just have to take their chance. I predict panic buying on a scale never seen before in this country. There will be fighting in the aisles of the supermarkets.

Appointment with Leonora De Witt on Friday 25th of this month at 6 p.m.

Tuesday January 15th

Midnight. We are at war with Iraq. I phoned my mother in Leicester and told her to keep the dog in. It is twelve years old and reacts badly to unexpected noises. She laughed and said, 'Are you going mad?' I said, 'Probably,' and put the phone down.

Wednesday January 16th

Bought sixteen bottles of Highland Spring water, in case water supply is cut off owing to bombardment by Iraqi airforce. It took me four trips from the Spar shop on the corner to the flat, but I feel more secure knowing I will not go thirsty during the coming *Blitzkrieg*.

Brown has not mentioned my beard for some days now. He is preoccupied with the effect that 'Operation Desert Storm' will have on the desert wildlife. I said, 'I'm afraid I regard Iraqi wildlife as being on the side of the enemy. I'm more worried about my dog, at home in Leicester.'

'Ever the parochial, Mole,' said Brown, in a lip-curling manner. I was quite insulted. Brown reads nothing, apart from journals on wildlife, whereas I have read most of the Russian Greats and am about to embark on *War and Peace*. Hardly parochial, Brown!

Thursday January 17th

I have hired a portable colour television, so I can watch the Gulf War in bed.

Friday January 18th

The spokesperson for the USA military is a man who calls himself 'Colon Powell'. Every time I see him, I think of intestines and the lower bowel. It detracts from the gravity of the War.

Saturday January 19th

Bert Baxter rang me up at the office today. (I will kill whoever gave him the number.) He wanted to know 'when you and my favourite gal are comin' to see me?' His 'favourite gal' is Pandora. Why doesn't Bert just *die* like other pensioners? His quality of life can't be up to much. He is nothing but a burden to others (me).

He was entirely ungrateful when I dug a grave for his dog, Sabre, last year, though I challenge anyone to dig a neater hole in compacted soil with a rusty garden trowel. If I'd had a decent spade at my disposal, then, *naturellement*, the grave would have been neater. The truth is that I hated and feared Sabre. The day the wretched Alsatian died was a day of rejoicing for me. No more smelling its noxious breath. No more forcing Bob Martin's conditioning tablets between its horrible vicious teeth.

Bert burbled on about the war for a while, and then asked me if I had heard my old enemy Barry Kent on *Stop the Week* this morning. Apparently, Kent was publicizing his first novel, *Dork's Diary*. I am now utterly convinced there cannot be a God. It was me that encouraged Kent to write poetry, and now I find out that the ex-skinhead, frozen peabrain has written a novel, *and got it published!!!*

Pandora told me this evening that Kent made Ned Sherrin, A. S. Byatt, Jonathan Miller and Victoria

Mather laugh almost continuously. Apparently the phone lines at the BBC were jammed with listeners asking when *Dork's Diary* will be published (Monday). This is absolutely and totally the last straw. My sanity hangs by a fragile thread.

Sunday January 20th

I was passing Waterstone's bookshop when I saw what appeared to be Barry Kent standing in the window. I lifted my hand in greeting and said, 'Hello, Baz,' then realized that the smirking skinhead was only a cardboard cut-out. Copies of *Dork's Diary* filled the window. I'm not ashamed to say that curses sprang from my lips.

As I flicked through the pages of the slim volume, my eye was caught not only by the many obscenities with which the book is littered, but by the name – 'Aiden Vole' – given to one of the characters. This 'Aiden Vole' is obsessed with matters anal. He is jingo-istic, deeply conservative and a failure with women. 'Aiden Vole' is an outrageous caricature of me, without a doubt. I have been slandered. I shall see my solicitor in the morning. I shall instruct him or her (I haven't actually got a solicitor yet) to demand hundreds of thousands of pounds in damages. I couldn't bring myself actually to buy a copy of the book. Why should I add to Kent's royalties? But I noticed as I left the shop that Kent is giving a reading from *Dork's Diary* on Tuesday evening at 7 p.m. I will be in the audience. Kent will leave Waterstone's a broken man when I have finished with him.

Monday January 21st

The Cubicle, DOE

Just listened to Kent on *Start the Week* on my portable radio. He has certainly extended his vocabulary. Melvyn Bragg said that the Aiden Vole character was 'wonderfully funny' and asked if he was based on anybody real. Kent laughed and said, 'You're a writer, Melv; you know what it's like. Vole is an amalgam of fact and fantasy. Vole stands for everything I hate most in this country, after the new five-pence piece, that is.' The other guests – Ken Follett, Roy Hattersley, Brenda Maddox and Edward Pearce – laughed like drains.

Spent the rest of the morning looking through the Yellow Pages for a solicitor with a name I can trust. Chose and rang 'Churchman, Churchman, Churchman and Luther'. I am seeing a Mr Luther at 11.30 a.m. on Thursday. I am supposed to be visiting the Newport Pagnell newts on Thursday morning with Brown, but he will just have to face them alone. My reputation and my future as a serious novelist are at stake.

Alfred Wainwright, who wrote guides to the fells of the Lake District, died today. I once used Mr Wainwright's maps when I attempted to do the 'coast to 'coast' walk with the 'Off the Streets' Youth Club. Unfortunately, I developed hypothermia within half an hour of leaving the Youth Hostel at Grimsby and my record-breaking attempt had to be abandoned.

Tuesday January 22nd

Review of *Dork's Diary* in the *Guardian*:

'A coruscating account of *fin de siècle* provincial life. Brilliant. Dark. Hilarious. Buy it!' Robert Elms

Box Room 10 p.m.
Couldn't get in to see Kent; all the tickets were sold. Tried to speak to him as he entered the shop, but couldn't get near to him. He was surrounded by press and publicity people. He was wearing sunglasses. In January.

Wednesday January 23rd

Beard coming along nicely. Two spots on left shoulder blade. A slight pain in anus, but otherwise I am in superb physical condition.

Read long interview in the *Independent* with Barry Kent. He told lies from start to finish. He even lied about the reason for his being sent to prison, claiming he was sentenced to eighteen months for various acts of violence, when I know very well that he got four months for criminal damage to a privet hedge. I have faxed the *Independent*, putting the record straight. It gave me no pleasure to do this, but without the Truth we are no better than dogs. Truth is the most important thing in my life. Without Truth we are lost.

Thursday January 24th

Lied on the phone to Brown this morning and told him that I could not visit the Newport Pagnell newt habitat on account of a severe migraine. Brown ranted on about how he had 'never taken a day off work in twenty-two years'. He went on to brag that he had 'even passed several massive kidney stones into the lavatory at work'. Perhaps that explains why the lavatory basin is cracked.

I was late for my appointment with Mr Luther, the solicitor, though I left the flat in plenty of time – another time warp or memory-loss – a mystery, anyway. As I told Luther (in great detail) about Kent's slander of me, I noticed him yawning several times. I expect he was up late; he looks the dissolute type. He was wearing braces covered in pictures of Marilyn Monroe.

Eventually he raised his hand and said, 'Enough, I've heard enough,' in an irritable sort of way. Then he leaned across his desk and said, 'Are you vastly rich?'

'No,' I replied, 'not vastly.'

He then asked, 'Are you desperately poor?'

'Not desperately. That's why I . . .'

Luther interrupted before I could finish my sentence, 'Because unless you are vastly rich, or desperately poor, you can't possibly afford to go to court. You don't qualify for Legal Aid and you can't afford to pay a barrister a thousand pounds a day, can you?'

'*A thousand pounds a day*?' I said, absolutely aghast. Luther smiled, revealing a gold back molar.

I remembered my grandma's advice, 'Never trust a man with a gold tooth.' I thanked Mr Luther politely but coldly and left his office. So much for English justice. It is the worst in the world. As I passed the waiting room, I noticed a copy of *Dork's Diary* on the coffee table, next to copies of *Amnesty* and *The Republican*.

Got home to find a note from Leonora De Witt informing me that she is unable to keep our appointment tomorrow. Why? Is she having her hair done? Is double-glazing being installed in her consulting room? Have her parents been found dead in bed? Am I so unimportant that my time is a mere plaything to Ms De Witt? She suggested a new appointment: Thursday 31st January at 5 p.m. I left a message on her Ansafone, agreeing to the new arrangement, but announcing my displeasure.

Saturday January 26th

I was awake all last night, watching 'Operation Desert Storm'. I feel it's the least I can do – after all, it is costing HM Government thirty million pounds a day to keep Kuwait a democracy.

Sunday January 27th

According to the *Observer* today, Kuwait is not and has never been a democracy. It is ruled by the Kuwaiti Royal Family.

Bluebeard laughed when I told him. 'It's all to do with *oil*, Adrian,' he said. 'Do you think the Yanks would be in there if Kuwait's main product was *turnips*?'

Pandora bent down and kissed the back of his withered neck. How she could allow her young, vibrant flesh to come into contact with his ancient, wrinkled skin, I'll never know. I had to go into the bathroom and take deep breaths and control the urge to vomit. Why slobber over *him* when she could have *me*?

My mother rang at 4 p.m. I could hear my young stepfather, Martin Muffet, hammering in the background. 'Martin's putting some shelves up for my knick-knacks,' she shouted over the row. Then she asked me if I had read the extracts from *Dork's Diary* in the *Observer*. I was able to answer truthfully. 'No,' I said. 'You should,' said my mother. 'It's totally brilliant. When you next see Baz, will you ask him for a free copy, signed to Pauline and Martin?'

I said, 'It is highly unlikely that I will see Kent. I do not move in the same illustrious circles as him.'

'Which illustrious circles *do* you move in, then?' asked my mother.

'None,' I answered truthfully. Then I put the phone down and went to bed and pulled the duvet over my head.

Monday January 28th

Britain's Jo Durie and Jeremy Bates won the mixed doubles in Melbourne. This surely points to a renaissance in British tennis.

> *Pandora's Little Pussy*
> I love her little Pussy
> Her coat is so warm
> But if I should stroke her
> She'll call the police and identify me in
> A line-up
> And do me some harm

Wednesday January 30th

Shocked to hear on Radio Four that King Olav the Fifth of Norway was buried today. His contribution to the continuing success of the Norwegian leather industry is something that is little appreciated by the vast majority of the Great British Public. Prince Charles was England's graveside representative.

Borrowed *Scenes from Provincial Life* by William Cooper from the library. I only had time to choose one book, because a 'suspicious package' was found in the Romantic Fiction section and the library was evacuated.

Sink blocked again. Plunged for the duration of *The Archers*, but to no avail.

Thursday January 31st

I didn't arrive at the consulting room on Thames Street until 5.15 p.m. Leonora De Witt was not pleased.

'I'll have to charge you for the full hour, Mr Mole,' she said, seating herself in an armchair which was covered in old bits of carpet. 'Where would you like to sit?' she asked. There were many chairs in the room. I chose a dining chair which was standing against a wall.

When I was seated, I said, 'I was under the impression that our sessions were to be under the auspices of the National Health Service.'

'Then you were gravely mistaken,' said Ms De Witt. 'I charge thirty pounds an hour – under the auspices of the private enterprise system.'

'*Thirty pounds an hour!* How many sessions will I need?' I asked.

She explained that she couldn't possibly predict, that she knew nothing about me. That it depended on the cause of my unhappiness.

'How do you feel at the moment?' she asked.

'Apart from a slight headache, I feel fine,' I replied.

'What are you doing with your hands?' she said quietly.

'Wringing them,' I replied.

'What is that on your brow?' she asked.

'Sweat,' I answered, taking out my handkerchief.

'Are your buttocks clenched, Mr Mole?' she pressed.

'I suppose they are,' I said.

'Now answer my first question again, please. How do you feel at this moment?'

Her large brown eyes locked into mine. I couldn't avert my gaze.

'I feel totally miserable,' I said. 'And I lied about the headache.'

She talked at length about the *Gestalt* technique. She explained that it was possible to teach me 'coping mechanisms'. Apart from Pandora, she is probably the loveliest woman I have ever spoken to. I found it hard to take my eyes off her black-stockinged feet, which were slipped into black suede shoes with high heels. Was she wearing tights or stockings?

'So, Mr Mole, do you think we can work together?' she said.

She looked at her watch and stood up. Her hair looked like a midnight river pouring down her back. I eagerly affirmed that I would like to see her once a week. Then I gave her thirty pounds and left.

Friday February 1st

Just returned from Newport Pagnell. My nerves are shot to pieces. Brown drove like a man possessed. At no time did he exceed the speed limit, but he drove onto the kerb, scraped against hedgerows and on the motorway section of our journey he left only a six-inch gap between our fragile Ford Escort and the monolithic juggernaut in front of us.

'It saves precious fuel if you can stay in the lorry's slipstream,' he said by way of explanation. The man is an environmental fanatic. He spent last Christmas Day classifying seaweed at Dungeness. I rest my case. Thank God for the weekend. Or *le weekend*, as our fellow Europeans say.

Saturday February 2nd

Viscount Althorp, Princess Diana's brother, has confessed to his thin wife and the rest of the world that he had an affair in Paris. Prince Charles and Princess Diana must have been horrified to find out that there was an adulterer in the family. He should be stripped of his title immediately. The Royal Family and their close connections should be above such brutish instincts. The country looks to them to set the moral standard.

Had bath, shampooed beard, cut fingernails and toenails. Put hot oil on hair to nourish it and give it shine and the outward illusion of health.

11.45 p.m. Bert Baxter has just telephoned. He sounded pathetic. Pandora was out and in a moment of weakness I agreed to go and visit him in Leicester tomorrow. Wrote a note to Pandora, left it on her pillow.

Pandora,

Baxter rang in considerable distress, something about killing himself – I intend to visit him tomorrow. He intimated to me that he wished to see you too. I plan to rise at 8.30 to catch the train, or, should you wish to accompany me, my alternative *modus operandi* will be to rise at nine and be driven by you in your motor car, thus arriving in Leicester at approximately 11 a.m. Would you please inform me of your decision by the method of slipping a note under my door? Please do not disturb me tonight with the sounds of your wild love-making. The walls of my box room are very thin and I am sick of sleeping with my Sony Walkman on.

Adrian

Sunday February 3rd

At 2.10 a.m., Pandora burst into my box room and hurled abuse at me. She flung my note to her into my face and screamed, 'You pompous *nerd*, you pathetic *dork*! "*Modus operandi*"! 'Be driven by you in your motor car"! I want you out of this box room and out of my life, *tomorrow*!'

Bluebeard came in and led her away and I lay in bed and listened to them murmuring together in the kitchen. What brought on such an unprovoked outburst?

At 3.30 a.m. they went into Pandora's bedroom. At 3.45 a.m. I put Dire Straits into my Sony and turned the volume up to full.

Didn't wake until midday. Phoned Bert and said I was unable to visit him owing to being awake all night with intestinal pains. I could tell Bert didn't believe me. He said, 'You're a bleedin' liar. I've just spoken to my gal Pandora. She rang me on her car phone. She looked in your room before she set out for Leicester and she said you were sleepin' like a new-born.'

'Why didn't she wake me then?' I asked.

''Cos she 'ates the bleedin' sight of you,' said the diplomatic one.

Monday February 4th

Inexplicably late for work by twenty-three minutes. Brown was practically frothing at the mouth. Also accused me of stealing postage stamps. He said, 'Every penny is needed by the DOE if our wildlife is to be preserved.' As if! Are the badgers and foxes and tad-poles and lousy, stinking newts going to pop their clogs because I, Adrian Mole, made use of two second-class postage stamps paid for out of my taxes in the first place? No, Brown. I don't think so.

Tuesday February 5th

Pandora still in Leicester. Trimmed beard around mouth. Swallowed clippings. One lodged at back of throat; annoying.

Wednesday February 6th

Brown came into my cubicle today and demanded to see my 'A' level certificates! He had heard on the office grapevine that I had failed 'A' level Biology three times.

The only person in Oxford – apart from Pandora – who knows about my triple failure is Megan Harris, Brown's secretary. I confessed to her whilst in a drunken and emotional state at the DOE Christmas Party last year. She alone knows that my job as a Scientific Officer Grade One was granted to me under false pretences. Has Megan blabbed? I must know.

I told Leonora De Witt my family history tonight. It's a tragic story of rejection and alienation, but Leonora simply sat and picked balls of fluff from her sweater, which drew my attention to the shape of her comely breasts. It was obvious that she was not wearing a bra. I wanted to leave my chair and sink my head into her bosom. I went into some detail about my parents' deviant behaviour, but the only time she showed obvious interest was when I mentioned my dead grandfather, Albert Mole, whom I have to thank for my middle name.

'Did you see his dead body?' she asked.

'No,' I replied. 'The Co-op undertaker had screwed the coffin lid down and nobody could find the screwdriver at Grandma's house, so . . .'

'Continue,' ordered Leonora. So I did. Through fat, hot tears. I told about my feeling of exclusion from 'normal' life; of how I long to join my fellow human beings, to share their sorrows, their joys, their sing-songs in pubs.

Leonora said, 'People sing awful songs in pubs. Why do you feel a need to join in singing those mawkish lyrics and banal tunes?'

'I stood outside such pubs as a child,' I said. 'Everybody sounded so happy.'

Then the alarm went off on her watch and it was time to cough up thirty quid and leave.

On my way home I went into a pub and had a drink. I also initiated a conversation about the weather with an old man. There was no singing, so I went home.

Thursday February 7th

I asked Megan outright this morning. I approached her in the corridor as she was being scalded by the Autovent tea/coffee/oxtail soup machine. She admitted that she had let it 'slip out' that I was totally unqualified for my position. Then she swore me to secrecy and informed me that she and Brown have been having an affair since 1977! Brown and the lovely Megan! Why do women throw themselves at worn-out old gits like Brown and Cavendish, and ignore young, virile, bearded men like me? It defies logic.

Megan was eager to talk about her affair with Brown. Apparently he had sworn to leave Mrs Brown in 1980, but has not yet done so. I feel sorry for Mrs Brown every time she comes into the office. It is not her fault that she looks like she does. Some women have got good dress sense and some women haven't. Mrs Brown obviously does not know that pop socks should only be worn under trousers or long skirts. Also, somebody should tell her that warts can be cured nowadays.

Friday February 8th

Pandora is back in Oxford, but not speaking to me much, apart from the bare facts that Bert is no longer suicidal. She bought him a kitten and also installed a cat flap in his back door. Brown asked me again for my Biology 'A' level certificate. I looked at him enigmatically and said, 'I think you'll find that Megan has the information you require.' God, blackmail is an ugly word. I hope Brown doesn't force me to use it.

I have thrown my condom away. It had exceeded its 'best before' date.

Monday February 11th

Megan came into my cubicle today, sobbing. Apparently Brown forgot her birthday, which was yesterday. Alack, alas! It looks as if I am cast into the role of Megan's only confidant. I put my arms around her and kissed her. She felt lovely and soft and squashy. She pulled away quite soon, however, and said, 'Your beard is scratchy and horrible.'

But was my beard the *real* reason?

Does my breath stink? Does my body stink?

Who can I trust to tell me the truth?

I can certainly see what Brown sees in Megan, but I will never in a billion years see what she sees in him. He is forty-two, thin, and wears atrocious clothes from 'Man at C&A'. Megan says he is good in bed. Who is she trying to kid? Good at what in bed? Doing jigsaws? Sleeping? Perhaps she means that he is unselfish with the duvet? If Brown is good in bed, then I am a tractor wheel.

Tuesday February 12th

Tried to visit newt habitat in Northamptonshire, but 'wrong kind of snow' caused Class 317 engine to fail. Was forced to sit in freezing carriage whilst buffet bar attendant gave out continuous announcements in annoying adenoidal voice. Was pleased when buffet car ran out of all supplies and closed. Got back to Oxford at 10.30 p.m., to find message from Megan. Rang her to find out that she and Brown had had a row; their affair is over. I was distraught. This means I no longer have a hold over Brown. It could signal the end of my career with the DOE.

Wednesday February 13th

Brown/Megan affair is on again. Apparently Brown cycled round to Megan's flat in the early hours, after telling Mrs Brown he was going bat-watching. Their reconciliation was very passionate.

I cannot imagine anything in the world more distasteful than seeing Brown in a state of orgasmic pleasure. Apart from *being* with Brown in a state of orgasmic pleasure.

Bought new condom – spearmint flavoured.

Also bought bunch of bananas. Megan says they are very good for those, like me, who suffer from an irritable bowel.

Thursday February 14th

Valentine's Day card from my mother as usual. Megan in tears again. Brown forgot. Bought economy box of tissues at lunchtime for Megan's sole use. I can't afford to keep wasting Kleenex on her. Bluebeard has sent Pandora a disgracefully extravagant bouquet (it is disgusting when people are starving), and at seven o'clock this evening he called with champagne, an Art Nouveau brooch and a pair of satin pyjamas. Then, as if that wasn't enough, he took her out for dinner in a hired car with uniformed driver! Most unacademic behaviour.

Cavendish behaves more like a pools winner than a professor of Linguistics at an ancient seat of learning.

Left to myself, I ate a simple meal of bread, tuna and cucumber and went to bed early. I am reading *English Love Poems*, edited by John Betjeman. Valentine's Day is a ridiculous charade, the ignorant masses are manipulated by the greetings card companies into forking out millions – and for what? For the illusion of being loved.

Friday February 15th

A Valentine's Day card! Signed 'A Secret Admirer'! I sang in my bath. I walked to work without touching the pavement! Who is she? The signature told me that she is educated and uses a felt-tip pen, like me.

Leonora had her hair pinned up today; she was wearing silver earrings so long that they brushed her slim shoulders. She was wearing a scooped-neck black top. A bra strap was visible. Black lace. She occasionally pushed it back inside her top. Every time she did so her sparkling bracelet fell down her arm towards her elbow. I am not in love with Leonora De Witt. But I am obsessed with her. She invades my dreams. She made me talk to an empty chair and pretend that it was my mother. I told the chair that it drank too much and wore its skirts too short.

Saturday February 16th

I finally took my library books back today: *A Single Man* by Christopher Isherwood, *English Love Poems* by John Betjeman, *Scenes from Provincial Life* by William

Cooper and *Notes from the Underground* by Dosto-evsky. I owed seven pounds, eighty pence in fines. My least favourite librarian was on duty at the desk. I don't know her name, but she is the Welsh one with the extroverted spectacles.

After I'd written out my cheque and handed it to her, she said, 'Do you have a cheque card?'

'Yes,' I replied. 'But it's at home.'

'Then I'm afraid I cannot accept this cheque,' she said.

'But you know me,' I said. 'I've been coming here once a week for eighteen months.'

'I'm afraid that I don't recognize you at all,' she said and handed me my cheque back.

'This beard is quite recent,' I said coldly. 'Perhaps you could try to visualize my face without it.'

'I don't have time for visualization,' she said. 'Not since the cuts.'

I showed her a small photograph of myself that I carry in my wallet. It was taken pre-beard.

'No,' she said, after giving it a cursory glance. 'I don't recognize that man.'

'But that man is *me*!' I shouted. A queue of people had built up behind me and they were listening avidly to the exchange. The librarian's spectacles flashed in anger.

'I have been doing the job of three people since the cuts began,' she said. 'And you are making my job even more difficult. Please go home and find your cheque card.'

'It is now 5.25 p.m. and the library closes in five minutes,' I said. 'Even Superman couldn't fly back in time to pay the fines, choose four books and leave before the doors close.'

Somebody behind me in the queue muttered, 'Get a bleedin' move on, Superman.'

So I said to the spectacled one, 'I'll be back tomorrow.'

'Oh no you won't,' she said, with a tiny smile. 'Due to the cuts this library doesn't open again until Wednesday.'

On my way home I railed internally against a government that is depriving me of new reading matter. Pandora has forbidden me to touch her books ever since I left a Jaffa cake inside her Folio Society edition of *Nicholas Nickleby*; Julian's books are in Chinese and I'm finding the last hundred pages of *War and Peace* heavy going. There is no way I can afford to buy a new book. Even a paperback costs at least a fiver.

I have to cough up thirty pounds a week for Leonora. I have even had to cut down on my consumption of bananas. I am down to one a day.

I have been forced to read my old diaries. Some of the entries are incredibly perceptive. And the poems have stood the test of time.

Sunday February 17th

Pandora spoke to me today. She said, 'I want you to leave. You stultify me. We had a childhood romance, but we are both adults now: we have grown in different directions and the time has come to part.' Then she added, cruelly, I thought, 'And that bloody beard makes you look absolutely ridiculous. For God's sake, shave it off.' I went to bed shattered. Read page 977 of *War and Peace*, then lay awake staring into the darkness.

Monday February 18th

I looked into the newsagent's on my way to work. I saw the following advertisement, written in a reasonably educated hand, on a Conqueror postcard:

Large sunny room to let – in family house.
Fire sign preferred. Use of W machine/dryer.
£75pw inclusive to N/S male professional. Ring Mrs Hedge.

I rang Mrs Hedge as soon as I got to my cubicle. She asked for my date of birth. I told her it was April 2nd, which excited the response, 'Aries, good. I'm Sagittarius.'

I went to see her at 7 p.m. and inspected the room. 'It's not very sunny,' I said.

She said, 'No, but would you expect it to be on an evening in February?'

I like the cut of her jib. She is oldish (thirty-five to thirty-seven, I would guess), but has not got a bad figure, although it's hard to tell with the clothes women wear nowadays. Her hair is lovely; treacle-coloured, like Pandora's used to be before she started mucking about with Colour-Glo. She was wearing quite a bit of make-up and her mascara had smudged. I hope this is not a sign of sluttishness. She was recently divorced and needs to let the room in order to continue paying the mortgage. Apparently the Building Society (my own, coincidentally) has turned nasty.

She invited me to test the bed. I did so and had a sudden vision of myself and Mrs Hedge engaging in vigorous sexual intercourse. I said aloud, 'I'm sorry.'

Naturally Mrs Hedge was completely in the dark as to the reason for my apology and said, '"Sorry"? Does that mean you don't like the bed?'

'No, no,' I gibbered. 'I love you; I mean, I love the bed.'

I was concerned that I hadn't made a good impression, so I rang Mrs Hedge when I got home (in an effort to impress her) and informed her that I was a writer; would the scratching of my pen in the small hours bother her?

'Not at all,' she replied. 'I am visited by the Muse myself in the night occasionally.'

You can't walk on the pavement in Oxford without bumping into a published or unpublished writer. It's no wonder that the owner of the stationery shop where I buy my supplies goes to the Canary Islands twice a year and drives a Mercedes. (He drives a Mercedes in *Oxford*, not the Canary Islands, though of course it is perfectly feasible that he has the use of a Mercedes *in* the Canary Islands as well. But I doubt, given the comparative infrequency of his visits, if he actually *owns* a Mercedes in the Canary Islands though I suppose it could be leased.) I don't know why I felt the need to explain the Canary Islands/Mercedes confusion. I suppose it may be another example of what Leonora calls my 'childish pedantry'.

Tuesday February 19th

My mother rang in a panic at 11.00 p.m., to ask if Martin Muffet, my young stepfather, had turned up at the flat. Quite frankly, I laughed out loud. Why would Muffet want to visit *me*? He knows I disapprove of my mother's foolhardy second marriage. Apart from the age difference (which is as wide as the mouth of the Amazon), they are physically and mentally incompatible.

Muffet is a six foot six bag of bones, who thinks the Queen works hard and that Paddy Ashdown is incapable of telling a lie. My mother is five foot five and squeezes herself into clothes two sizes too small for her and thinks that Britain should be a republic and that our first president should be Ken Livingstone, the well-known newt lover. On my last visit, I noticed that young Mr Muffet was far less attentive to my mother than of late. I expect he is regretting his mad rush into matrimony.

My mother said, 'He went to London this morning, to visit the Lloyd's building for his Engineering course.'

My mother's grasp of the geographical layout of the British Isles has always been minimal. I informed her of the distance from the Lloyd's building in the City of London to that of my box room in Oxford.

She said in a pathetic voice, 'I thought he might have popped in on his way back to Leicester.'

She phoned back at 2 a.m. Muffet was trapped in an underground train in a tunnel for six hours, or so he said.

Thursday February 21st

This time Leonora invited me to imagine that the chair was my father. She gave me an African stick and I beat the chair until I lay limp and exhausted and physically unable to lift the stick again.

'He's not a bad bloke, my dad,' I said. 'I don't know why I went so berserk.'

Leonora said, 'Don't talk to me, talk to him. Talk to the chair. The chair is your father.'

I felt stupid addressing the empty chair again, but I wanted to please Leonora, so I forced myself to look the upholstery in the eye and said, 'Why didn't you buy me an anglepoise lamp when I was revising for my GCSEs?'

Leonora said, 'Good, good, take it further, Adrian.'

'I hate your Country and Western cassettes,' I said.

'No,' Leonora whispered. 'Deeper, darker, an earlier memory.'

'I remember when I was three,' I said. 'You came into the bedroom, yanked my dummy out of my mouth and said, "*Real* boys don't need a dummy."'

I then grabbed the stick from where it was lying on the floor and once again began to beat the chair. Dust flew.

Leonora said, 'Good, good. How do you *feel*?'

I said, 'I feel terrible. I've wrenched my shoulder beating that chair.'

'No, no,' she said, irritably. 'How do you feel *inside*?'

I cottoned on.

'Oh, at peace with myself,' I lied. I got up, gave my therapeutic dominatrix the thirty quid and left. I needed to buy some Nurofen before the late-night chemist closed. I was in agony with my shoulder.

Friday February 22nd

Another split in the Newport Pagnell newts. There are now three separate habitats. Something fishy is happening in the newt world. Brown is phoning newt experts worldwide, droning on about this phenomenon.

Mrs Hedge has interviewed other potential tenants, but has chosen me! I was racked all night by erotic dreams, concerning me, Brown, Megan and Mrs Hedge. I am ashamed, but what can I do? I can't control my subconscious, can I? I was forced to go to the launderette, though it is not my usual day.

Saturday February 23rd

Norman Schwarzkopf was on television tonight, pointing a stick at an incomprehensible map. Why he was dressed in army camouflage is a mystery to me:

a) there are no trees in the desert
b) there were no trees in the briefing room
c) he is obviously too important to go anywhere near the enemy; he could go around dressed like Coco the Clown and still not be shot at

Tuesday February 26th

Visited Mrs Hedge today, to finalize arrangements for renting the room and to discuss our tenancy agreement. She had a picture of the charred head of an Iraqi soldier who was found dead in a vehicle held against her fridge by a Mickey Mouse magnet. I averted my eyes and asked her for a drink of water.

Wednesday February 27th

Yesterday evening I informed Pandora that I am moving out of the flat at the weekend. I had hoped that she would fall on my neck and beg me to stay, but she didn't. At 1 a.m. I was woken by the sound of a champagne cork popping, glasses clinking and wild, unrestrained laughter from Pandora, Cavendish and Julian. The Infernal Triangle.

Thursday February 28th

Leonora did most of the talking tonight. She told me that I expect too much of myself, that I have impossibly high standards. She told me to be kind to myself and made me draw up a list of ten things I enjoy doing. Every time I banish a negative thought about myself, I am allowed to treat myself.

She asked if I can afford the occasional self-indulgence. I confessed that I have savings in the Market Harborough Building Society. She gave me a piece of paper and a child's crayon and told me to write down ten treats.

Treats

1) Reading novels
2) Writing novels
3) Sexual intercourse

4) Looking at women
5) Buying stationery
6) Eating bananas
7) Crab paste sandwiches
8) Watching boxing on television
9) Listening to Tchaikovsky
10) Walking in the countryside

I asked Leonora what her treats were.

She said in a husky low voice, 'We're not here to talk about me.' Then she smiled and showed her beautifully white teeth and said, 'We have a few things in common, Adrian.'

I felt a throb of sexual desire surge through me.

'I too like to watch the boxing on television,' she said. 'I'm a Bruno fan.'

Friday March 1st

At breakfast this morning, I asked Cavendish if he would help me to move my things to Mrs Hedge's. He has got a big Volvo estate. He said, 'Can't think of anything I'd rather do, Aidy.' He offered to move me immediately, but I said, 'Tomorrow morning will do. Some of us have to *work*?'

He laughed and said, 'So you think teaching Linguistics is a soft option, do you, Aidy?'

I said, 'Yes, as a matter of fact, I do. I doubt if *work* is a four-letter word to you.'

'Speaking as a professor of Linguistics,' he snarled, 'I can assure you that work is indeed a four-letter word.' As he reached for the ashtray, his dressing gown fell open, revealing withered nipples and grey matted chest hair. I was almost physically sick. I could hardly swallow my Bran Flakes.

Took the portable TV back to the shop. On my return, I wrote a poem to Pandora and slipped it under her door. It was my last-ditch attempt to seduce her away from Cavendish.

Pandora! Let Me! by A. Mole
Let me stroke your inner thighs
Let me hear your breathy sighs
Let me feel your silky skin
Let me make your senses spin
Let me touch your soft white breast
Let us stop and have a rest.
Let me join our beating hearts
Let me forge our private parts
Let me delve and make you mine
Let me give you food and wine
Let me lick you with my tongue
Let me do whatever's wrong
Let me watch you take your pleasure
Let me dress you in black leather
Let me fit you like a glove
Let me consummate our love.

At 1 a.m. Pandora pushed a note under my door.

Adrian,
   If you continue to send such filth to me, I will, in future, pass it on to the police.
   Pandora

Saturday March 2nd

As I packed my belongings, I reflected that I have not acquired much in my life. A basic wardrobe of clothes. A few hundred books. A Sony Walkman. A dozen or so cassettes. My own mug, cup, bowl and plate. A poster by Munch, a cactus, a magnifying mirror on a stand, a bowl for bananas, and a lamp. It is not much to show for a year and a half of toil at the DOE. True, I have got £2,579 saved in the Market Harborough Building Society, and £197.39 in Nat West, but even so.

   I found the blue plastic comb I have been searching for since last year. It was on top of the wardrobe. Why? How did it get there? I have never climbed on the wardrobe to comb my hair. I suspect Julian. He is a big fan of Jeremy Beadle's.

11 p.m. Too tired to write much, just to put it on the record that I am lying in Mrs Hedge's bed. It is very comfortable. My new address is now:

8 Sitwell Villas
Summertown
Oxford.

Sunday March 3rd

I didn't know where I was when I woke up, then I remembered. I smelt bacon cooking, but I didn't go downstairs. I felt like an intruder. I got up, tiptoed to the bathroom, got dressed, made my bed, then sat on the bed listening to sounds from below. Eventually, driven by hunger, I went downstairs. Mrs Hedge was not there. The breakfast plates were still on the kitchen table. The kitchen pedal bin was overflowing. There were eggshells on the floor. The cupboard under the sink was full of filthy yellow dusters. The fridge was full of little saucers containing mouldy leftovers. The grill pan was unwashed. The *Observer* was speckled with tinned tomato juice.

It is as I feared: Mrs Hedge is a slut. The phone rang non-stop. Took messages: 'Ted phoned.' 'Ian rang.' 'Martin called.' 'Call Kingsley back.' 'Julian rang: Are you going to the launch on Tuesday?'

I was mopping the kitchen floor when Mrs Hedge returned. She was carrying a large shrub and four tins of Carlsberg.

'Christ,' she said. 'It looks like I've struck lucky. Do you like housework, Mr Mole?'

'I find it difficult to tolerate disorder,' I said.

She went out into the garden to plant the shrub, then sat on the patio on an iron chair, swigging Carlsberg out of the tin. She didn't seem to notice the cold. When it started to rain, she came into the house, got a golfing umbrella from the jar in the hall, and went back out again. I went up to my room to work on my novel, *Lo! The Flat Hills of My Homeland.*

When I next went downstairs, there was no sign of Mrs Hedge. I was pleased to see three tins of Carlsberg still left in the fridge. She may be a slut and an eccentric, but, thank God, she is not yet an alcoholic.

Monday March 4th

Mrs Hedge was still in bed when I got back from work. The kitchen was a disgrace. The Carlsberg was gone from the fridge. She must have drunk them in bed! It is the only conclusion.

Wednesday March 6th

Went to Pandora's to pick up my post. Nothing exciting. Letters from the Market Harborough Building Society, *Reader's Digest* and Plumbs, a firm promoting stretch covers. How did Plumbs get hold of my name and address? I have never shown the slightest interest in soft furnishings. Pandora has turned my box room into a study. I opened a file on her desk marked, 'Lecture Notes'. Didn't understand a word. They were written in what was probably Serbo-Croat.

Thursday March 7th

I walked into the bathroom tonight without knocking. Mrs Hedge was in the bath, shaving her legs. I will buy a bolt for the door tomorrow. I'd guess she is at least 38C.

Friday March 8th

Mrs Hedge said, 'Feel free to invite your friends round, Mr Mole.' I told her that I hadn't got any friends. I walk alone.

When I told Leonora the same thing, she said, 'Before our next session, please try to speak to a stranger; smile and initiate a conversation; and make a new female friend.'

Saturday March 9th

There was a stranger in the kitchen when I came down. He was eating Marmite on toast. He said, 'Hi. I'm Gerry.'

I smiled and said, 'Good morning. I'm Adrian Mole.'

That was the extent of our social intercourse. I found it difficult to initiate a conversation with a man wearing a woman's negligee and nothing else.

I made myself a cup of tea and left.

I wish I was back in my box room.

Monday March 11th

Mr Major on the news. He said, 'I want us to be where we belong, at the very heart of Europe, working with our partners in building the future.'

A peculiar thing: Mr Major cannot say the word 'want' to rhyme with 'font', which is the correct English pronunciation. For some reason, he says 'went'. I suspect that this disability stems from childhood. When little John lisped, 'I want some sweeties,' etc., etc. Did his father leap down from his trapeze and shout, 'I'll give you *want*!'? Or shout, 'Say *want* again and I'll beat you black and blue,' thus leaving little John sobbing into the sawdust of the Big Top and unable to pronounce that little English word?

My heart goes out to him. He is obviously in urgent need of therapy. It seems to me that we have both suffered for having embarrassing fathers. I will bring the subject up when I next see Leonora.

Tuesday March 12th

Brown slipped down a grassy bank and bruised his coccyx at the weekend. He was collecting owl droppings. He has been incapacitated and is lying on a plank on his bedroom floor. Ha! Ha! Ha! Ho! Ho! Ho! Three cheers!

Wednesday March 13th

Brown's deputy, Gordon Goffe, is throwing his weight (twenty stone) about. He is conducting an enquiry into 'postage stamp pilfering'. This is just my luck. I was about to send the opening chapters of my novel *Lo! The Flat Hills of My Homeland* off to Faber and Faber today. I shall have to fork out for the stamps myself. Once they have read these chapters, they will be panting for the rest.

Thursday March 14th

The Birmingham Six have been released from prison.

Gordon Goffe is lumbering around the offices, carrying out spot checks on our drawers. Megan was found to have an illicit box of DOE ballpoints. She has received an oral warning. No session with Leonora this week. She is attending a conference in Sacramento.

Friday March 15th

Barry Kent was on *Kaleidoscope* reading from *Dork's Diary*. The little I heard was nihilistic rubbish. Goffe barged into my cubicle and said that I was not allowed to listen to Radio Four during office hours. I pointed out that Mr Brown had never objected.

Goffe said, 'I am not Mr Brown,' a statement so stupid that I was lost for an answer. I've got an answer now, at three minutes past midnight, but it is obviously too late.

Saturday March 16th

Called round to Pandora's flat for my letters. Nothing of interest: circular for thermal underwear; *Reader's Digest* competition entry form – prize: a gold bar; Plumbs catalogue, offering discount on mock velvet curtains. I am twenty-four next month and I must confess, dear journal, that I had expected by now to be in correspondence with interesting and fascinating people. Instead, the world seems to think of me as a person who gets up in the morning, puts on his thermal underwear, draws his mock velvet curtains and settles down to read his new copy of *Reader's Digest*.

The cat looked thin, but was pleased to see me. I gave it a whole tin of cat food. Pandora was out, so

I had a good look around the flat. Her underwear drawer is full of disgusting sex aids. Bluebeard is obviously not up to it.

Sunday March 17th

Had an interesting talk about the Russian elections with the girl in the local newsagent's this morning. Then, as she handed me my *Sunday Times*, she remarked (joking, I presume), 'It's very heavy. Would you like me to help you carry it home?'

'No,' I jocularly replied. 'I think I can just about manage.' Though, as I took it, I pretended to buckle under its weight. How we laughed.

She is quite pleasant-looking in a sort of un-assuming sort of way.

6.00 p.m. On rereading the above, I think I have been unfair to the girl in the newsagent's. A gingham nylon overall is not the most flattering of garments. And I didn't see her legs, as they were behind the counter at all times.

I have just read the *Sunday Times* books section and was appalled, astonished and disgusted to see that *Dork's Diary* is at number ten in the hardback bestseller list today!

Monday March 18th

Called in at the newsagent's for a packet of Polos on the way to work. The girl joked that I was paying for fresh air, i.e. the hole! This hadn't occurred to me before, so I handed the Polos back to her and said, 'Okay, I'll have Trebor Mints instead.' Again, we laughed uproariously. She has certainly got a good sense of humour. Legs still behind the counter. Brown still malingering at home. Goffe still rampaging in the office. Leonora will be pleased to hear about the girl in the newsagent's.

Tuesday March 19th

A letter from Pandora, my first at Sitwell Villas:

Sunday, March 17th
Adrian,

I have asked you many times to return the front door key to this flat. You have not yet done so. I'm afraid I must give you an ultimatum. Either the key is in my possession by 7 p.m. on Tuesday night, or I call out a locksmith, have the lock changed and send the bill to you. The choice is yours. I will no longer tolerate you:

a) interfering in the cat's feeding pattern;

b) snooping in my underwear drawer; or

c) helping yourself to food from the refrigerator when I am not there.

As I have said, I will continue to redirect your post (such as it is) and relay any messages that I consider to be urgent.

At 6.59 p.m., I pushed an envelope containing the key, a ten-pence piece and a terse note under the door of Pandora's flat. The note said:

Pandora,

a) In my opinion, the cat is too thin and appears to be lacking in energy;

b) I vividly remember you saying that 'Suspenders, etc. are symbols of women's enslavement to men's lust.' Ditto vibrators;

c) The pot of crab paste in the refrigerator was *mine*. I purchased it on February 20th this year. I have the receipt to prove it. I admit that I did help myself to a slice of bread. I enclose, as you cannot fail to see, a ten-pence coin, as remuneration for the slice of granary.

Wednesday March 20th

How do I get the legs out from behind the counter?

Thursday March 21st

Her name is Bianca. A strange name for somebody working in a newsagent's. They are usually called Joyce. I saw her carrying boxes of crisps from a delivery lorry into the shop. Legs okay, but ankles a bit bony, so, on a scale of one to ten, only five.

9.00 p.m. Leonora was in a strange mood tonight. She was annoyed because I was fifteen minutes late. I pointed out to her that she would be paid for the full hour.

She said, 'That's not the point, Adrian. Our sessions together are carefully structured. I insist that you are punctual in future.'

I replied, 'My chronic unpunctuality is one of my many problems. Shouldn't you be addressing it?'

She crossed her shapely legs under her black silk skirt and I saw a flash of white. From that point on I was helpless and could only nod or shake my head in answer to her questions. Speech was beyond me. I felt that if I opened my mouth I would utter crude inarticulate protestations of lust, which would frighten her and signal the end of our time together.

Ten minutes before the end of our session she said, 'You are displaying typically regressive behaviour at the moment, shall we take advantage of it?'

I nodded and she encouraged me to talk about my earliest memories. I remembered being bitten by a dog and my grandma applying iodine to the wound. I also remember my (now dead) grandad kicking the dog round the kitchen.

Then it was time to fork out £30 and leave.

Saturday March 23rd

Mrs Hedge asked me if she should marry Gerry, sell up and move to Cardiff. I advised against it. I have only just settled in, found out how to work the grill pan, etc. I can't face looking for alternative accommodation. Anyway, why ask me? I've only spoken to the ugly brute a few times.

Sunday March 24th

The lavatory seat was up, so I guessed that Gerry was *in situ*. I went to buy my newspaper from Bianca and, on my return, sure enough, Gerry and Mrs Hedge were in the kitchen eating eggs and bacon. Mrs Hedge didn't look pleased to see me. I threw a few Rice Krispies into a bowl and took them up to my room. But, by the time I'd got upstairs, they had stopped snapping and crackling and popping, which annoyed me considerably. I loathe soggy cereals.

Monday March 25th

Gerry is now a fixture. I am like a cuckoo in the nest.
A gooseberry in the strawberry patch. A piranha in
the goldfish bowl. Conversation stops when I enter the
kitchen or sitting room and they are there. I wanted
to watch the Oscar ceremony on television tonight,
but Gerry snatched the remote control and kept it on
his lap, thus denying me the pleasure of *seeing* that
gifted and modest actor Jeremy Irons win an Oscar
for Britain. I had to hear this wonderful news on Radio
Four and visualize Mr Irons's delight myself. Whoever
said that the 'pictures are better on the radio' was
completely wrong.

Tuesday March 26th

I have asked Bianca to give me prior warning, should a
suitable-sounding postcard arrive at the shop offering
accommodation. She agreed. I think she finds me
personable. Haste has changed the meaning of the
above sentence: postcards cannot walk into a newsagent's and talk suitably. Leonora cancelled tonight's
appointment. 'An emergency,' she said.

Am I not an emergency? My sanity hangs by a
gossamer thread. Leonora is the only barrier between
me and the public ward in a lunatic asylum. How will

she live with herself if I am admitted foaming at the mouth and struggling inside a straitjacket?

Wednesday March 27th

Mr David Icke, who is a famous Leicester person, has revealed that he is a 'channel for the Christ spirit'. He went on television and told the goggling press that his wife and daughter were 'incarnations of the archangel Michael'. He blamed the planet Sirus for bringing earthquakes and pestilence to the world. Gerry and Mrs Hedge mocked him and said he is barmy, but I'm not so sure. We Leicester people are known for our level heads. Perhaps Mr Icke knows something that we ordinary mortals cannot even guess at.

Thursday March 28th

Bianca studied Astronomy in the sixth form. She said this morning, 'There is no such planet as Sirus.' But, as I pointed out to her, 'David Icke did say that Sirus was *undiscovered*, so naturally no reference *would* be found to it in the books, would it?'

A queue formed, so we were forced to break off our discussion. I called in on my way home from work, but Bianca was busy – some old git was complaining about his newspaper bill.

Friday March 29th

The more I think about David Icke's predictions, i.e. that the world will end unless it 'purges itself of evil', the more it makes sense. He is a successful man, who was employed by the BBC, no less! He was also a professional goalkeeper for Hereford City. We should not be too quick to scoff. Columbus was once mocked for remarking that the world was round. Something that was verified by the first US astronauts.

My mother rang tonight to ask me what I want for my birthday next week. I told her to get me the usual, a book token. She went on to say that Leicester was agog about David Icke, and that 'there has been a run on turquoise track suits' (worn by Mr Icke's followers). She said she felt sorry for his mother. Apparently, Mr Icke claimed he was born on the planet Sirus, whereas his mother said in the *Leicester Mercury* that she distinctly remembers giving birth to him in the Leicester General Maternity Hospital.

I ran out of bananas tonight. I had to walk to the outer suburbs before finding an off-licence that stocked them.

Saturday March 30th

Posted two birthday cards to myself. I put second-class stamps on, so they should get here by Tuesday morning.

Spring

Monday April 1st

A man with a Glaswegian accent rang me in my cubicle
this morning and said, 'I have just finished reading
the opening chapters of your novel *Lo! The Flat Hills
of My Homeland* and I want to publish it next year.
Would an advance of £50,000 be acceptable?'

I stammered out, 'Yes,' and asked to whom I was
speaking.

'*A. Fool!*' laughed the imposter, and slammed the
phone down.

How cruel can you get? For fifteen seconds, I had
achieved my ambition. I was a professional writer
living in my own house. I'd learned to drive. I had a
car in the garage. I had a Rolex watch and a Mont
Blanc pen. There was an air ticket to the USA in the
pocket of my cashmere coat. Fan letters bristled inside
my leather briefcase. Invitations to literary events were
stacked on the mantelpiece. Then my dream was shattered by the hoaxer and I went back to being simple
Adrian Mole, who was halfway through writing a
report on newt movements, in a cubicle in a DOE
building in Oxford. I suspect Goffe.

Tuesday April 2nd

Birthday cards from Mother, Rosie, Father, Grandma, Mrs Hedge and Megan. Six cards in all. Not bad, I needn't have posted two to myself.

Presents
1) Ten pound book token from mother.
2) W. H. Smith voucher from father (fiver).
3) 2 pairs of socks from Mrs Hedge (white).
4) Cactus plant from Megan (obscene).

No surprise party. No candles to blow out. No singing. No Leonora until Thursday.

Wednesday April 3rd

I am twenty-four and one day old. *Question*: What have I done with my life? *Answer*: Nothing.

Graham Greene died today. I wrote to him four years ago, pointing out a grammatical error in his book *The Human Factor*. He didn't reply.

Thursday April 4th

I trimmed my beard this morning. Mrs Hedge screamed when I came out of the bathroom. When she recovered, she said, 'Christ, you look like the Yorkshire Ripper.'

I had a terrible session with Leonora. I went into her room with the self-esteem of an anorexic aphid and came out feeling worse.

My low self-esteem on entering Leonora's room was due to an acrimonious phone conversation I'd had with my mother earlier. She had rung the office to ask me if I would like to go to a party given by Barry Kent to celebrate the success of *Dork's Diary*. The venue is the North East Leicester Working Men's Club, and half of Leicester has been invited.

I said to my mother, 'I would sooner wash a corpse.'

My mother accused me of petty jealousy, and then had a tantrum and recited my faults: arrogance, overweening pride, snobbery, pretension, phoney intellectualism, wimpishness, etc., etc.

I recited this to Leonora who said, 'I suggest that you take on board what your mother is saying. I also suggest that you *go to the party*.' She said that she had bought five copies of *Dork's Diary*: for her husband, Fergus; for her best friend, Susan Strachan; for her therapist, Simon; for her supervisor, Alison; and for herself. I was totally gobsmacked. When Leonora said that it was time to go, I refused to leave my chair.

I said, 'I can't bear the thought of you enjoying Barry Kent's work.'

Leonora said, 'Tough, give me thirty pounds and leave.'

I said, 'No, I am totally sexually obsessed by you.

I think about you constantly. I have revealed my innermost feelings to you.'

Leonora said, 'Yours is a standard reaction. You'll get over it.'

I said, 'Leonora, I feel betrayed. I refuse to be treated like an example from a text book.'

Leonora stood up and tossed her magnificent head and said, 'Ours is a professional relationship, Mr Mole. It could never be anything else. Come and see me next Thursday.'

'Okay,' I said. 'Take your thirty pieces of silver.'

I flung a Market Harborough Building Society cheque made out for thirty pounds onto the desk and left, slamming the door.

If my father had allowed me to abandon that dummy in my own time, I'm convinced I would now be enjoying perfect mental health.

Saturday April 6th

Am I the only person in Britain who has an open mind re the David Icke sensation? Bianca described him as a 'barmpot' this morning – but as I pointed out to her, Jesus himself was reviled in his day. The press were against him and the money-lenders slagged him off to all and sundry. Also, Jesus was a bit of an eccentric as regards clothes. He would not have won a 'Best Dressed Palestinian of the Year Award'. But, had track suits been around in Christ's day, he would almost certainly have opted for the comfort and wash-ability of such garments.

Sunday April 7th

Dork's Diary is now at number eight. Glanced through my *Illustrated Bible Stories* tonight and was startled to find on page 33 (Raising Lazarus) that Jesus is wearing turquoise robes!!!

Monday April 8th

Brown is back, but he is wearing a noisy surgical corset, which is quite useful (the noise, not the corset), because Megan is seeing Bill Blane (Badger Dept) on the side. I like Bill. He and I discussed David Icke at the Autovent today. Bill agrees with me that Sirus could have been overlooked by the astronomers. It could well have been hidden behind another, bigger planet.

The emir of Kuwait has promised to hold parliamentary elections next year. He has announced that women will be allowed to vote. Good for you, Sir!

Tuesday April 9th

John Major has been cross-examined by the press about his 'O' levels. I hope this won't remind Brown about my own, non-existent, Biology 'A' level. Why, oh why, couldn't I have been born an American? College students there are given multiple choice type exams. All the dumbos have to do is put a tick against what they think is the right answer.

Example: Question: Who discovered America?
 Was it: a) Columbus?
             b) Mickey Mouse?
             c) Rambo?

Wednesday April 10th

Bill Blane has asked me to go for a drink after work tomorrow. This could be the start of a new friendship.

Thursday April 11th

Bill wanted to talk about Megan. In fact, he talked about her all night. I couldn't get a word in edgeways, apart from saying, 'Same again?' when it was my turn to buy a round. I drank far too much (three pints) and in my muddled state started walking back to

Pandora's flat before realizing my mistake and turning my steps towards the Hedge household.

Friday April 12th

Worked on *Lo! The Flat Hills of My Homeland* tonight. Started Chapter Eleven:

As he skirted the top of the hill, he looked east and saw the city of Leicester glowing in the dying embers of the setting sun. The tower blocks reflected the scarlet rays and bounced them against the factory chimneys and the Royal Infirmary multi-storey car park. He sighed with the glorious anticipation of knowing that he would soon be tramping the reconstituted concrete streets of his home town. He could have entered the city by a more discreet route – turned off the motorway at Junction 23 – but he preferred this, the route of the sheep drovers, and anyway, he hadn't got a car.

He had been away too long, he thought. He had grown tired of the world and its attractions. Leicester was where his heart was. He strode down the hill, his eyes were wet. The wind, perhaps? Or the pain of absence? He would never know. The sun slipped away behind the grand edifice of the Alliance and Leicester Building Society headquarters and he felt the stealthy black fingers of night collect around him. Soon it was dark. Still he descended. Down. Down.

Not many people know that Leicester lies in a basin, he ruminated. No wonder it is the bronchitis centre of the world, he thought. Before long, he had descended the hill and he was on flat ground.

I think this is probably the best writing I have ever done. It is magnificent. I hope I can maintain this standard throughout the novel.

Saturday April 13th

Notes on *Lo!*:

a) Should I give my hero a name? Or should I continue to call him '*he*', '*him*', etc.?

b) Should the narrative be stronger? At the moment, not much happens. *He* leaves Leicester, then comes back to Leicester. Should the reader know what *he* does in between?

c) Should *he* have sex, or go shopping? Most modern novels are full of references to one or the other – the reading public obviously relishes such activities.

Descriptions (to be slotted in somewhere):

The tree bent in the wind, like a pensioner at Land's End.

The fried egg spluttered in the frying pan like an old man having a tubercular coughing fit in a 1930s National Health Service hospital.

Her breasts were as full as hot air balloons. Her face was infused with anger, her eyes flashed like a manic lighthouse whose wick needed cleaning.

The tea was welcome. *He* sipped it gratefully, like an African elephant which has previously found its waterhole to be dry, but then remembered, and walked to, another.

From now on, I shall write down these thoughts and ideas as they come to me. They are far too good to waste. Publication looks to be within my grasp.

Sunday April 14th

Woke at 8.30, had breakfast: cornflakes, toast, brown sauce, two cups of tea. Collected *Sunday Times* and *Observer*. Bianca not there. *Dork's Diary* has gone to number seven. Changed into blazer. Walked round Outer Ring Road, came back. Brushed and hung up blazer. Lay on bed. Slept. Woke up, put on blazer, went out, had pizza in Pizza Hut. Came back, lay on bed, slept. Woke, had bath, changed into pyjamas and dressing gown. Cut toenails, trimmed beard, inspected skin. Tidied tapes into alphabetical order, Abba to Warsaw Concerto. Went downstairs. Mrs Hedge in kitchen, in tears at kitchen table. 'I've got nobody to confide in,' she cried. Made crab paste sandwiches. Went to bed. Wrote up journal.

I can't go on like this; I'd have more of a social life in prison.

Monday April 15th

Went to see DOE doctor, Dr Abrahams. I told him I was depressed. He told me he was depressed. I told him that my life was meaningless, that my ambitions remained unrealized. He told me that his dream was to become the Queen's gynaecologist by the age of 44. I asked him how old he was. He told me that he was 45. Poor old git. He gave me a prescription for my depression. I asked the chemist if there were any side effects.

She said, 'Well, there's lack of concentration. Your physical movement may be reduced. You'll notice an increase in heart rate. There'll possibly be sweating and tremors, constipation and perhaps difficulty in urinating. Bit depressing, really, isn't it?'

I agreed with her and tore the prescription into pieces.

Wednesday April 17th

Rocky gave me a lift to work this morning in his limo. We discussed Pandora, how arrogant she is, etc. Rocky said, 'But, y'know, Aid, I'll always love the girl, she's, y'know, kinda like *unique.*'

I congratulated Rocky on his use of the word 'unique'.

Rocky told me that Carly Pick, his girl friend, is teaching him new words.

I said, 'So, she's extending your vocabulary, is she?' But he looked at me blankly, from which I inferred that she hadn't been at it for long.

When the car drew up outside the DOE, I was pleased to see that Brown was looking out of his office window. He ducked out of sight, but he couldn't have failed to see me exiting from the limousine. It won't hurt Brown to know that I mingle with the rich and powerful.

Robert Maxwell has saved the *Mirror*. He is a saint!

Thursday April 18th

The Newport Pagnell newts seem to have settled down, thank God. The road plans are finalized and construction is due to start next month.

Mrs Brown came to the office today. She had lost her handbag in the Ashmolean Museum. Brown was entirely unsympathetic. Before he closed his office door, I heard him say, 'That's the second time this year, you stupid cow.' He would not have spoken to Megan like that. Mrs Brown is very pretty. It's just that her clothes are horrible. It's as though there is a lunatic living in her wardrobe who orders her what to wear every morning. She can get away with looking ridiculous in Oxford. People probably assume that she is just another barmy professor, but she would be a laughing stock in Leicester.

Saturday April 20th

Mrs Hedge crying again this morning. I must away from this Vale of Tears. I need cheerful people around me.

Bianca handed me a card this morning. It said, in mad handwriting:

ROOM TO LET
Academic household willing to let room free to tolerant person of either gender, in return for light household duties/babysitting/cat-sitting. Would suit working person with most evenings free. Please ring Dr Palmer.

I rang immediately from the phone box outside the newsagent's. A bloke answered.

DR PALMER: Christian Palmer speaking.
ME: Dr Palmer, my name is Adrian Mole. I've just seen your postcard in the newsagent's.
DR P: When can you start?
ME: Start what?
DR P: Looking after the bloody kids.
ME: But you don't know me.
DR P: You sound okay and you've already proved you can

use a telephone. So you can't be a total simpleton.

Have you got all your faculties: four limbs, eyesight?

ME: Yes.

DR P: Ever been done for molesting kiddie-winkies?

ME: No.

DR P: Got any particularly nasty personal habits?

ME: No.

DR P: Good. So when can you start? I'm on my own here. My wife's in the States.

The telephone receiver was dropped. Suddenly I heard Palmer shout, 'Tamsin, put the top back on that bottle of bleach! Now!'

He came back on the phone and gave me his address in Banbury Road.

I went into the newsagent's and asked Bianca what newspapers and magazines Palmer read. This is a sure sign of character. It was a baffling list:

Newspapers: the *Observer*, the *Daily Telegraph*, the *Sun*, the *Washington Post*, the *Oxford Mail*, the *Independent*, the *Sunday Times*, *Today*.

Magazines: *Time Out, Private Eye, Just Seventeen, Vogue, Brides, Forum, Computer Weekly, Woman's Own, Paris Match, Gardening Today, Hello!*, the *Spectator*, the *Literary Review, Socialist Outpost*, the *Beano, Angler's Weekly, Canoeist, Viz, Interiors, Goal!*

I stopped her and said, 'Palmer's newspaper bill must be enormous. How does he pay it?'

'Infrequently,' she replied.

Sunday April 21st

Dr Palmer is tall and thin and wears his hair like Elvis Presley did during his silver-cloaks-in-Los-Angeles phase. His first words to me were, 'On your way to a fancy dress party?' He laughed and fingered the lapels of my blazer.

I mumbled something neutral and he asked, 'Is that beard *real*?'

I assured him that I had grown it myself and he said, 'How old are you?'

I answered, 'Twenty-four,' and he laughed a strange laugh, like a dog's bark, and said, '*Twenty-four*: so why the hell do you want to walk round looking like bloody Jack Hawkins?'

'Who's Jack Hawkins?' I asked.

'He's a film star,' he replied. 'Everybody's heard of Jack Hawkins.' He looked annoyed for some reason. Then he said, 'Well, unless you're twenty-four, that is.'

We were still standing on the doorstep of his decrepit house. A line of dirty, unrinsed milk bottles stood on the step. A little kid of unknown sex ran up the hall and tugged at Palmer's trousers. 'I've done a great big one! Come and look, Daddy!' it said.

We all three went into a gigantic room which seemed to be a kitchen, living-room and study combined. In the middle of the floor stood a potty in the shape of an elephant. Dr Palmer looked in the potty and exclaimed, 'Tamsin, that is a truly wonderful piece of shit.'

I averted my eyes as he carried the potty out of the room. Then I heard him shouting, 'Alpha! Griffith! Come and see what Tamsin's done!' There was a thundering on the stairs. I looked into the hall and saw two other androgynous children looking into the potty, saying, 'Wow!' and 'Mega shit!'

I adjusted my blazer in the mirror over the large fireplace and thought that the Dr Palmer household was unsuited to one of my temperament. I do not like to hear little children swear and I prefer them to be dressed in proper clothes and to have hairstyles which give a clue to their sexual orientation. However, when Dr Palmer came back from emptying the potty, I was pleased to see that he was drying his hands, which indicated to me that he knew the fundamentals of hygiene. I agreed to inspect the free room. We climbed the stairs, followed by Tamsin, Griffith and Alpha, who spoke to each other in a language I was not familiar with.

'Is it Welsh they're speaking?' I asked.

'No,' Palmer laughed. 'It's Oombagoomba. It's their own language. They're wearing their Oombagoomba clothes.'

I looked at the rags and bits of cloth and shawls, etc. with which the kids were festooned and was relieved to find out that it was not their usual mode of dress. I too used to have my own made-up language (Ikbak), until my father beat it out of me during a long car journey to Skegness.

The 'free room' turned out to be the whole of the attic floor. It had a kitchen at one end, and a private bathroom at the other. There was a proper desk. I could imagine reading the proofs of *Lo!* at that desk.

'You can do what you like up here,' said Palmer, 'apart from serial killing.'

'Are you a teacher?' I ventured.

'No,' he said. 'I'm leading a research project on popular culture. We are trying to establish why people go out to pubs, discos, bingo sessions, to the cinema, that sort of thing.'

'It's to enjoy themselves, isn't it?' I said.

Palmer laughed again. 'Yeah, but I've got to stretch that very simplistic answer into a three-year study and a seven-hundred page book.'

As we went down the stairs, I mentioned to Dr Palmer that as well as being an excellent tenant, I am also a novelist and a poet.

He groaned and said, 'So long as you *never* ask me to look at your manuscripts, we'll stay the best of friends.'

He made me a cup of coffee after grinding up some beans and he told me a bit about his wife, Cassandra, who is in Los Angeles directing a film about mutilation. She sounds horrific, although he claims to miss her. I am too tired and confused to write more. Dr Palmer has told me he must know by Wednesday if I want the room. He's got to go out on Friday to a darts competition.

Monday April 22nd

Should I go, or should I stay?

Can I stand babysitting for three children, four nights a week?

I could save £75 a week. In a year, that is . . .? As usual, when faced with mental, or even physical, arithmetic, my brain has just left my body and walked out of the room.

Thank God for calculators. Nine hundred pounds! It's not as if I would be sacrificing my social life. I haven't got one and, with a bit of luck, Mrs Palmer will stay in America, or fall over Niagara Falls, or something.

Thursday April 25th

Rang Palmer from the office and told him that I would be moving in tonight. Rang Pandora; asked if Cavendish would help me to move.

'Moving?' she said. 'Again?' Then, 'You make more moves than a tiddlywink.'

Rang Mrs Hedge, asked her to take my Y-fronts out of the washer and hang them on my bedroom radiator to dry. Mentioned that I would be moving on.

She said, 'Everybody does, eventually.'

Rang my mother and gave her my new address in case of a family tragedy. She yakked on for half an hour about President Gorbachev's threat to resign and predicted that the USSR was in danger of collapse. I cut in eventually and said, 'I no longer take an interest in world events. There is nothing I can do to influence them, so why bother?'

Rang Grandma, in Leicester. Had a long chat about Princess Diana. Grandma doesn't think she's been looking happy lately. I voiced my own concern. Diana is too thin.

Rang Market Harborough Building Society to notify change of address.

Rang Waterstone's. Pretended to be irate reader; threatened to sue them for selling pornography, i.e. *Dork's Diary*.

Rang Megan. Pretended to be Brown. Said, 'God, I love you, Megan,' in his horrible squeaky voice.

Eventually, Brown burst in and demanded that I get off the phone. I sincerely hope he hasn't been listening outside the door.

I had a compulsion to visit Leonora again. She agreed to see me immediately. She was wearing a white dress. She looked like a sacrificial virgin. I wanted to deflower her, but I found myself talking about Bianca.

Leonora leant forward in her chair, displaying her dark cleavage. I found myself saying that I was quite interested in Bianca, although I found her lack of cleavage disappointing.

Leonora said, 'But could you love Bianca?'

I said, 'The idea is ridiculous. The thought of *her* doesn't keep me awake at night, but the thought of *you* does.'

Leonora sighed and said, 'I suggest you cultivate this friendship with Bianca. I am a married woman, Adrian. Your obsession with me is typical of a therapist/client relationship. It is called transference. You must face the truth about your feelings.'

I said, 'The truth about my feelings is that I don't love you. I just want to go to bed with you.'

Leonora said, 'Thirty pounds please.'

I felt like a client paying a whore.

Friday April 26th
Moving Day

Cavendish and Palmer are old friends. When they saw each other, they did that arms-clasped-on-each-other's-shoulders, then grin-and-shake, which so many men in Oxford seem to go in for these days. As I removed my possessions from the back of the Volvo and tried to stop Tamsin, Griffith and Alpha from interfering, I heard Cavendish and Palmer laughing like madmen in the living-room. I'm not sure, but I think I heard the word 'blazer' mentioned. The children spoke Oombagoomba all night until their father returned at 11.30 p.m. They flatly refused to go to bed, or to converse with me in English. Instead, they lay under the massive pine table on a pile of cushions and jabbered away in that made-up lingo. It was like being abroad; if you closed your eyes.

Saturday April 27th

Bought *The White Hotel* by D. M. Thomas this morning. If it is even half as good as *The Great Babylon Hotel* by Arnold Bennett I will be more than satisfied. When Christian saw me take it out of the carrier bag, he raised his eyebrows and said, 'Don't leave it lying around. Alpha's got a reading age of thirteen.'

I said, 'You should encourage your child to read.'

Christian snapped, '*The White Hotel* is a bit heavy for a kid who still believes that fairies live at the bottom of the garden.'

I must say this surprised me. I went down to the bottom of the garden yesterday. It is covered in rusting toys and stinking garden rubbish. It is hardly Fairyland.

At 11.30 p.m., I opened *The White Hotel*, read for ten minutes, then got out of bed and bolted the door. It must never fall into Alpha's hands.

Monday April 29th

Babysat. Christian is at the semi-final of a darts competition with his dictaphone and clipboard. Do the big-bellied darts players realize that they are taking part in a research project? I doubt it. They all seem to have tunnel vision, which I suppose is an advantage if you play darts for a living.

Christian told me today that Bianca was enquiring about me, asking if I'd settled in. He told her that the kids like me. I wish he'd told me. Christian asked me why I don't ask Bianca for a date. I answered nonchalantly that I was too busy. But, dear journal, the truth is that I'm afraid *she might refuse.* My ego is but a frail and fragile thing and furthermore am I sure I want to commit myself to a person who works in a newsagent's shop?

Notes on Bianca:

Negative

1. She is pleasant-looking but certainly not a head-turner, unlike Leonora, who is capable of stopping the traffic.
2. When I mentioned that my walk to work was 'pleasantly Chekhovian', largely due to the blossoming cherry trees, she looked at me blankly and asked me what 'Chekhovian' meant.
3. Her hips do not look capable of bearing a child.
4. She wears Doc Marten boots.

5. She is a Guns 'n' Roses fan.

Positive
1. She is kind, especially to the children who linger over the sweets section in the newsagent's.
2. I seem to be able to make her laugh.
3. Her skin looks like white silk. I have a strange desire to stroke her face whenever I am close to her.

Tuesday April 30th

I'm glad April is over. It is a bitter-sweet month. The blossom is out, but the wind still swells around and flaps the bottoms of your trousers unless you tuck them into your socks.

Beard bushy now. Food gets caught in it. Brown pointed out a piece of egg white at 9.30 a.m. I ate my boiled egg at 7.39 this morning. Since that time, I have spoken to, or been seen by, at least thirty people. Why did no one else point out that I had egg white in my beard? It is not as if it was a *small* piece. As egg white goes, it was quite a large piece, and as such, impossible to overlook. I will have to buy a small hand mirror and check my beard regularly after meals. I cannot risk such social embarrassment happening again.

Wednesday May 1st

Babysat. Griffith asked me to help him with his model of a Scud missile, which he is making out of a toilet roll tube and cut-up bits of washing-up liquid bottle. I pointed out to him that I am a pacifist.

Griffith (six) said, 'If your sister was being threatened by a gang of vicious thugs, would you stand by and do nothing?'

I said, 'Yes.' Griffith doesn't know my sister Rosie. She is quite capable of seeing off a gang of vicious thugs.

Christian was back from his karaoke evening by 11 p.m. Apparently, he'd been forced to sing 'Love is a Many Splendoured Thing' in order to keep his cover. So his research project *is* an undercover operation. That explains why Christian changes out of his ragged denims and into his Sta-Pressed polyesters before joining his unsuspecting fellow low-culture vultures.

Thursday May 2nd

Read through the whole of *Lo! The Flat Hills of My Homeland* manuscript so far. It is crap from start to finish.

Friday May 3rd

Perhaps I was too harsh last night. *Lo!* has passages of sheer brilliance. About five.

Saturday May 4th

Left *Lo!* on kitchen table overnight. No comment from Christian this morning, though Alpha said, 'You've spelt "success" wrong on page four. It's got two c's and two s's.' Christian didn't even look up from his *Sun*.

If there's one thing I can't bear, it's a precocious child. It's completely unnatural. I was tempted to tell Alpha that any fairy living in the Hell Hole at the bottom of her garden should have a tetanus jab, but I didn't.

I received the new Plumbs catalogue this morning, offering me four tapestry-look cushions with frilled edges at the bargain price of £27.99. How did they track me down? The envelope came direct from Plumbs to the Banbury Road. Are they watching me?

Sunday May 5th

Put blazer on and went for my customary Sunday walk around the Outer Ring Road at 2 p.m. Some old git in a Morris Minor stopped and asked me for directions to the Oxford Bowling Club. As if *I'd* know! Returned to find house full of Christian's friends having what he described as a 'fondue party'. They were dipping raw vegetables into a stinking pot of what looked like yellow emulsion paint. I declined to join them.

Monday May 6th

Bianca was passing as I left for work this morning, so we walked part of the way together. As we crossed at the lights, her hand brushed mine. An electric shock passed through me. I apologized and put my hand in my raincoat pocket to prevent another such occurrence. She took off her Sony headset and invited me to listen to her Guns 'n' Roses tape. After five minutes I handed it back to her. I couldn't stand the din.

Tuesday May 7th

Bianca was there again outside the house this morning. I don't know why she keeps coming down this road. It's not on her route to work.

Babysat. The kids went to bed at 9.30 p.m., after I'd read them the first three chapters of *Lo!* For once, they seemed quite tired, yawning, etc.

Wednesday May 8th

Bianca there yet again, tying the laces on her Docs. She told me that she gets bored in the evenings – she hasn't got that many friends in Oxford. She misses the cinema especially, but she is fed up with going on her own. She went on and on about Al Pacino. She has seen *Sea of Love* eleven times. I haven't seen it once. Personally, I can't stand the man. I told her that I too haven't seen a film in ages. When she left me and went into the newsagent's, she looked irritable. Pre-menstrual, probably.

Thursday May 9th

Babysat. At 7.30 p.m. I offered to read more of *Lo!* to the kids, but they said, as one, that they were very tired and wanted to go to bed! I had a peaceful night washing my working wardrobe and shampooing my beard. Christian got back at 1 a.m. after observing a fight in an Indian restaurant. I advised him to put his trousers in cold water to soak overnight. Turmeric is one of the most stubborn stains known to man. It is a pig to shift once it has gained a hold.

Monday May 13th

A terrible scandal at lunchtime today! Megan Harris and Bill Blane were caught in the act of photocopying their private parts! They would have got away with it, had the machine not jammed. They have both been suspended on full pay, pending an internal enquiry. I am quite pleased. It has saved me from having to photocopy two hundred pages of Newport Pagnell newt drivel.

Tuesday May 14th

It is totally unfair. Because of Bill's suspension, I have been given responsibility for the entire Badger Department. Brown threw the badger case histories on my desk and said, 'You're a friend of Bill's. Sort this out.'

Just because Brown was the one to force the photo-copy room door open yesterday, there's no need to take it out on me. He may have lost a mistress and a secretary, but he must remember what he learned on his managerial training course and keep his head.

Wednesday May 15th

Up at dawn to catch taxi to badger set. I must learn to drive. On the return journey, the taxi driver kept complaining about the smell. I had the fresh badger droppings in a sealed DOE jar, so how the aroma came in contact with the taxi driver's nose is a mystery to me. Personally, I found the fresh air 'pine tree' hanging from the roof of his taxi to be much more olfactorily offensive.

Friday May 17th

I am already up to my ears in newts and badgers, and now Brown is hinting that I may also be given responsibility for *natterjack toads*! He is obviously trying to force me into resigning or having a nervous breakdown due to overwork.

Photocopies of Megan's and Bill's private parts are being passed around the office. I think this is absolutely disgusting – a total invasion of their private lives, not to mention their private parts. Anyway the copies are so blurred that it is impossible to tell which is Bill's and which is Megan's. That photocopier never did work properly.

Bianca came round with Palmer's newspaper bill tonight. I answered the door and would have invited her in, but I didn't want her to think that sexual intercourse was on my mind – though, of course, it was. It's never off my mind. She had obviously gone to some trouble with her clothes, for a change. She was wearing tight denim jeans, high-heeled ankle boots and a white shirt which was tucked into a brown leather belt. She had recently washed her hair. I could smell Wash 'n' Go – the shampoo I use myself. It was on the tip of my tongue to ask her if she would come in for coffee, but something held me back.

She didn't seem to want to move off the doorstep – she kept talking about how fed up she was with having nothing to do in the evening. I was forced to stand in a cold wind, wearing only a shirt and trousers. This could result in a severe chill. I must check my temperature over the next few days.

Sunday May 19th

As predicted, I woke up yesterday feeling feverish, so I had three tablespoons of Night Nurse (though it was only 8.30 in the morning) and went back to sleep. Today, Christian knocked on my door at 12.30 p.m. and asked if I could watch the kids for three hours while he attended a 'Stag Strip' at a Working Men's Club. I reluctantly agreed and dragged myself out of bed.

I myself, personally, have never watched a strip show. I wouldn't know how to arrange my facial features. Would I watch with studied indifference like

TV detectives when they are forced to interview scumbag low-life in strip joints? Would I smile and laugh as though *amused* by the sight of a young woman taking her clothes off? Or would I swallow frequently, pant and goggle my eyes and reveal to onlookers that I am sexually excited? I fear the latter.

When Christian returned, he went upstairs. The shower was running for at least three quarters of an hour. I suspect he was symbolically cleansing himself.

Today was an Oombagoomba day, so I didn't – indeed, *couldn't* – talk to the kids.

The Chancellor, Norman Lamont, is going to sue a sex therapist for damages. But *how* did she damage you, Lamont? The British people should be told.

A letter from *Reader's Digest* arrived on Saturday, informing me that my name has been shortlisted out of many hundreds of thousands to receive a huge cash prize! All I have to do is agree to subscribe to the *Reader's Digest* magazine! It is easy to sneer at *Reader's Digest*, but it has to be said that they are an extremely handy way for busy bibliophiles to keep abreast of matters literary.

Plumbs have also written to me, offering to supply a lace circular tablecloth, plus a plywood circular table, should I not already have one. I must say I was quite tempted by both.

Thursday May 23rd

Christian held a drinks party last night and Cavendish and Pandora came round. I tried to engage Pan in conversation, but every time I did, I could see her eyes looking past me over my shoulder. Am I such boring company?

At 8 o'clock, Bianca turned up in a shiny, tight black dress. I introduced her to Pandora. Pandora said to her, 'That's a great dress, Bianca. God, don't you love lycra? What did we do without it?' They then yakked on about lycra for half an hour. In my opinion, Pandora's expensive education has been entirely wasted.

There must have been at least fifty people in the living-room/kitchen/study at one point. The majority of them were graduates, but you would never have known it from their conversation. The main topics were, in order:

1) *The Archers*
2) Football (Gazza)
3) Lycra
4) University cuts
5) Princess Diana
6) Alcoholism
7) The Oxford murder
8) Oats
9) Rajiv Gandhi being burnt
10) The Gossard Wonderbra

Call themselves intellectuals! My efforts to talk about my book, *Lo! The Flat Hills of My Homeland*, were met with cool indifference. Yes! The so-called 'best brains' in the land listened to me for a few minutes, then made feeble excuses to leave my company. At one point, just as I was telling him about my hero's apprenticeship to a cobbler in Chapter Eleven, a man called Professor Goodchild moved away, saying: 'Please spare me the sodding details.'

Yet only minutes later, I overheard him talking about his fish tank and how best to clean it.

Bianca left at 11.30 in the company of a dubious-looking type in a black leather jacket. He is something big in astrophysics, apparently, though in my opinion he looked like the type of moron who wouldn't know which end of a telescope to put his eye to.

As we were cleaning up after the party, Christian said, 'Adrian, take a tip from me, throw that bloody blazer away. Buy yourself some fashionable, young man's clothes!'

I replied (quite wittily, I thought), 'Lycra doesn't suit me.' He looked puzzled for a moment, then continued to wash the glasses.

Pandora also commented unfavourably, saying, 'That fucking awful blazer: give it to Oxfam, for Christ's sake.'

Perhaps I will.

I lay awake for hours imagining Bianca and the astrophysicist gazing at the stars together. Would he trust her with his telescope?

Friday May 24th

A household on my route to work has acquired an American pit bull terrier. On the surface, it seems to be a friendly beast. All it does is stand and grin through the fence. But in future I will take a different route to work. This is a considerable inconvenience to me, but I cannot risk facial disfigurement. I would like the photograph on the back of the jacket of my book to show my face as it is today, not hideously scarred. I know that plastic surgeons can work miracles, but from now on I am taking no chances.

Brown was in a foul mood today. He has had a letter from Megan's solicitor. She is threatening to sue him for defamation of character, unless she is reinstated immediately. I hope Brown caves in. Megan's replacement, Ms Julia Stone, is one of those superior types who never lose their money in chocolate machines in railway stations.

Saturday May 25th

Oxford is full of sightseers riding on the top deck of the tourist buses and walking along the streets gazing upwards. It is extremely annoying to us residents to be asked the way by foreigners every five minutes. Perhaps it is petty of me, but I quite enjoy sending them in the wrong direction.

I have just remembered! When I gave my blazer to the Oxfam shop yesterday, my condom was in the top pocket. This means that, should a sexual opportunity arise today, I will be unprepared. It also means that I can no longer go into the Oxfam shop – at least, not until Mrs Whitlow, the volunteer helper I gave it to, dies or retires. Mrs Whitlow has often congratulated me on being a 'decent, clean-living young man', though I have given her absolutely no grounds for thinking so.

Monday May 27th

Why do the banks have to close just because it is a Bank Holiday? It is a day when people want to *spend* money, isn't it? Borrowed £5 from Christian for Durex and bananas.

Tuesday May 28th

I have just finished Chapter Twelve of *Lo! The Flat Hills of My Homeland*, 'The Dog It Had To Die':

He closed the front door of his mother's house with a sigh. He had left her slumped on the kitchen table surrounded by brimming ashtrays and empty Pilsner cans. Upstairs, his father was injecting heroin into his collapsed veins. The family pet, an American pit bull terrier, looked out from the front window of the squalid terraced house and growled, showing its fearsome jaws. He walked down the street and tossed off greetings to the stunted neighbours. A couple fornicated in an alley, their eyes dead, their motions automatic. He wept internally. Anguish gripped his soul. He rued the day he had been born. Then, suddenly, a shaft of sunlight fell across his path. He stood, mesmerized. Was it a sign, a portent, that his life would improve from now?

He turned and went back to the house. He opened the front door. The dog, Butcher, growled at him, so he strangled it until the dog lay dead at his feet. He felt Evil, but at the same time strangely Good. The dog had been nothing but a nuisance and nobody ever took it for a walk. His conscience was clear.

Wow! Powerful writing, or what? I believe Dostoevsky would be proud of me. Canine murder is surely a first in English fiction. I expect I'll get a few letters from English dog lovers when *Lo! The Flat Hills of My Homeland* is published, but I shall write back and point out that I am an artist and must go where my pen takes me.

Wednesday May 29th

Julia Stone and I had a brief conversation at the Autovent machine today, while my oxtail soup was pouring into my plastic cup. She asked me not to use the ladies' lavatory again. I pointed out to her that the men's lavatory had run out of toilet paper, but she said if I continued to 'invade female space', she would report me for sexual harassment. She also said that she had checked the post book and that I used more postage stamps than any other member of staff.

I told her in cold tones – though not as cold as my oxtail soup – that I wrote more letters, therefore I needed more stamps. But I fear I have made an enemy.

Ms Julia Stone is a daunting woman. My throat constricts whenever I have to talk to her. Lipstick might help. Her, not me.

Christian returned from the Golden Gate nightclub with a black eye. His crime was to look at a yob. Yes, the yob accused Christian of 'looking' at him. This is a frightening example of the disintegration of British society. Yobs used to *enjoy* people looking at them. From now on, I shall avert my eyes whenever I see a yobbish person approaching me.

After Christian had stopped fussing with his eye and gone to bed, I sat at the kitchen table and tried to get some sex into *Lo! The Flat Hills of My Homeland*.

Chapter Thirteen: Deflowering
He lay in bed in his Parisian bedroom. Fifi began to remove her lycra dress. His breathing rate increased. She stood revealed before him, her chest strained beneath her Gossard Wonderbra, her knickers were clean and nicely ironed. He reached out for her, but she said to him in her French accent, 'No, no, *mon amour*, I am thinking you must wait.'

His ardour increased as he noticed that her bottom was smooth and had no pimples. He groaned and . . .

It's no good. I can't write about sex. Not even French sex in Paris.

Saturday June 1st

Two letters, one from Plumbs, offering me a set of matching towels with my personal monogram embroidered on the hems; the other from Sharon Bott.

Dear Adrian,
  I hope you are well   long time no see   I saw your mum in town and we had a talk   she said how much Glenn looked like you   I said yes and she said is he our Adrians Sharon I must know   she just came out with it like that   I din't know what to say   I have got to confess I was seeing someone else at the time as I was seeing you I din't want to double time you Adrian but you was sometimes moody and I wanted some laffs I was only young. Glenn is going to school now and is a big boy. My mum says you should pay some money but I said no mum it would not be fair cause I dont no if Glenn is Adrians or not   Your mum gave me this address to write to you   I hope they're is not to many spelling mistakes and that but I never write anything now since I left school their is no need I saw Baz on the telly did you   He has done alright for himself I have not got a bloke now sinse Daryl run off with the video and

£35 I had saved for the gas   I have put a bit of wait on but I am going to go to Waitwatchers and get it off   You mum said she would babysit   she is so good to me.

Cheers,

Sharon

Sunday June 2nd

I spoke to my mother this morning and ordered her to keep her nose out of my affairs. She said, 'Glenn is the *result* of one of your affairs,' and put the phone down. From then on, I got the engaged signal.

I was enraged by my mother's interference. How dare *she* pontificate about *anybody*'s morals? I know for a fact that she was not a virgin on her wedding night. Grandma told me.

And anyway, my mother should not have spoken in the plural. I have not had *affairs*. I have had *an* affair. In the singular. With Sharon Bott, a simpleton who cannot differentiate between 'they're', 'there' and 'their' and is a virtual stranger to the comma and full stop. She probably thinks that a semi-colon is a partial removal of the intestines.

Memo to self: Is the kid mine? Blood test? Letter of denial?

2 *a.m.* Wrote to Sharon.

3 *a.m.* Destroyed the letter. (My reply to her must be carefully crafted. I need time to read up on the law relating to paternity.)

Tuesday June 4th

Thank God, Prince William has made a full recovery after being bashed on the head by a golf club. When I think how close we came to losing our future King, my heart stands still. Well, not literally *still*, it doesn't *stop*, but I'm glad the kid is better. I phoned Grandma in Leicester. She wanted to know why Prince Charles didn't pick his son up from the hospital. She said, 'Doesn't he know that it is traditional in our English culture?' She thinks that the monarchy is losing touch with the common herd and she complained bitterly that the Royal Yacht *Britannia* costs thirty-five thousand pounds a week to run.

5.00 *p.m.* The *Oxford Mail* has just informed me that the emir of Kuwait has yet to announce the date for democratic elections to be held in his country. Puzzling, considering all the trouble and expense the allies went to only recently. Get a move on, emir! I'm also informed by the *Oxford Mail* that the Royal Yacht *Britannia* costs thirty-five thousand pounds *a day!* *A day!* I phoned Grandma immediately and put her right. She was disgusted.

Query: Why does the emir of Kuwait spell his name with a small 'e'?

Friday June 7th

I spent the morning writing a report on a projection of newt births and the early afternoon on a report on the distribution of badgers. But I fear some of the paperwork has got mixed up. As I was photocopying the reports, I noticed that I had muddled a few facts. However, Brown was shouting down the corridor for the reports, so what could I do? His management meeting was due to start at 4 p.m., so I had no choice but to hand him the papers.

Saturday June 8th

Wrote to Sharon:

Dear Sharon,

How very nice to hear from you after all this time.

I'm afraid that there is no chance at all that I can be the father of your child, Glenn.

I have recently had my sperm counted and I was informed by the Consultant Spermatologist that my sperms are too weak to transform themselves into a child. This is a personal tragedy to me, as I had planned on having at least six children.

You mention in your letter that you were double-timing me. I was most upset to read this – our relationship was not ideal, I know; we came from different backgrounds: me: upper working/lower middle; you: lower working/ underclass. And, of course, our educational attainments are worlds apart, not to mention our cultural interests. But despite these differences, I had thought that we rubbed along quite well sexually. I see absolutely no reason why you should have betrayed me and sought out another sexual partner. I confess that I am devastated by your revelation. I feel cheap and used. I would be most obliged to you if you would stop seeing my mother. She is addicted to human dramas of any kind. She thinks of herself as a character in a soap opera. I suggest that you should go to Weight- watchers (not *Wait*watchers, by the way), and hire yourself a competent child-minder. My mother is not to be trusted with young children: she dropped me on my head at the age of six months, whilst taking a boiled egg out of a saucepan.

Anyway, Sharon, it was very nice to hear from you.

Regards,

Adrian

PS. Who were you double-timing me with? Not that it matters, of course. I have had a constant stream of lovers since our relationship ended. It is simple curiosity on my part. But I would like to know the youth's name, though it is not in the least important. Don't feel obliged to let me know. I just think it may help you to get it off your chest. Guilt can eat away at you, can't it? So would you please

write to me and let me know the youth's name? I think you
would feel better about yourself.

Sunday June 9th

I spent the day quietly, working on Chapter Fourteen
of my novel.

He looked at the young boy, who was poking a stick at a
natterjack toad. 'Stop!' he cried. 'It is one of an endangered
species. You must be kind to it.' The young child stopped
poking at the toad and came to hold his hand.

'Who are you?' lisped the child. He longed to shout, 'I
am your *father*, boy!' but it was impossible. He looked at
Sharon Slagg, the boy's mother, who weighed twenty-one
stone and had numerous split ends. How could he have
once enjoyed sexual congress with her?

He let go of the boy's hand and said, 'I am nobody, boy.
I am a stranger to you. I am simply a person who loves the
planet we live on – including the dumb creatures that we
share our planet with.'

With that, he walked away from his son. The boy
exclaimed, 'Please, stranger, don't go.' But he knew he must,
before Sharon Slagg looked up from *Damage*, the book she
was reading on the park bench. The boy said, 'I wish you
were my father, stranger, then I too would have a daddy to
come to parents' evenings.'

He thought his heart would break. Sobbingly, he walked

away across the grass until the boy was the size of an ant in the distance.

I don't mind admitting that this piece of writing had me wiping my eyes. God, I'm clever. I can tug at the heart strings like no other writer I know. I do feel that my book is now vastly improved by these additions. It still lacks narrative thrust (or does it?), but nobody can say that it doesn't engage the reader's emotions.

Thursday June 20th

Bianca came round tonight to borrow a cup of Basmati rice. She has stopped going out with the Stargazer: she said his breath smelled constantly of kiwi fruit.

She is a nicely spoken girl, with quite an extensive vocabulary. I asked her why she was serving in a newsagent's. She said, 'There are no jobs for qualified engineers.'

I was totally gobsmacked to learn that Bianca has an upper second degree in Hydraulic Engineering – from Edinburgh University. Before she left with the rice, I asked her to mend the leaking shower in my room. She said she would be pleased to come round tomorrow night and see to it for me. She asked if she should bring a bottle of wine with her. I said there was no need. She looked disappointed. I sincerely hope she is not an alcoholic or a heavy drinker who needs a 'nip' before she can do a job of work.

I am making good progress on the novel. I took out my epic poem *The Restless Tadpole* tonight. It is amazingly good, but I can't spare the time to finish it. The novel has to come first. There is no money in poetry. Our Poet Laureate, Ted Hughes, has been wearing the same jacket in his photograph for the past twenty years.

Friday June 21st

Bianca came round *avec* tool box, but *sans* wine. She hung about after she'd fixed the shower and talked about how lonely she is and how she longs to have a regular boy friend. She asked me if I have a regular girl friend. I replied in the negative. I sat in the armchair under the window and she lay on my bed in what an old-fashioned kind of man could have interpreted as a provocative pose.

I wanted to join her on the bed, but I wasn't sure how she would react. Would she welcome me with open arms and legs? Or would she run downstairs screaming and ask Christian to call the police? Women are a complete mystery to me. One minute they are flapping their eyelashes, the next they are calling you a sexist pig.

While I tried to work it out, a silence fell between us, so I started to talk about the revisions I am making to my book. After about twenty minutes, she fell into a deep sleep. It was a most awkward situation to be in.

Eventually, I went downstairs and asked Christian to come and wake her up. He sneered and said, 'You're unbelievably stupid at times.' What did he mean? Was he referring to my inability to fix my own shower head, or to my timidity regarding sex?

When Bianca woke up she looked like a sad child. I wanted to put my arms round her but before I could she had grabbed her tool box and run down the stairs without saying goodnight.

Saturday June 22nd

Had a most satisfactory shower this morning. The force of the water has improved considerably.

2.00 p.m. Worked on Chapter Fifteen. I have sent *him* to China.

11.30 p.m. I have brought *him* back from China. Can't be bothered to do all that tedious research. I just got him walking along the Great Wall, then flying back to East Midlands Airport. I went down to the kitchen to make myself a cup of hot chocolate and told Christian about my hero's trip to China. Christian said, 'But you told me that he is a pauper. Where would he get the money for his air ticket?' God, how I hate pedants!

1.00 a.m. Insert for Chapter Fifteen:

What was this on the mat? He bent down and picked up a letter from the *Reader's Digest*. On the front of the expensively papered envelope was written 'OPEN AT ONCE'. He obeyed. Inside was a letter and a cheque for one million pounds! He was fabulously rich! 'How shall I spend it all?' he asked the cat. The female cat looked back at him inscrutably. 'China?' he said. 'I'll have a day trip to China!'

I hope this satisfies my pedantic landlord and my most critical of readers.

Sunday June 23rd

At breakfast, I told Christian how my hero got the money to go to China. He now wants to know what my hero does with the *remaining* money. There is no pleasing him.

12 noon

Chapter Sixteen: A Gratuitous Act
The beggar outside Leicester bus station stared in disbelief as £999,000 showered down onto his head. *He* walked away, a pauper once again.

5.00 p.m. Saw Bianca walking towards me as I was returning from my perambulations around the Outer

Ring Road this afternoon. She was wearing shorts and a T-shirt: her legs, apart from the ankles, looked superb, long and slim. I hurried towards her. To my astonishment, she crossed over the road and ignored me. So much for Christian telling me that she fancies me! It's certainly a good job I didn't join her on the bed the other night. I could be in prison now, on a sexual assault charge.

The next time I go to the library I will try to find a book that explains to the intelligent layman how women's brains work.

Summer

Wednesday July 3rd

Brown reminded me today that I have two weeks' holiday entitlement which I will lose unless I take it within the next two months.

Rang my travel agent. Told her I want two weeks in Europe in a four star hotel with half board, but for no more than £300. She promised to ring back if anything turned up in Albania. I said, 'Not Albania, I hear the food is inaudible.' After I'd put the phone down, I remembered that the word for bad food is, of course, 'inedible'. I hope I'm not suffering from an early onset of senile dementia. Word-loss is an early signal.

Friday July 5th

The travel agent rang today. Unfortunately, the call was put through to Brown's office, where I was being reprimanded because of a mix-up over the newt and badger reports. The Department of Transport had received the erroneous intelligence that a family of badgers had appeared on the route of the projected Newport Pagnell bypass. Naturally, I was constrained by Brown's presence, so I was unable to concentrate on what the travel agent was saying.

I said that I would ring her back, but she said, 'You must book it *now* if you want it.'

I said, 'Book what?'

She said, 'Your holiday. A week on the Russian lakes and rivers, and a week in Moscow. A fortnight for £299.99, full board.'

'Go ahead,' I said.

Saturday July 6th

Rang 'Easy-pass' Driving School and booked a free lesson as advertised in the *Oxford Mail*. I take to the road on Thursday, July 18th.

I have taken driving lessons before, but have been badly let down by my previous instructors. They were all incompetent.

Sunday July 7th

Babysat while Christian went to bingo. He won £7.50 and was near to winning the area prize of £14,000. He only needed two fat ladies.

Monday July 8th

Worked on *Lo!* Shall I give *him* a name? If so, what shall it be? It needs to express his sensitivity, his courage, his individualism, his intellectual vigour, his success with women, his affinity with nature, his proletarian roots.

Tuesday July 9th

How about Jake Westmorland?

Wednesday July 10th

Maurice Pritchard?

Thursday July 11th

Oscar Brimmington?

Friday July 12th

Jake Pritchard?

Saturday July 13th

Maurice Brimmington?

Sunday July 14th

A decision will have to be made soon. I can't move on with my book until it has. Christian prefers 'Jake Westmorland'. However, the man in the greengrocer's likes the sound of 'Oscar Brimmington'. Whereas a bus conductor, whose opinion I sought, was very keen on 'Maurice Westmorland'.

Monday July 15th

Spent the day babysitting. I got the kids to test me on the Highway Code. Somebody kept ringing the house tonight. A woman. All she said was, 'Hello.' But when I asked who was calling she put the phone down. It sounded like Bianca, but why should she behave in such a childish manner?

Tuesday July 16th

Brown had to have his surgical corset adjusted at the Radcliffe Hospital this morning, so I took the opportunity to go into his office and look at my file: 'MOLE – ADRIAN.'

FORESIGHT – NONE

PUNCTUALITY – POOR

INITIATIVE – NONE

RELIABILITY – QUITE GOOD

HONESTY – SUSPECTED OF PILFERING POSTAGE
   STAMPS

ACCEPTANCE OF RESPONSIBILITY – POOR

RELATIONS WITH OTHERS – QUITE GOOD

I believe his 'A' level Biology qualification to be
   bogus.

Wednesday July 17th

Dear Mr Brown,

It is with great regret that I write to inform you of my intention to resign from the Department of the Environment. I will of course serve out my statutory two months' notice. I have been unhappy for some time now with how the department is run. I feel that my talents have been wasted. Collecting badger faeces was not in my original job description.

Also, in my opinion, the protection of animals has reached ludicrous levels. The beasts have more rights than I do. Take bats. If I were to hang upside down and defecate in a church, I would be taken away to an institution. Yet bats are *encouraged* by conservationists such as yourself,

Mr Brown. It's no wonder that our churches are empty of parishioners.

I remain, sir,

Adrian Mole

At 10.00 a.m. I wrote the above letter, put it into an envelope and wrote 'FOR THE ATTENTION OF MR BROWN'.

At 11.00 a.m., after staring down at the envelope for a full hour, I put it under my blotting pad. Thinking perhaps that I could brazen it out regarding the bogus 'A' level.

At midday, while I was at the Autovent, the envelope disappeared. I searched my cubicle but found nothing, apart from my little blue comb.

At 1.00 p.m., I was summoned to Brown's office and told to clear my desk and leave the premises immediately. He gave me an envelope which contained a cheque for £676.31 = two months' pay plus holiday money less tax and National Insurance.

Who delivered my resignation letter? I suspect the Sexually Harassed One.

So, like three and a half million of my fellow citizens, I am without work.

1 a.m. Christian got me drunk tonight. I had two and a half glasses of Vouvray and a pint of draught Guinness in a can.

Thursday July 18th
Driving Lesson

Stayed in bed until 2 p.m. My driving instructor is a woman called Fiona. She is old (47) and has got lots of loose skin around her neck, which she pulls at in times of crisis. I did *tell* her that it is over a year since I was behind the wheel. I did *ask* if I could practise first on Tesco's Megastore out-of-town car park, but Fiona refused and forced me to drive on real roads with real traffic. So what happened at the roundabout was not my fault. Fiona should have been quicker with the dual controls.

Friday July 19th

A letter from Faber and Faber:

Dear Mr Mole,

I am afraid that I am returning your manuscript, *Lo! The Flat Hills of My Homeland*.

It is a most amusing parody of the English *naïf* school of fiction.

However, we do not have a place for such a book on our list at the moment.

Yours sincerely,
Matthew Evans

After reading the letter six times, I tore it in pieces. Mr Evans will be sorry one day. When my work is being auctioned in hotel rooms, I will instruct my agent to disqualify Mr Evans from the bidding.

There was no reason to get up, so I stayed in bed all day, wondering if there was any point in going on. Pandora despises me, I am out of work and I am incapable of driving a car in a straight line. At 7 p.m. I got out of my bed and rang Leonora. A man answered the phone: 'De Witt.'

'It's Adrian Mole,' I said. 'Could I speak to Leonora?'

'My wife's dressing,' he said; which threw me for a while. Images of Leonora in various lingerie outfits flashed into my mind.

'It's an emergency,' I managed to croak out. I heard him put the receiver down with a crack and shout, 'Darling, it's for you. Something about moles.'

There was a muttered oath, and then Leonora came on the phone.

'Yes?'

'Leonora, I'm in despair. Can I come round and see you?'

'When?'

'Now.'

'No, I'm giving a dinner party at eight and the first course is an asparagus soufflé.'

I wondered why she would think I was remotely interested in her menu.

'I need to talk to you,' I said. 'I've lost my job, my

novel's been rejected and I crashed the driving school car yesterday.'

'They are all life experiences,' she said. 'You will come out of this a stronger man.'

I heard her husband shouting something in the background. Then she said, 'I have to go. Why don't you talk to that girl, Bianca? Goodbye.'

I did as I was told. I went and stood outside Bianca's house and looked up at her flat. Nobody went in or came out.

After watching for an hour I went home and got back into bed. I hope the De Witts and their guests all choked on their asparagus soufflé.

Saturday July 20th

Cassandra Palmer turned up on the doorstep this afternoon. Christian's face turned white when he saw his wife. The children greeted her politely, but without much enthusiasm, I noticed. She looks as though she wrestles in mud for a living. I loathed her on sight. I cannot stand big women who shave their heads. I prefer them with hair.

Her first words to me were, 'Oh, so *you*'re the cuckoo in the nest.'

Sunday July 21st

The dictatorship of Cassandra started this morning. Our household is not allowed to drink tap water, coffee, tea or alcohol, nor to eat eggs, cheese, chocolate, fruit yoghurt, Marks & Spencer's lemon slices . . . etc., etc. The list goes on forever. There are also things we mustn't say. I happened to mention that Bianca's boss, the newsagent, is a fat man. Cassandra snapped, 'He's not fat, he's dimensionally challenged.'

I laughed, thinking this was a good joke, but Cassandra's mouth turned into a grim slit and with horror I realized she was serious.

Christian remarked to his wife over lunch that he was losing his hair, 'going bald' were his words. Once again, Cassandra snapped into action.

'You're a little follicularly disadvantaged, that's all,' she said, as she inspected the top of her husband's head.

I cannot share this house with that woman, or *her* language. It is not as though she is pleasant to look at. She is as ugly as sin, or, as she might put it, she is facially impaired.

Monday July 22nd

I asked Bianca if she would keep a lookout for suitable accommodation. She agreed, though there is nothing to keep me here in Oxford any more, apart from my unrequited love for Dr Pandora Braithwaite.

Tuesday July 23rd

Dr Braithwaite
Since you gained your Ph.D.
You have had no time for me.
You loved me once, you could again.
Pandora, give up other men!
You swore to love me for all time.
As long as Moon and June would rhyme.
Please marry me and be my wife.
For you I'll sacrifice my life.
I'll stay at home, I'll cook and clean
In the background, never seen.
When you return from brainy toil,
I'll have the kettle on the boil.
While you translate from Serbo-Croat,
I will shake our coco doormat.
I'll gladly wash your duvet cover,
If only I can be your lover.

I put the poem through Pandora's door at 4 a.m. This is my last-ditch attempt to sound out Pandora's true feelings for me. Leonora has said that I must move on emotionally. What will Pandora's reaction be?

Wednesday July 24th

I found this letter on the doormat.

Dear Adrian,

You woke me at 4 a.m. with your clumsy manipulation of my letter box. Your poem caused my lover and me much merriment. I hope, for your sake, that it was *meant* to be funny. If it was *not*, then I urge you to seek further psychiatric advice from Leonora. She told me that you have stopped seeing her regularly. Is it the cost?

I *know* you can afford £30 a week. You don't drink, or smoke, or wear decent clothes. You cut your own hair, you don't run a car. You don't gamble or take drugs. You live rent-free. Withdraw some money from your precious Building Society and *get help*.

Regards,
Pandora

PS. Incidentally, I am *not* a Ph.D., as you state in your poem. I am a D. Phil. A subtle but important difference here in Oxford.

So that's it. If Pandora came to me tomorrow, begging to be Mrs A. A. Mole, I would have to turn her down. I have moved on. It's Leonora I must see. Must.

Thursday July 25th

5.15 p.m. I have just phoned Leonora and insisted that she gives me an emergency appointment. I said I had something momentous to tell her. She agreed reluctantly.

5.30 p.m. I burst into Leonora's room this evening and found her with another client, a middle-aged man who was sobbing into a Kleenex (woman trouble, I suppose). I was ten minutes early and Leonora was furious and ordered me to wait outside. At 6.30 p.m. precisely, I knocked on her door and she shouted, 'Come.' She was still in a bad mood and so I tried to make conversation and asked her what had upset the sobbing middle-aged man. This angered her even more. 'What is said to me in this room remains confidential,' she said. 'How would *you* feel if I talked about *your* problems to my other clients?'

'I don't like to think about you having other clients,' I confessed.

She sighed deeply and curled a hank of black hair around her finger. 'So what's the momentous happening?' she said eventually.

'I've moved on from Pandora Braithwaite,' I said, and I told her about the poem and Pandora's reaction to it and my reaction to Pandora's reaction. At that moment, a tall, dark man wearing a suede shirt came in. He looked surprised to see me.

'Sorry, darling. I can't find the small grater, for the parmesan.'

'Second drawer down, darling, next to the Aga,' she said, looking up at him in rapt adoration.

'Terribly sorry,' he said.

When he'd gone out, I stood up and said, 'How dare your husband interrupt my consultation with his petty domestic enquiries?'

Leonora said, 'My husband didn't know you were here. I squeezed you in, if you remember.' Her tone was carefully measured, but I noticed that a vein was pulsating on the side of her temple and that she was wringing her hands.

'You should learn to express your anger, Leonora. It's no good for you to bottle it up,' I said.

She then said, 'Mr Mole, you are not making progress with me. I suggest you try another analyst.'

'No,' I said. 'It's you I want to see. You're my reason for living.'

'So,' she said. 'Think what you're saying. Are you saying that without me you would commit suicide?'

I hesitated. Noises of pans banging and glasses tinkling came up from the basement, as did a delicious smell that made my mouth water. For some reason I blurted out, 'Could I stay to dinner?'

'No. I never socialize with my clients,' she said, looking at her slim, gold watch.

I sat down and asked, 'How mad am I, on a scale of one to ten?'

'You're not mad at all,' she said. 'As Freud said, "It

is impossible for a therapist to treat either the mad or those in love.'"

'But I *am* in love. With you,' I added.

Leonora sighed very deeply. Her breasts rose and fell under her embroidered sweater.

'That is why I think that seeing another therapist would be a good idea. I have a friend, Reinhard Kowolski, who has a superb reputation . . .'

I didn't wait to hear any more about Herr Kowolski. I left her room and put three ten pound notes on the hall table, next to the laughing Buddha and walked out into the street.

I felt angry, so I decided to express my anger and I kicked an empty Diet Coke can all the way home.

When I got to the attic, I laid out all my job-searching clothes ready for the morning. Then I lay on my bed with the *Oxford Mail* and ringed all the likely looking jobs in the situations vacant columns.

There was nothing that required one 'A' level in English.

Friday July 26th

Went to the Job Centre, but the queue was too long, so returned to find Cassandra in the kitchen, examining the children's books, pen in hand. She picked one up and changed *Winnie the Pooh* to *Winnie the Shit*. 'I hate ambiguity,' she explained, as she snapped the cap back on her Magic Marker.

Saturday July 27th

Saw Brown in W. H. Smith's, buying the current wild-life magazines. He smiled and said, 'Enjoying your life of leisure, Mole?'

I forced a smile to my lips and said, 'On the contrary, Brown, I am working as hard as ever. I am a middle manager at the Book Trust in Cambridge, at £25,000 a year, plus car. I got the position thanks to my having English Literature at "A" level.' Brown stormed off, forgetting to pay for his magazines. He was stopped on the pavement by a security guard. I didn't hang around to watch Brown's humiliation.

Sunday July 28th

Stayed in room all day, out of Cassandra's way. She is insisting that everyone in the house meditates for half an hour each morning. Christian has stopped doing his research into popular culture. Cassandra objected to the smell of cigarette smoke on his clothes when he returned from his low-class haunts. If she is not careful, she will wreck his academic career.

I am living on my savings, but I cannot continue to do so. The State will have to keep me – after all, I didn't ask to be born, did I? And one day the State will be glad it supported me. When I am a high-rate taxpayer.

However, before I throw myself on its mercy, I am going to tramp the streets of Oxford tomorrow and look for a job, any job that doesn't involve driving or working with animals.

Next year, I will have lived for a quarter of a century and as yet I have made no mark on the world – apart from winning a *Leicester Mercury* literary prize when I was seventeen.

If I died tomorrow, what would be written on my tombstone?

> Adrian Albert Mole
> Unpublished novelist
> and pedestrian
>
> Mourned by few
> Scorned by many
> Winner of the *Leicester Mercury*
> 'Clean Up Leicester' Essay Prize

Tuesday July 30th

Why do beggars *always* want money for a cup of tea? Don't any of them drink coffee?

Wednesday July 31st

Why didn't palace flunkies arrange for Princess Diana to be kept dry at the open-air Pavarotti concert last night? If she develops pneumonia and dies, the country will be plunged into crisis and Charles will be devastated with grief. He obviously adores her. Somebody's head should roll.

Thursday August 1st

Dear Adrian,

I was sorry to read about your poor cwallity seed   the person I was seeing on the side was barry kent   I feel better now it is off my chest.

Yours sinserely,
    Sharon

Barry Kent! I should have known! He is an amoral, talentless turd! He is lower than a cesspit. He has the prose style of a *Daily Sport* leader writer. He wouldn't know what a semi-colon was if it fell into his beer. The little I have read of *Dork's Diary* forced me to the conclusion that Kent should be arrested and charged with criminal assault on the English language. He deserves to burn in everlasting hell with a catherine wheel tied to his cheating penis.

Friday August 2nd

Dear Sharon,

Many thanks for your commiserations regarding my 'seed', as you put it. May I suggest that you get in touch with Barry Kent (who, as you know, is now both *rich* and famous) and ask him to contribute to Glenn's upbringing? The least Kent can do is to send Glenn to a private school, thus giving his child an excellent start in life.

I remain,

Yours,

Adrian

PS. I am absolutely sure that Barry will be thrilled to hear that he has a child.

PPS. Eton is quite a good private public school.

Sunday August 4th

Cassandra announced at breakfast that she has taken the locks off the bathroom and lavatory doors. 'Inhibitions about nakedness and bodily functions are the reason why the English are no good at sex,' she said. She looked pointedly at her husband, who blushed and rubbed the side of his nose.

The Queen Mother is 91 today. I suppose she doesn't think it is worth getting her teeth seen to now. I can see her point.

Monday August 5th

Contacted Foreign Parts, the travel agents, about my Russian cruise and explained that I have been made redundant and would like to cancel and have my money back. The travel agent told me that it was impossible and told me to refer to the small print on my documents. I peered in vain and eventually went to Boots and bought a pair of 'off the peg' reading spectacles for £7.99. The travel agent was right; I will have to go.

Tuesday August 6th

Christian told me (shamefaced) that Cassandra requires my attic room. She is opening a reincarnation centre where people can get in touch with their former selves. She wants me out of the attic by mid-September. I couldn't help myself. I burst out, 'Your wife is a cow!' Christian said, 'I know, but she used to be a kitten.'

So, no job and, when I get back from the Russian cruise, nowhere to live.

Thursday August 8th

Dear John Tydeman,

The last time I wrote to you, it was to apologize for clogging up the BBC's fax machines with my 700-page novel, *Lo! The Flat Hills of My Homeland*. You sent it back to me (eventually) and said, and I quote: 'Your manuscript is awash with consonants, but vowels are very thin on the ground, thin to the point of non-existence.'

You will, I am sure, be delighted to hear that I have now reinstated the vowels and have spent this year rewriting the first sixteen chapters, and I would value your comments on them. They are enclosed with this letter. I know you are busy, but it wouldn't take you long. You can read them in the BBC's coffee lounge during your coffee breaks, etc.

I remain, Sir,

Yours,

Adrian Mole

10.30 p.m. I have seen Leonora for the last time. She has dismissed me from my post as her client. I over-played my hand and declared my love for her. In fact, it wasn't so much a declaration, it was more of a proclamation. It was probably heard all over Oxford. Her husband heard it because he came into the room with a tea towel and a little blue jug in his hand and asked Leonora if she was all right.

'Thank you, Fergus, darling,' she said. 'Mr Mole will be leaving soon.'

'I'll be outside if you need me,' he said, and left, leaving the door slightly open.

Leonora said, 'Mr Mole, I am calling a halt to our professional relationship, but before you leave I would like to reassure you that your problems are capable of being solved.

'You expect too much of yourself,' she said, leaning forward sympathetically. 'Let yourself off the hook. Be *kind* to yourself. You've expressed your worries about world famine, the ozone layer, homelessness, the Aids epidemic, many times. These are not only your problems. They are shared by sensitive people all over the world. You can have no control over these sad situations – apart from donating money. However, over your personal worries, lack of success with your novel, problems with women, you do have a certain amount of control.' Here she stopped and she looked as though she wanted to take my hand, but she didn't.

'You are an attractive, healthy young man,' she said. 'I have not read your manuscript, so I can't comment on your literary talent or otherwise, but what I do know is that there is somebody out there who is going to make you happy.'

I turned on my dining chair and looked out of the window. 'Not literally out there, of course,' she snapped, following my glance. She stood up, shook my hand and said, 'There will be no charge for this session.'

I said, 'It isn't transference: it's true love.'

'I've heard that at least twenty times,' she said, softly. She rose to her feet. Her rings sparkled under the light and she shook my hand. As I left, I passed her husband, who was still drying the little blue jug twenty minutes later. A suitable case for treatment if ever I saw one.

'I intend to marry your wife one day,' I said, before closing the front door.

'Yes, that's what they all say. Cheerio.' He smiled and went towards Leonora and I closed the door on a painful – and expensive – period of my life.

Friday August 9th

Adrian,

What the fuck are you playing at, getting Sharon Bott to write to me and ask for money to send her sprog to fucking Eton? I'm down here at Jeanette Winterson's place, trying to finish my second novel and I can do without all this fucking rubbish.

Baz

Saturday August 10th

I looked in the Job Centre window today. There were three vacancies in the window. One for a 'mobile cleansing operative' (road sweeper?), one for a 'peripatetic catering assistant' (pizza delivery?) and one for a 'part-time clowns enabler' (!). I didn't exactly reach excitedly for the Basildon Bond on my return to Stalag Cassandra.

Sunday August 11th

Went to the newsagent's. Bianca is back from Greece. She has got a fantastic tan. She was wearing a low-cut white tee shirt, which displayed her breasts. They looked like small, ripe, russet apples. I asked her facetiously if she had had a holiday romance. She laughed and admitted that she had – with a fisherman who had never heard of Chekhov. I asked if she was going to continue the romance. She gave me a strange look and said: 'How would you *feel* about it if I did, Adrian?'

I was about to reply when a member of the underclass thrust a *Sunday Sport* into her hands, so the moment was lost.

10.00 p.m. How do I feel about Bianca's holiday romance? I'm always pleased to see her, but I can't stop comparing her to the lovely Leonora: Bianca is a Malteser: Leonora is an Elizabeth Shaw gold-wrapped after dinner mint.

Tuesday August 13th

I leave for Russia on Thursday. I bought myself a new toiletry bag – it's time I treated myself. I hope there are some decent women of childbearing age aboard.

I spent the evening packing. I decided not to take any books. I expect there will be a library on the ship, well stocked with the classics of Russian literature in good translations. I hope my fellow passengers are cultured people. It would be intolerable to have to share the dining room and decks with English lager louts. I decided to include a huge bunch of semi-ripe bananas amongst my luggage. I am used to eating a banana a day and I have heard they are in short supply in Russia.

Saturday August 17th

River camp – Russia
It is 7.30 p.m. There is no cruise ship. There are no passengers. Each member of our party is paddling their own canoe. I am crouched inside a two-man tent. Outside are swarms of huge, black mosquitoes. They are waiting for me to emerge. I can hear the river throwing itself over the rapids. With a bit of luck, I will die in my sleep.

The man I have been sharing my tent with, Leonard Clifton, is out chopping trees down with a machete, borrowed from Boris, one of our river guides. I sincerely hope that one of Clifton's trees falls on his horrible bald head. I cannot stand another night listening to his interminable anecdotes about the Church Army.

I told Boris earlier today that I would give him all my roubles if he would arrange for me to be airlifted to Moscow. He paused from repairing the hole in my canoe and said, 'But you must paddle now to the river's end, Mister Mole; there is no inhabitations, peoples or telephonings here.'

On my return to civilization, I will sue Foreign Parts for every penny they've got. At no time did they mention that I would be paddling a canoe, sleeping in a tent, or drinking water from the river. The worst privation of all is that *I have got nothing to read*. Clifton lent me his Bible, but it fell overboard at the last rapids. As I watched it sink, I shouted 'My God, my God, why hast thou forsaken me?' To the bewilderment of the rest of the group and of myself, I must admit.

Monica and Stella Brightways, the twins from Barnstaple, are outside leading the singing of 'Ten Green Bottles'. Leonard and the rest of the gang are joining in lustily.

10.00 p.m. Tent. I have just returned from the forest, where I was forced to urinate into the darkness. I stood with the others round the fire for a moment, drinking black tea.

Monica Brightways had a serious argument with

the scoutmaster from Hull. She claimed she saw him take two slices of black bread from the sack at lunch-time. He denied it vehemently and accused her of hogging the camp fire. Everyone took sides, apart from me, who loathes them both equally.

Capsized eleven times earlier today. The rest of the hearties were furious with me for holding them up. It is all right for them. They are all members of the British Canoe Union. I am a complete novice and crossing a lake in a force-nine gale is something out of my worst nightmare. The Waves! The Wind! The Water! The lowering black Russian sky! The Danger! The Fear!

I pray to God we may soon come to our journey's end. I long for Moscow. Though I will have to stay in my hotel room; the mosquitoes have attacked my face unmercifully. I look like the Elephant Man on acid.

Midnight The drinking of vodka is now taking place. From my tent I can hear every word. The Russians are maudlin. Every time they talk about 'our souls', the English snigger. I crave sleep. I also crave hot water and a flushing lavatory.

Moscow! Moscow! Moscow!

Wednesday August 21st

Moscow train
The lavatory on the train defies description. However, I'll try. After all, I am a novelist.

Imagine that twenty buffalo with loose bowels have been trapped inside the lavatory for two weeks. Then try to imagine that an open sewer runs across the floor. Add an IRA prisoner on dirty protest. Then concoct a smell by digging up a few decomposed corpses, add a couple of healthy young skunks and you come quite near to what the lavatory looks and smells like.

Leonard Clifton is writing to President Gorbachev to complain.

I said, 'I think Gorbachev has other things on his mind at the moment, such as preventing civil war and feeding his fellow citizens.'

A harmless remark, you might think, but Clifton went mad. He screamed, 'You have ruined my holiday, Mole, with your pathetic whingeing and nasty, cynical comments.'

I was totally gobsmacked. Nobody in the group came to my defence – apart from the Brightways twins, who had already informed the group at frequent intervals that they 'loved all living things'. So anything they had to say was irrelevant. They no doubt equate my life with that of a lugworm.

Thursday August 22nd

Hotel room – Moscow

I am staying in the 'Ukraina', near the Moskva River. It looks like a hypodermic syringe from outside. Inside, it is full of bewildered guests of all nationalities. Their bewilderment stems from the hotel staff's reluctance to pass on any information.

For instance, hardly anybody knows *where* meals are being served, or even *if* meals are being served.

For breakfast this morning I had a piece of black bread, four slices of beetroot, a sprig of fresh coriander and a cup of cold, black tea.

An American woman in the queue behind me wailed to her husband, 'Norm, I gotta have juice.'

Norm left the queue and went up to a group of loitering waiters.

I watched him mime an orange, first on the tree and then off the tree. The waiters watched him impassively, then turned their backs on him and huddled around a portable radio. Norm returned to the queue. His wife shot him a contemptuous look.

She said, 'I just gotta have some fruit in the morning. You *know* that, Norm. You know how my system seizes up.'

Norm pulled a face indicating that he remembered *exactly* what happened to his wife's system when it seized up. I thought fondly about the bunch of bananas upstairs in my room.

They were worth their weight in gold.

At nine-thirty, most of our group gathered in the foyer of the hotel ready to start our visit to Red Square. I lurked behind a pillar, dabbing TCP onto the fourteen mosquito bites which disfigured my face.

The Barnstaple twins, Monica and Stella Brightways,

kept us waiting for ten minutes, claiming that they had to wait for the lift to ascend to where their room was on the nineteenth floor. Eventually we set off in a bus which seemed to have an interior exhaust pipe next to my seat at the back. I coughed and choked on the diesel fumes and made a futile attempt to open the window. The coach driver was wearing a Gorbachev badge and seemed to be in a bad mood. Our coach parked on the edge of Red Square and we got out and gathered around our Intourist guide, Natasha. She held up a red and white umbrella, and we followed behind like moronic sheep. When we got to the Square, it became obvious that something was happening, a protest march or a demonstration of some kind was taking place. I lost sight of the red and white umbrella and became lost in the crowd. I heard an ominous rumbling behind me, but was unable to move.

An old lady in a headscarf shook her fist towards the noise. She screamed something in Russian. Spittle flew out of her mouth and landed on my clean sweater. Then the crowd parted and the rumbling grew nearer and the tracks of a Russian army tank clanked past an inch away from my right shoe. The tank stopped and a young man clambered aboard and began to wave a flag. It was the hammer and sickle flag I'd been used to seeing everywhere. The crowd roared its approval. What was happening? Had Moscow Dynamo won at football? No, something more important was taking place.

A young woman who wore too much blue eye-shadow said to me, 'Englishman, today you have witnessed the end of Communism.'

'I nearly got run over by a tank,' I said.

'A proud death,' she said. I reached into my pocket for a banana to boost my blood-sugar level. I started to peel it. The young woman's eyes filled with tears. I offered her a bite, but she misinterpreted my gesture and shouted something in Russian. The crowd roared and cheered. She then turned and told me she was shouting 'Bananas for all under Yeltsin!' The crowd began to chant. Then the young woman ate my banana.

'A symbolic gesture, of course,' she said.

When I returned to my room, I found a hefty young Russian woman sitting on a chair outside the door. She was wearing a low-cut brown lamé minidress.

She said, 'Ah, Mr Mole, I am Lara. I come to your room, to sleep, of course.'

I said, 'Is this part of the Intourist programme?'

Lara said, 'No. I am, of course, in love with you.'

She followed me into my room and went to the bunch of bananas on the bedside table. She looked down at them with lust in her eyes and I understood. It wasn't me she wanted: it was the bananas. I gave her two. She went away. Intercourse with her might have done me some harm. She had thighs like Californian redwoods.

Friday August 23rd

I lay awake most of the night, scratching at my mosquito bites and regretting my hasty decision and wondering how news about my bananas had spread. The next day the streets were full of rioting Muscovites and we were confined to the hotel.

After lunch (black bread, beetroot soup, a wizened piece of meat, one cold potato), I returned to my room to find that my bananas had gone. I was outraged.

I complained to Natasha, but she only said, 'You had *ten* bananas?' She looked misty-eyed and then snapped, 'You should, of course, have put them in the hotel safe. They will be changing hands on the black market by now.'

I found Leonard Clifton in the gloomy basement bar. There had been a coup against Gorbachev and then a counter-coup by Boris Yeltsin.

'This is bad news for Soviet Communism,' he said, 'but good news for Jesus.'

England! England! England!

I long for my attic room.

Monday September 2nd

Oxford

I am in bed, exhausted and hideously deformed. Why do mosquitoes exist? Why? Cassandra said they are 'a vital component of the food chain'. Well, I Adrian Mole, would gladly *pull* the chain on them. And, if the food chain collapses and the world starves, so be it.

I have written to Foreign Parts, threatening to report them to ABTA unless I receive *all* my money back, plus compensation for the double trauma suffered from the mosquitoes and the revolution.

Tuesday September 3rd

Christian passed by Foreign Parts today. He said it looked deserted. There was a pile of unopened letters on the doormat inside the shop.

Thursday September 5th

A reply from John Tydeman, Head of Drama, BBC Radio.

Dear Adrian,

To be perfectly honest, Adrian, my heart sank when I returned from holiday and saw that your manuscript, *Lo! The Flat Hills of My Homeland* had landed on my desk yet again. You say in your letter, 'I expect you are busy'. Yes, I damned well *am* busy, incredibly so.

What exactly is a 'coffee break'? I've never had a 'coffee break' during the whole of my long career with the BBC.

I drink coffee at my desk. I do not go to a 'coffee break' lounge where I loll about on a sofa and read handwritten manuscripts, 473 pages long. My advice to you (without reading your wretched MS) is to:

1) Learn to type
2) Cut it by at least half
3) Supply a SAE and postage. The BBC is suffering from a cash crisis. It certainly cannot afford to subsidize your literary outpourings.
4) Find yourself a *publisher*. I am *not* a publisher. I am the Head of Radio Drama. Though sometimes I wonder if I am Marjorie Proops.

I am sorry to have to write to you in such terms, but in my experience it is best to be frank with young writers.

> Yours, with best wishes,
> John Tydeman

Poor old Tydeman! He has obviously gone mad. 'Sometimes I wonder if I am Marjorie Proops' (!) – perhaps the Director General should be told that his Head of Radio Drama is suffering from the delusion that he is an agony aunt.

And he admitted that he hadn't even read the re-edited *Lo! What do we licence-payers pay for?*

Dear Mr Tydeman,

I would appreciate it if you could send my MS back, ASAP. I do not want it circulating around the corridors of the BBC and being purloined by a disaffected freelance producer, anxious to make his or her mark on the world of broadcasting.

Adrian Mole

PS. Allow me to inform you, sir, that you are *not* Marjorie Proops.

Saturday September 7th

Spent most of the day in a futile search for a reasonably priced room. As I made my weary way back home, I passed Foreign Parts. There was a note on the door:

This business is closed. All enquiries to Churchman, Churchman, Churchman and Luther, Solicitors.

I didn't take down the telephone number. It was already in my filofax, under 'S'. A middle-aged couple *were* taking the number down, though. They were due to depart tomorrow on a cycling holiday in 'Peter Mayle Country', Provence. They were facing the awful realization that they were not going to see the famous table on the infamous terrace, and possibly take tea with Pierre Mayle plus *femme*.

As the couple walked away, I heard her say to him: 'Cheer up, Derek, there's always the caravan at Ingoldmells.' A fine woman, indomitable in the face of disaster. Mr Mayle has been cheated of meeting a true Brit.

Sunday September 8th

I have decided to go with Jake Westmorland.

Chapter Seventeen: Jake – A Hero of Our Time

Jake stood on top of the tank in Red Square. What a good job I took Russian at school, instead of French, he thought. Then, quieting the multitudes by a small gesture of his hand, he spoke.

'I am Jake Westmorland,' he shouted. The revolutionary hordes bellowed their grateful recognition. A sea of banners waved joyously. The sultry Russian sunlight glinted on the dome of St Basil's Cathedral as Jake tried to quieten the crowds and begin his speech. The speech that he hoped would prevent the disintegration of the Soviet Union . . .

Monday September 9th

I have written eleven speeches for Jake and thrown them all in the bin. None of them was capable of changing the course of world history.

. . . But before Jake could make the speech that would almost certainly have saved the Soviet Union, a shot rang out and Jake fell off the tank and into the arms of Natasha, his Russian mistress. She threw Jake over her shoulder and the silent crowd parted to let them through.

Thursday September 12th

Cassandra has ordered me to be out of the house by noon on Saturday! The lousy, stinking undergraduates have hogged all the private rented accommodation. I had no choice but to throw myself on the mercy of Oxford Council. But the Council official I spoke to today maintained that I am 'intentionally homeless' and refused to help me. I have started collecting cardboard boxes. Either to pack my belongings in, or to sleep in – who knows?

Friday September 13th

Christian has taken the children to see his mother in Wigan. He is a spineless coward. The hideous Cassandra is walking around the house in her absurd clothes, singing her ludicrous rapping songs. I asked her tonight if I could store my books in the attic until I've found a place of my own. She replied, 'Books?' as though she'd never heard the word before.

I said, 'Yes, *books*. You know, those things with cardboard covers stuffed with paper. People read them, for pleasure.'

Cassandra snorted contemptuously. 'Books belong in the past, together with stiletto heels and Gerry and the Pacemakers. This is the nineties, Adrian. It's the age of technology.'

She went to her word processor and pressed a button. A series of little green men wearing Viking helmets filled the screen and began to fight with little red men wearing baseball caps, who came out of a cave. Cassandra leaned eagerly towards the screen. I sensed that our conversation was over and left the room.

Query: Is the world going mad, or is it me?

Saturday September 14th

8.30 a.m.

Options
1) Pandora (no chance)
2) Bianca (possible)
3) Mother (last resort)
4) Bed and breakfast (expensive)
5) Hostel (fleas, violence)
6) Streets

11.30 a.m.

1) Pandora turned me down flat. She is a true *Belle Dame sans Merci*.
2) Bianca is away attending a Guns 'n' Roses convention in Wolverhampton. Left note at newsagent's.
3) My mother is out gawping at a new crop circle just outside Kettering.

4) The cheapest B&B is £15.99 a *night*!
5) There is nothing under 'Hostel' in the phone book.
6) I hit the road at high noon.

11.35 p.m. Leicester. Bert Baxter's house
So, it has come to this. I am reduced to sleeping on a
Put-U-Up in a pensioner's living-room, which stinks
of cats. Baxter is charging me £5 for tonight, plus £2.50
for bacon and eggs. My mother's house is locked and
dark, and the key is not in its usual place under the
drain cover. In normal circumstances I would have
broken the small pantry window and climbed in,
but my mother has had a security system installed.
Delusions of grandeur, or what?

My father, supposedly penniless, is on holiday in
Florida with a rich divorcee called Belinda Bellingham.
I know I could go to my grandma's but I can't bear
her to find out that I am unemployed and homeless.
The shock could kill her. She has my GCSE certificates
framed on the hall wall. My 'A' level English certificate
is in a silver frame on the mantelpiece in her front
room. Why give such anguish to an elderly diabetic?

Monday September 16th

1.35 a.m. I am now trying to sleep on the sofa-bed in
my mother's living-room. As I write, the television
in my mother's bedroom is blaring. The washing
machine is on its spin cycle. The dishwasher is

shrieking and somebody is taking a shower. Subsequently, the water pipes are banging all over the house. My stepfather, Martin Muffet, has just gone upstairs with his DIY toolbox. Does nobody sleep in this house?

Tuesday September 17th

My grandma knows all. My mother has told her everything. She is disgusted. I hope she never finds out that Bert Baxter gave me a bed for the night.

Wednesday September 18th

G knows about B&B at BB's. She saw BB in C&A.

Friday September 20th

A postcard of Clifton Suspension Bridge came this morning.

Dear Adrian,
   I've only just got your message! Sorry I didn't see you before you left. That Cassandra is a sad woman all right!
   I've never been to Leicester. Is it nice? Hope so for your sake!
   There's a floor here for you if you fancy coming back to Oxford! I know where I can borrow a double mattress.

Let me know soon, please!

Love,

B.

The exclamation marks gave me some pain. Could I share a floor with a woman who was so profligate with them? And what would the sleeping arrangements be? This 'double mattress' she mentioned. Was it for me only? If so, why a double? I presume she has an adequate bed of her own. I decided to write an ambiguous reply, keeping my options open, but committing myself to nothing. My mother, who had brought the postcard to me in bed, wanted to know *everything* about 'B'. Height, weight, build, colouring, education, class, accent, clothes, shoes. 'Is she nice?' Have I 'slept with her'? 'Why not?' The Spanish Inquisition would be nothing compared to my mother. Nothing.

Dear Bianca,

It was most kind of you to write to me and offer the use of a double mattress and your floor.

I confess to you that when I asked you for your help in solving my temporary difficulty regarding my lack of accommodation, I was in somewhat of a panic.

I am surprised that you responded as you did. Ours has not been a long acquaintanceship. For all you know, I could have severe character faults or a psychotic personality.

I would urge caution in the future. I would not like to see you taken advantage of. I am not sure about my future plans. Leicester has a certain *je ne sais quoi*: it is quite pleasant in the autumn, when the fallen leaves give the pavements a little colour.

Yours,

Best wishes,

Adrian

Sunday September 22nd

I was looking forward to a traditional Sunday dinner with Yorkshire pudding and gravy, etc. But my mother informed me at 1.00 p.m. that she doesn't *do* Sunday dinner any more. Instead, we were driven four miles in Muffet's car to a 'Carvery' where we paid £4.99 a head to be served with slices of cardboard and dried up vegetables by a moronic youth in a chef's hat. My sister Rosie spilt Muffet's half pint of Ruddles all over our table. I tried to come to the rescue with half a dozen beer mats – but the beer mats refused to soak up any beer. They repelled all liquid. In the end, the moronic one threw us a stinking dishcloth.

Query: What is the purpose of modern beer mats? Are they now merely symbolic, like the crucifix?

6.00 p.m. My mother has informed me that I have got to pay her board of 'a minimum of thirty-five pounds a week, or you're out on your ear'. Does blood count for nothing in 1991?

Tuesday September 24th

My grandma has said I can move in with her, rent free, providing I cut the grass, wind the clocks and fetch the shopping. I agreed immediately.

Wednesday September 25th

I read the first three chapters of *Lo!* aloud to Grandma tonight. She thinks it is the best thing she has ever heard. She thinks that the publishers who rejected it are barmy. And she has got nothing but contempt for Mr John Tydeman. She recently wrote to him to complain about the sex in *The Archers*. She claims that he didn't reply personally. Apparently he got a machine to do it for him.

Sunday September 29th

Archers omnibus. Egg, bacon, fried bread, the *People*. Roast beef, roast potatoes, mashed potatoes, cabbage, carrots, peas, Yorkshire pudding, gravy. Apple crumble, custard, cup of tea, extra strong mints, *News of the World*. Tinned salmon sandwiches, mandarin oranges and jelly, sultana cake, cup of tea.

Monday September 30th

Chapter Eighteen: Back to the Wolds
Jake settled back in the rocking chair and watched his
grandmother making the corn dolly. Her apple cheeks
glowed in the flames from the black leaded range. The
copper kettle sang. The canary in the cage by the window
trilled along with it. Jake sighed a deep, contented sigh.
It was good to be back from Russia and all that unpleas-
antness with Natasha. Here, he could truly relax, in his
grandma's cottage on the Wolds.

Autumn

Autumn

Tuesday October 1st

My father brought Mrs Belinda Bellingham round to meet me at Grandma's house tonight. I was totally gobsmacked; she is a posh person! My father has started to pronounce his aitches religiously and to say 'barth' instead of 'bath'. And he has also discovered manners: every time my grandma came into the room, he leapt out of his chair.

Eventually she snapped, 'Sit *down*, George. You're up and down like a window cleaner's ladder.'

Mrs Bellingham is blonde and pretty, with those cheekbones that denote centuries of wise breeding. I thought she was very pale, considering she had just spent two weeks in the sun. Later in the evening, I found out that she lives in fear of skin cancer. Apparently she spent her holiday running from one patch of shade to another. Mrs Bellingham is the managing director of 'Bell Safe' – a burglar alarm company. My father starts work next Monday as Mrs Bellingham's sales director. They tried to persuade my grandma to allow them to install a burglar alarm at cost price, but she refused, saying, 'No, thank you. If I have to go out, I turn the volume up on Radio Four and leave my front door open.'

Mrs Bellingham and my father exchanged scandalized glances. Grandma continued, 'And I've never been burgled in sixty years, and anyroad up, if I had an alarm on the front of the house, folks'd know I've got something valuable, wouldn't they?'

There was an awkward pause, then my father said, 'Well, Belinda, I'll see you home, shall I?'

He fetched her coat and held it out while she put it on. He has obviously been having lessons in social etiquette. When they'd gone, my grandma shocked me by saying, 'Your dad's turned into a right brown-nosing bugger, hasn't he?'

Perhaps she is suffering from the early symptoms of senile dementia. I have never heard her swear before.

Sir Alan Green, the Director of Public Prosecutions, has been caught talking to a prostitute and has resigned. Under the 1985 Sexual Offences Act, a man seen approaching a woman more than once can be stopped by the police. This is news to me. I shall certainly be more careful whom I approach in the street from now on.

Friday October 4th

Grandma and I have scoured the house from top to bottom today. Grandma has a fixation about germs. She is convinced that they are lying in wait for her, ready to pounce and bring her down. I blame the television advertisement for a lavatory cleaner which depicts 'germs' the size of gremlins, who lurk about in the 'S' bend, chuckling malevolently. Although I've seen this advertisement hundreds of times, I simply can't remember what the product is called.

Query: Is television advertising effective?

Later, Grandma sat down and watched the Labour Party singing 'We Are the Champions' as the finale to their conference in Brighton. Not many of the shadow cabinet knew the words. I hope Freddie Mercury wasn't watching – it would have stuck in his teeth, not to mention his craw.

Sunday October 6th

Turning the pages of my *Observer* today, I saw Barry Kent's ugly face staring out at me. Apparently he is a new member of a place called the Groucho Club. I read the accompanying article avidly. It is exactly the sort of place I would like to be a member of. Should I ever reach that goal, I shall tell the manager (Liam) the truth about Kent's past and have him blackballed.

Elizabeth Taylor has married a bricklayer with a bad perm. He is called Larry Fortensky. Michael Jackson's ape, Bubbles, was the best man.

Chapter Nineteen: Time to Move On
Jake slipped out of the cottage as the village church struck

midnight. He ran stealthily down the lane and towards the minicab which was waiting, as instructed, by the post office. As he threw his rucksack into the back of the car and climbed in after it, he sighed with relief. He never again wanted to see the apple cheeks of his grandmother and he vowed to burn the next corn dolly he came across.

'Put your foot down!' Jake barked to the minicab driver. 'Take me to the nearest urban conurbation.'

The minicab driver's brow was furrowed. 'What's an urban conurbation when it's at 'ome?' he said.

Jake snapped, 'Okay, dolt! You want specifics, take me to the Groucho Club.'

At the mention of the magic words, the cab driver's shoulders straightened. The dandruff stayed on his scalp. He had waited years to hear the words, 'Take me to the Groucho Club'. He looked at Jake with a new respect and he did as he was told. He put his foot down on the clutch and the minicab sped away from the Wolds and towards the great metropolis where, in the Groucho, the Great were no doubt quaffing the house wine and exchanging witticisms. Jake hoped Belinda would be there, at the bar, showing her legs and laughing hysterically at one of Jeffrey Bernard's jokes.

Monday October 7th

Barry Kent is making a film for BBC2 about his 'roots'. The television cameras were in the Co-op, blocking the aisles. I couldn't get to the cat food, so I complained to the manager (who, incidentally, didn't look a day older than seventeen). He replied, 'Barry Kent's comin' here in person this afternoon.' It was as though he were talking about royalty.

I said, 'I don't give a toss. I want three tins of Whiskas, *now*!' The boy manager went off and, in crawling tones, asked the cameraman to pass him three tins of cat food. With what I thought was ill grace, the cameraman obliged and, after paying the starstruck child, I left the shop.

Tuesday October 8th

My mother has been persuaded to give a talk to camera about 'the Barry Kent she once knew'. I urged her to tell the truth, about the bullying, lying, scruffy, thick youth we knew and despised.

But my mother said, 'I always found Barry to be a sensitive child.' The director made her stand by her overflowing wheelie bin in the side yard.

My mother said, 'Shouldn't I be made-up, by a proper make-up artist?' Nick, the director, said, 'No, Mrs Mole, we're going for actuality.' My mother touched the cold sore on her lip and said, 'I'd counted on a bit of camouflage to hide this.' A strong light was turned on her, which showed every line, wrinkle and bag on my mother's face.

Then the director shouted, 'Go!' and my mother went. To pieces. After seventeen attempts, BBC2 gave up, packed their gear and went off. My mother ran upstairs and threw herself on the bed. There is nothing so pitiful as a failed interviewee.

Saturday October 12th

Kent is still poncing around the neighbourhood. I saw him being filmed walking up our street. He was wearing a floor-length overcoat, cowboy boots and dark glasses. I ducked out of sight. I have no wish to be publicly identified as the dork in *Dork's Diary*.

I took the dog for a walk to the field where Pandora used to ride Blossom, her pony. It tired very quickly. I had to carry it back.

I saw Mrs Kent, Barry's mother, on the way home. She was walking her pit bull terrier. I asked her if she had registered the beast yet (as required by law).

She said, 'Butcher wouldn't hurt a fly.'

I said, 'It's not flies I'm worried about. It's the tender flesh of small children.'

She changed the subject and told me that Barry had bought her the council house she now lives in. This made me laugh quite a lot. The Kents' house is a byword for squalor in our neighbourhood. They chop the internal doors up for firewood every winter.

Sunday October 13th

Finished Chapter Nineteen tonight.

Jake was sick of being interviewed. He ordered the journalists to leave the Groucho Club and leave him alone. He turned to Lenny Henry and said, 'Let's have a drink, Len.' Lenny smiled his thanks and Jake snapped his fingers. A waiter came running immediately and bent deferentially towards Jake. 'A bottle of champagne – a big one – and make that three glasses,' for Jake had just seen one of his best friends, Richard Ingrams, of *News Quiz* fame, come through the hallowed swing doors. 'Hey, Rich, over here!' shouted Jake. There was a sound of scuffling coming from the reception area. Jake turned his head round to see Liam, the manager, throwing Kent Barry, the failed writer, out of the club and into the gutter.

Monday October 14th

Dear Bianca,
    After further reflection, can I take you up on your offer? It would be most convenient for me to spend a few days sleeping on your floor in Oxford. Quite honestly, I cannot tolerate another moment living with my family. It isn't just the noise level and the constant bickering; it's the small things – the encrusted neck of the HP Sauce bottle; the slimy soap dish; the dog hairs in the butter.

You can telephone me on the above number, any time, night or day. Nobody sleeps in this house.

All my very best wishes,
Adrian Mole

Tuesday October 15th

My sister Rosie told me that she hated me this morning. Her outburst came after I suggested that she comb her hair before going to school. My mother got out of bed and came downstairs. She lit her second cigarette of the day (she smokes the first in bed) and immediately took Rosie's side. She said, 'Leave the kid alone.'

I said, 'Somebody has to maintain standards in this house.'

My mother said, 'You can talk. That beard looks like a ferret's nest. I don't know how you can bear to have it so near to your mouth. A public health inspector would close it down.'

During the ensuing row, nasty things were said on both sides, which I now regret. I accused her of being a neglectful mother, with loose morals. She counter-attacked by describing me as 'a fungus-faced dork'. She said she had secretly read my *Lo!* manuscript and thought it was 'crap from start to finish'. She said, 'in the unlikely event of it being published, I hope you will use a pseudonym, because, to be honest, Adrian, I couldn't stand the public shame.'

I put my head on the kitchen table and wept.

My mother then put her arm around me and said, 'There, there, Adrian. Don't cry. I didn't mean it, I think *Lo! The Flat Hills of My Homeland* is a very interesting first attempt.'

But it was no good. I wept until dehydration set in.

10.00 p.m. Why hasn't Bianca phoned? I used a first class stamp.

Thursday October 17th

Drew more money out of the Market Harborough Building Society. My dream of being an owner-occupier has receded even further into the realms of fantasy.

I have received a postcard of the Forth Bridge, with no address but posted in London.

Dear Adrian,

I'm going to London to try for a proper job. I've got an interview with British Rail. In a rush. Please reply c/o my friend Lucy:

Lucy Clay
Flat 10
Dexter House
Coghill Street
Oxford

She has promised to pass on any messages.

I hope you are well and happy. I miss you!

Love,

B.

PS. How about a London floor when I find one?

Friday October 18th

Chapter Twenty: The Reckoning

Jake pushed the earth wire out of the lawnmower plug, then screwed the plug together again. He could hear his mother on the telephone to her new lover (a schoolboy called Craig).

He waited for her to finish cooing her endearments down the phone and re-emerge on the terrace. 'I've cut half the lawn, mother,' he shouted, 'but I've got to go to the barber's now.'

His mother frowned and dropped ash all down her cashmere dress. 'But Jake, darling,' she remonstrated. 'You know I hate to see a job half done.' She went towards the lawnmower.

Jake chuckled inwardly. He had banked on this trait of his mother's. As he passed through the french windows, he heard the hover-mower whir into life, to be followed immediately by the high-pitched scream.

Jake immediately felt guilty, then comforted himself by thinking that he had advised his mother time after time to install a circuit breaker; advice she had foolishly chosen to ignore.

Sunday October 20th

It was my father's access day today. He came to take Rosie out to McDonald's as usual. While she looked for her shoes, my father and I talked man to man about my mother. We agreed that she was an impossible person to live with. We had a good laugh about Martin Muffet, who was in the back garden building a lean-to conservatory with the assistance of his Black and Decker work bench. We agreed that, since marrying my mother, Muffet has aged ten years.

I congratulated my father on capturing Mrs Belinda Bellingham, and confessed that I didn't have much luck with women. My father said, 'Tell them what they want to hear, son, and buy them a bunch of flowers once a fortnight. That's all there is to it.'

I asked him if he intended to marry Mrs Bellingham, but before he could answer, my mother staggered into the room carrying a large cardboard box which contained the swag she'd bought from a car boot sale. She'd bought a painting of Christ on the cross; an ashtray with two scottie dogs painted on it; an aluminium toast rack; twenty-seven bent candles; a chenille tablecloth; a Tom Jones LP; six cooking apples; and a steering wheel. As she excitedly unpacked the junk onto the kitchen table, I saw my father looking at her with what I can only describe as lovelight in his eyes.

Monday October 21st

Bianca rang, but I was out cutting Bert Baxter's disgusting toenails. My mother wrote down a telephone number where I could contact Bianca, but then lost it almost immediately. We searched the house, but failed to find the scrap of paper. I expect the dog ate it. It has recently taken to scoffing whole pages of the *Leicester Mercury*, a sign of its increasing neurosis or a vitamin deficiency – who knows? Nobody can afford to take it to the vet to find out.

Tuesday October 22nd

I sent a postcard of Leicester Bus Station to Bianca c/o Lucy Clay:

Dear Bianca,

Thank you for your postcard of the Forth Bridge.

I was most surprised to hear that you were leaving Oxford and going to the 'Smoke', as the cockneys say.

I wish you luck in your search for a 'proper' job. Keep me posted. I have had no luck yet, but I keep trying.

It is very difficult living here with my family. There is a total clash of lifestyles. I strive to be tolerant of the noise and disorder, but it is hard, very hard.

Yours,

With very best wishes,

Adrian

Mrs Bellingham has offered me a job selling security devices. It is evening work. I have to call on nervous householders after dark and put the fear of God into them until they sign up for a burglar alarm or security lights. I said I would think about it.

Mrs Bellingham said in her careful voice, 'There are three million unemployed. Why do you need to think about it?'

I said I hoped that beggars could still be choosers.

She is offering me £3.14 an hour. No commission, no insurance stamp, no contract of employment – cash in hand. I asked her if she objected to my belonging to a union. Her face went whiter than ever and she said, 'Yes, I'm afraid I do. Mrs Thatcher's greatest achievement was to tame the unions.' My father is a Thatcherite's lackey!

Thursday October 24th

I despise myself. I have only been working for two nights, but I have already sold a whole house security system, six car alarms, four peepholes and half a dozen bike locks. My method is simple. I get into the house and show the householders the portfolio that Mrs Bellingham has assembled. It consists of lurid stories cut out of the tabloid newspapers and police press releases. After leafing through this alarming document, it would take great insouciance for the householder to deny that more security in the home is a desirable thing.

Mrs Bellingham has instructed me to ask the question, 'Don't you think your family deserves more protection from the dark forces of evil that are at large in our community?'

So far only one person has said, 'No,' and he was the defeated-looking father of six teenage boys.

Monday October 28th

Shaved beard off. Mrs Bellingham said it made me look untrustworthy. I am completely in her power. If she ordered me to go to work wearing a Batman outfit, I would have to obey her. I have no legal rights of employment.

Thursday October 31st

At last! The economic recovery is on its way! The Confederation of British Industry has reported that they expect outputs and exports to increase in the years ahead. According to the CBI, manufacturers are expecting huge new orders. I broke this good news to my mother. She said, 'Yes, and the dog is getting married on Saturday and I'm its Matron of Honour.' Then she and Martin Muffet went off into one of their mad laughing fits.

Ken Barlow of *Coronation Street* fame has been on

trial for being boring. He was found 'Not Guilty' and awarded £50,000.

My mother has got a job as a security guard in the new shopping centre that has just opened in Leicester city centre. She looks like a New York City police-woman in her uniform. She told the security firm, 'Group Five', that she was *thirty-five years old*! She is now living in fear that her true age, forty-seven, will be revealed. Is everybody partially sighted at Group Five? Did her interview take place in a candlelit office? I asked her these questions.

She said, 'I bunged on rather a lot of Max Factor's pan-stick and sat with my back to the window.'

Friday November 1st

In view of my continuing success in flogging her security paraphernalia, Mrs Bellingham has raised my hourly rate from £3.14 to the heady sum of £3.25! Gee whiz! Fire a cannon! Release the balloons! Open the Bollinger! Issue a press release! Inform the Red Arrows!

Saturday November 2nd

Jake used his Swiss Army knife to dismantle the burglar alarm and in a matter of moments he had circumnavigated the padlocks, bolts and chains on the front door and was standing in the front hall of Bellingham Towers.

Upstairs, sleeping after an hour of arduous lovemaking, were the owners of the historic country house, Sir George and Lady Belinda, and their daughter, the Honourable Rosemary. Jake chuckled as he stuffed silver and *objets d'art* into a black plastic bag. He felt no guilt. He was robbing the filthy rich to feed the filthy poor. He was the Robin Hood of Leicestershire.

My mother claims that I look exactly like John Major, especially when I am wearing my reading glasses. This is total rubbish: unlike Mr Major, I have got lips. They may be on the thin side, but they are distinctly there. If I were Major, I'd have a lip transplant. Mick Jagger could be the donor.

Tuesday November 5th

Robert Maxwell, the mogul, has fallen overboard from his yacht, the *Lady Ghislaine*.

Went to Age Concern Community Bonfire Party. Pushed Bert Baxter there in his wheelchair. Baxter was asked to leave after half an hour because he was seen (and certainly heard) to throw an Indian firecracker into the bonfire. The organizer, Mrs Plumbstead, said apologetically, 'Safety has to be paramount.'

Baxter said scornfully, 'There were no such thing as *safety* when I were a lad.'

I pushed him home in silence. I was furious. Because of him, I missed the baked potatoes, sausages and soup. I had to wait for an hour for the district nurse to come and put him to bed.

Thursday November 7th

Kevin Maxwell has denied that his deceased father's businesses have financial problems.

Query: Would our banks lend £2.5 billion to a man with money problems?

Answer: Of course not! Our banks are respected financial institutions.

Sunday November 10th

To Grandma's for the Remembrance Day poppy-laying ceremony. I am proud of my dead grandfather, Albert Mole. He fought valiantly in the First World War so that I would not have to live under the tyranny of a foreign oppressor.

I cannot let the above sentence lie. The truth is that my poor, dead grandfather fought in the Great War because he was ordered to. He always did what he was told. I take after him in that respect.

Monday November 11th

A gang of Leicester yobs shouted out, 'Hey, John Major, how's Norma?' tonight, as I came out of the cinema. I looked around, thinking that perhaps the Prime Minister was visiting the Leicester Chamber of Commerce, or something, but there was no sign of him. I then realized, to my horror, that they were addressing their yobbish remarks to me.

Wednesday November 13th

A letter from Bianca.

Dear Adrian,

Thank you for your letter, which Lucy forwarded to me. As you can see from my address, I am living in London. I am renting a small room in Soho at the moment, but it is costing £110 per week, so I won't be here long!

I've got a job as a waitress in a restaurant called 'Savages'. The owner is a bit strange, but the staff are very nice. It would be lovely to see you when you're next in London. My day off is Monday. How is the novel going? Have you finished your revisions? I can't wait to read it in full!

Love,

Bianca (Dartington)

Thursday November 14th

Dear Bianca,

Many thanks for your letter of the 11th. I must confess that I was rather surprised to hear from you. I am hardly ever in London, but I may drop in and see you on my next visit. Isn't Soho a dangerous place in which to live? Please take care as you walk the streets. Personally, I am ossifying in this provincial hell.

Lo! is going very well. I have called my hero Jake Westmorland. What do you think?

Please write back.

Yours as ever,

Adrian

Friday November 15th

The New York Stock Exchange collapsed today. I hope this won't affect the interest rates of the Market Harborough Building Society.

Saturday November 16th

No reply from B.

Sunday November 17th

Why isn't there a Sunday delivery in this country? I expect it is because of objections from the established Church. Do the clergy imagine that God gives a toss if humans receive letters or not on a Sunday?

Monday November 18th

By second post. A postcard of Holborn Viaduct.

Dear Adrian,

No. Soho is not dangerous. I *love* Jake Westmorland. When are you coming to London?

Lots of love,
Bianca

Tuesday November 19th

I sent Bianca a postcard of the Clock Tower, Leicester.

Dear Bianca,

As it happens, I shall be in London next Monday. Would you like to have lunch? Please write or ring to confirm.

Very warm wishes,
Adrian

PS. I have shaved my beard off. It was the television pictures of Terry Waite that decided me.

Wednesday November 20th

Grandma's Christmas card arrived. The shops are full of Santa Clauses ringing bells and getting in the way of legitimate shoppers. My mother said that whilst on duty she saw an old lady shoplifting a Cadbury's Selection Box. I asked her what action she'd taken. She said, 'I turned and walked the other way.'

There is a rush on for burglar alarms. Everybody wants them fitted before Christmas when they fill their homes with consumer durables and Nintendo games.

Saturday November 23rd

A postcard from Bianca, of the original Crystal Palace.

Dear Adrian,

I have got to work on Monday. The office party season has started, but come down anyway. I will get off early. I look forward to seeing you. Come to 'Savages', Dean Street, at 2.30 p.m.

Love,

Bianca

Sunday November 24th

Freddie Mercury has died of Aids. There was no time for me to mourn, but I put 'Bohemian Rhapsody', which is one of my favourite records, on the record player.

I laid my wardrobe on my bed (or rather, the *contents* of my wardrobe) and tried to decide what to wear for my trip to London. I do not wish to be marked out as a provincial day-tripper by sneering metropolitans. Decided on the black shirt, black trousers and Oxfam tweed jacket. My grey slip-on shoes will have to do. Set my alarm for 8.30 a.m. I catch the 12.30 p.m. train.

Monday November 25th

Soho

I am in love with Bianca Dartington. Hopelessly, helplessly, mindlessly, gloriously, magnificently.

Tuesday November 26th

I am still here, in Soho, in Bianca's room above Brenda's Patisserie in Old Compton Street. I have hardly seen daylight since 3.30 p.m. on Monday.

Wednesday November 27th

Poem to Bianca Dartington:

> Gentle face,
> Night black hair,
> Natural grace,
> Love I swear.
> Marry me, be my wife,
> Make me happy, share my life.

Thursday November 28th

Phoned my mother and asked her to send my books to Old Compton Street. Informed her that I am now living in London, with Bianca. She asked for the address, but I wasn't falling for that. I hung up.

Friday November 29th

God, I love her! I love her! I love her! Every minute she is away, working at 'Savages', is torture for me.

Query: Why didn't I *know* that the human body is capable of such exquisite pleasure?

Answer: Because, Mole, you had not made love to Bianca Dartington – somebody who loves you body and soul – before.

Saturday November 30th

What did I ever see in Pandora Braithwaite? She is an opinionated, arrogant ball-breaker. An all-round nasty piece of work. Compared to Bianca, she is nothing, nothing. And as for Leonora De Witt, I can hardly remember her face.

I never want to leave this room. I want to live the whole of my life within these four walls (with occasional trips to the bathroom, which we have to share with a fire-eater called Norman).

The walls are painted lavender blue and Bianca has stuck stars and moons on the ceiling which glow in the dark. There is a poster of Sydney Harbour Bridge on the wall between the windows. There is a double bed with an Indian bedspread covered in cushions; a chest of drawers that Bianca has painted white; an old armchair covered in a large tablecloth. A wonky table, half painted in gold, and two pine chairs. Instead of a bedhead, we have got a blown-up photograph on the wall of Isambard Kingdom Brunel, Bianca's hero.

Every morning when I wake up, I can't believe that the slim girl with the long legs who is lying next to me is mine! I always get out of bed first and put the kettle on the Baby Belling cooker. I then put two slices of toast under the grill and serve my love with her breakfast in bed. I won't allow her to get out of bed until the gas fire has warmed the room. She catches cold easily.

I want to please her more than I want to please myself.

This morning, 'Stand By Me', sung by Ben E. King, was playing on Capital Radio.

I said, 'I love this song. My father used to play it.'

Bianca said, 'So do I.'

We danced to it, me in my boxer shorts and Bianca in her pink knickers with the flowers on.

'Stand By Me' is now our song.

Sunday December 1st

Went to the National Gallery today. We walked around the Sainsbury Wing like Siamese twins, fused together. We cannot bear to be apart for even a moment. The renaissance pictures glowed like jewels and inflamed our passion. Our mutual genitalia are a bit sore and bruised, but it didn't stop us making love as soon as we got back to the room. Norman next door banged on the wall and nearly put us off, but we managed to ignore him.

Monday December 2nd

I was putting my socks and shoes on this morning, when I noticed a strange expression on Bianca's face.

I said, 'What is it, darling?'

After a lot of cajoling, Bianca confessed that she

adored everything about me except my grey slip-on shoes and white towelling socks. As a mark of my love for her, I opened the window and hurled my only pair of socks and shoes into Old Compton Street. I was unable to go out all day as a consequence. I was a barefoot prisoner of love.

Late that afternoon, Bianca bought me three pairs of socks from Sock Shop, and one pair of dark brogues from Bally. They all fitted perfectly. The shoes are *serious*. I felt like a grown-up in them as I walked around the room. I then walked to the Nat West Bank in Wardour Street and removed £100 from the Rapid Cash machine. This is the most I have ever withdrawn in one go. I paid Bianca for the shoes (£59.99), which is also the most I have ever paid for a pair of shoes. Incidentally, it is now late evening and the grey slip-ons are still in the gutter. I *did* see a tramp try them on, but he scowled and took them off immediately, though they looked a good fit.

Wednesday December 4th

I telephoned my mother today and asked her why she hadn't sent my books on as I had asked.

She screamed, 'Mainly because you refused to give me your address, you stupid sod.' She then went on to say that she had asked our postman, Courtney Elliot, for an estimate of the cost of sending the books by Parcel Post. Apparently, he 'guestimated' (her word, not mine) that it would cost about a hundred quid! She said that my father is driving to London on Friday to attend a conference on Home Security. She said she would ask him to drop the books, and the rest of my worldly goods, off. I agreed reluctantly and gave her the address.

When Bianca had gone to work, I walked to Oxford Street and bought a dustpan and brush, a packet of yellow dusters, Mr Sheen, a floor cloth, some liquid Flash, a bottle of Windolene and a pair of white satin knickers from Knickerbox.

Bianca was thrilled when she returned at 3.00 p.m. to find our room cleaned and sparkling. Almost as thrilled as I was at 1.00 a.m. when she put the satin knickers on.

Friday December 6th

My father was in a foul temper when he got here tonight. The conference was in Watford, so he had to go considerably out of his way (backwards) in order to deliver my stuff. When he eventually found Old Compton Street, it was 9.30 p.m.

He parked outside on double yellow lines, with his hazard lights flashing. Together, we lugged the boxes of books and plastic bags of clothes four floors up to the room. When we'd finished, my father collapsed on the bed. His bald patch was glistening with sweat. I was glad that Bianca was at work. When he'd recovered, I went down to see him off. Mrs Bellingham had ordered him to be home at a reasonable time. He is obviously afraid of her. As we walked to the car, my father stopped, pointed to the gutter and shouted, 'What the bleeding hell is that?'

His Montego had been wheel-clamped. I thought he was going to break down and cry in the street, but instead he went berserk and kicked at the yellow clamp and shouted obscenities. It was highly amusing to the posing idiots who were drinking cappuccino in the cold wind on the opposite pavement.

I offered to go with him to the outer reaches of London, to start the long, bureaucratic process of declamping the car, but my father snarled, 'Oh, bugger off back upstairs to your cowing love nest.' He hailed a black cab and jumped in. As it turned into Wardour Street, I could tell that it wouldn't be long before my father was whining to the cab driver about his bad luck, his ungrateful son, his fearsome mistress and his feckless ex-wife.

Saturday December 7th

Spent a pleasant day cataloguing and then arranging my books on the bookshelves I constructed from three planks and nine old bricks I found in a skip in Greek Street. Cost? Nil. In the same skip, I found *Moral Thinking* by John Wilson. It was printed in 1970, before sex came into *The Archers*, however, so I suppose the morality may be out of date.

Bianca came home at lunchtime and asked if I wanted a job as a part-time washer-up in 'Savages'. It is cash in hand, off the books. I said, 'Yes.'

We went to see the Thames Barrier and talked about our future. We pledged that we would not let riches and fame divide us.

I start washing up on Monday.

Monday December 9th

Peter Savage, the owner of 'Savages', is certainly aptly named. I have never known a man with such a bad temper. He is rude to everybody, staff and customers. The customers think he is amusingly eccentric. The staff hate him and spend their meal breaks fantasizing about killing him. He is a tall, fat man with a face like a beef tomato. He dresses like Bertie Wooster and talks like Bob Hoskins of *Roger Rabbit* fame. He wears a CND tiepin on his Garrick Club tie.

Culturally, he is all over the place.

Tuesday December 10th

Savage was drunk at 10 a.m. At 12 noon he vomited into the yukka plant in the corner of the restaurant.

At 1 p.m. his wife came, abused him verbally and then carried him out to her car, helped by Luigi, the head waiter.

I am reading *The Complete Plain Words* by Sir Ernest Gowers. I am on page 143: *Clichés*. Far be it from me to say so, but I'm sure my writing style will improve by leaps and bounds.

Bianca startled me this evening by suddenly shouting, 'Please, Adrian, can't you stop that perpetual sniffing. Use a handkerchief!'

Wednesday December 11th

I toil over greasy pots and pans for £3.90 an hour, and the customers fork out £17 for a monkfish and £18 for a bottle of wine! Savage is obviously not as stupid as he looks.

Fogle, Fogle, Brimmington and Hayes, the advertising firm, held their Christmas party in 'Savages' at lunchtime. The restaurant was closed to ordinary customers. Bianca said that the managing director, Piers Fogle, told her that they were in a celebratory mood because they had just won a contract worth £500,000 on the strength of a slogan for an advertising campaign for condoms.

'What the well-dressed man is wearing' is to appear on billboards all over the country.

Their bill came to over £700. They gave Bianca and the other waitresses £5 each. I, the serf in the kitchen, got nothing, of course. Luigi put two fingers up to Fogle's back as he staggered out of the restaurant.

Saturday December 14th

We haven't made love for over twenty-four hours. Bianca has got cystitis.

Sunday December 15th

Bought *The Joy of Sex* in the Charing Cross Road. Cystitis is called 'The Honeymooners' Illness'. It can be caused by vigorous, frequent sex. Poor Bianca is in the toilet every ten minutes. Why is there *always* a price to pay for pleasure?

Monday December 16th

Savage was in court this morning, charged with assaulting a customer last April. He was fined £500 and ordered to pay costs and damages totalling my wages for five years. He came back to the restaurant with Mrs Savage and his lawyer to celebrate the fact that he hadn't been sent to prison, but after the champagne had been drunk and the tagliatelle consumed, Savage spotted a group of Channel Four executives on table eight and began to abuse them because they didn't show enough tobogganing on their sports programmes.

According to Bianca, Mrs Savage said, 'Darling, do be quiet, you're starting to get a little tedious.'

Savage shouted, 'Shut your mouth, you fat cow!'

She shouted, 'I'm a size *ten*, you callous bastard!'

The lawyer tried to conciliate, but Savage tipped the table up and Luigi ended up throwing his boss out of his own restaurant.

Personally, I would be happy to see Savage chained up in prison, on bread and water, with rats gnawing at his feet – and I'm a supporter of prison reform.

Tuesday December 17th

Experimented with making very gentle love. I was the passive partner.

Later, we had our first argument. Where are we spending Christmas Day and Boxing Day? In our room? At her parents'? At my parents'? Or with Luigi, who has invited us to his house in Harrow? We didn't shout at each other, but there was (and still is) a distinct lack of seasonal goodwill. Bianca turned her back on me in bed tonight.

Thursday December 19th

We woke up tangled together, as usual. Christmas wasn't mentioned, but love, passion and marriage were. We are going to spend Christmas with her parents in Richmond. Her father is going to pick us up on Christmas Eve. It will save me having to buy presents for my family.

Saturday December 21st

Tonight, Savage promenaded around the restaurant with a miniature Christmas tree on his head, complete with twinkling lights. He kissed all the women and blew cigar smoke at all the men. Luigi led him into the kitchen and propped him up against the sink. Savage then proceeded to tell me that his mother had never loved him and that his father had run away with an alcoholic nurse when he was eight. (When Savage *junior* was eight.) He broke down and wept, but I was too busy to comfort him. The cook was screaming for side plates.

Sunday December 22nd

Bianca stayed in bed today, tired out, poor kid, which gave me a chance to work on chapter twenty-one of *Lo! The Flat Hills of My Homeland*.

Jake ran his fingers down the length of her back. Her skin felt like the finest silk, even to his fingers, roughened by years of immersion in washing-up water. She sighed and squirmed into the flannelette sheet. 'Don't stop,' she said, her voice cracking like a whip. 'Don't ever stop, Jake . . .'

Tuesday December 24th
Christmas Eve

I braved the maddening crowds today and went out to buy Bianca's Christmas present. After tramping the streets for two hours, I ended up in Knickerbox and bought her a purple suspender belt, scarlet knickers, and a black lace bra. When the saleswoman asked me about size, I confessed I didn't know. I said, 'She's not Rubenesque, but she's not Naomi Campbell.'

The woman rolled her eyes and said, 'Okay, she's medium, yeah?'

I said, 'She looks a bit like Paula Yates, but with black hair.'

The woman sighed and said, 'Paula Yates breast-feeding or not breastfeeding?'

I said, 'Not breastfeeding,' and she snatched some stuff off the racks and gift-wrapped it for me.

I agonized in Burger King over whether or not to buy her parents presents. At four-thirty, I decided that, yes, I would ingratiate myself with them and bought her mother some peach-based pot-pourri. I phoned Bianca at 'Savages' and asked what I should get for her father. She said her father was fond of poetry, so I went and bought him a book of poems by John Hegley, called *Can I Come Down Now Dad?* which has a picture of Jesus on the cross on its cover. I also managed to track down a copy of *The Railway Heritage of Britain* by Gordon Biddle and O. S. Nock for Bianca.

Thursday December 26th
Boxing Day

Richmond

Bianca's mother is allergic to peaches; and her father, the Reverend Dartington, thought that the John Hegley book was in extremely bad taste. Also, I hate Bianca's brother and sister. How my sweet, darling Bianca could have come from such a vile family is a mystery to me. We slept in separate beds in separate rooms. We had to go to a wooden hut of a church on Christmas Day and listen to her father rant on about the commercialization of Christmas. Bianca and I were the only people to buy presents. Everyone else had given money to the Sudanese Drought Fund. Bianca bought me a Swatch watch and the *Chronicle of the Twentieth Century*, which will be an invaluable work of reference to me. I was very pleased. She was pleased with the Biddle and Nock.

Her brother, Derek, and her sister, Mary, obviously disapprove of our love affair. They are both unmarried and still live at home. Derek is thirty-five and Mary is twenty-seven. Mrs Dartington was forty-eight when Bianca was born.

There was no turkey, no drink and no celebration. It made me long for my own family's vulgarity.

This afternoon, we had to go for a walk alongside the river. Little kids were out in force, wobbling on new bikes and pushing prams with new-looking dolls inside. Derek has now taken a shine to me. He thought I was a fellow trainspotter; I quickly put him right. Bianca and I managed a quick embrace in the kitchen tonight before being interrupted by Mary, who came in looking for her constipation chocolate.

Mrs Dartington had a convenient 'turn' just before dinner and took to her bed. Bianca and I cooked the meal. We had salad, corned beef and baked potatoes. I cannot wait to get back to our room. I need Bianca. I need onions. I need garlic. I need Soho. I need Savage. I need air. I need freedom from the Dartingtons.

There are four beige car coats hanging up in the downstairs cloakroom.

Friday December 27th

The Reverend Dartington drove us back to Soho in martyred silence. Every time he stopped at a red light or pedestrian crossing, he drummed his fingers on the steering wheel impatiently.

Two days with her family have had a deleterious

effect on Bianca: she seems to have shrunk physically and regressed mentally. As soon as she got back into the room she burst into tears and shouted, 'Why didn't they *tell* me they were giving their Christmas presents to the Sudanese?'

I said, 'Because they wanted to claim the moral high ground and make you feel foolish. It's obviously a punishment because you are living in sin, in Soho, with a lowly washer-upper.'

An hour later, Bianca had sprung back in size and mental capacity. We made love for one hour, ten minutes. Our longest yet. It is quite useful having a stopwatch facility on my new Swatch.

Sunday December 29th

We went to Camden Lock today to buy Bianca a pair of boots. The whole area was thronging with young people who were both buying and selling. I said to Bianca, 'Isn't it nice to see the young out and about and enjoying themselves?'

She looked at me in a funny way and said, 'But *you* are young. You're only twenty-four, though sometimes I find it hard to believe.'

She was right, of course. I am young, officially, but I have never felt young. My mother said I was thirty-five on the day I fought my way out of her womb.

The cystitis is back. Bianca has reluctantly put the

satin knickers back in her underwear drawer and gone back to the cotton gussets.

I am reading a play, *A Streetcar Named Desire* by Tennessee Williams. Poor Blanche Dubois!

Winter

Wednesday January 1st 1992

'Savages' was closed last night, so we went to Trafalgar Square at 11.30 p.m. to see the New Year in. The crowd was like a drunken field of corn rippling and swaying in a storm. For over two hours I lost myself and went with the flow. It was frightening, but also exhilarating to find myself in a line doing the conga up St Martin's Lane. Unfortunately, the person in front of me had extremely fat buttocks. It was not an attractive sight.

When Big Ben struck twelve, I found myself kissing and being kissed by strangers, including foreigners. I tried to get to Bianca, but she was surrounded by a party of extrovert Australian persons who were all over seven foot tall. But finally, at 12.03 a.m. on the 1st of January, we kissed and pledged our troth. I can't believe I've got such a wonderful woman. Why does she love me? I live in fear that one day she will wake up and ask herself the same question.

We went to Tower Bridge today. It left me cold, but Bianca was enraptured by the structural design of the thing. I practically had to drag her away.

Thursday January 2nd

Got up at 3.30 a.m. and joined the queue outside Next in Oxford Street. The sale started at 9.00 a.m. I got into conversation with a man who had his eye on a double-breasted navy suit, marked down from £225 to £90. He is getting married to a parachute packer, called Melanie, next Saturday.

In my new black leather jacket, white T-shirt and blue jeans, I look like every other young man in London, New York and Tokyo. Or Leicester, come to think of it. For Leicester is at the very epicentre of the Next empire.

Bianca wanted to visit Battersea Power Station today and asked me to go with her, but I pointed out to her that *Lo!* was about to develop in a revolutionary direction and that I needed to work on Chapter Twenty-two.

She left the flat without saying a word, but her back looked very angry.

Jake pulled the collar of his Next black leather jacket up against the cruel wind that blew across the Thames. He stared down into the ebbing water. It was time he did something with his life other than help with famine relief in Sudan. He knew what it was. It was something he had fought against – God knows how he had fought! But the compulsion was overwhelming now. He had to do it. He had to write a novel . . .

Wednesday January 8th

President Bush vomited into the lap of the Japanese Ambassador at an official banquet in Tokyo tonight. We watched it on the portable television in the kitchen at 'Savages'. Mrs Bush shoved her husband under the table, then left the room. She didn't look too pleased. The television news showed the whole incident in slow motion. It was sickening. The Japanese people looked horrified. They are sticklers for protocol.

Savage has fired little Carlos for smoking a joint in the yard at the back of the restaurant. Savage then drank half a bottle of brandy, three bottles of Sol, stole various drinks from customers' tables and ended up fighting with the palm tree at the bar after accusing it of having an affair with his wife. Alcohol is certainly a dangerous drug in the wrong hands.

Wednesday January 15th

Jake sat in front of his state of the art Amstrad and pressed the glittery knobs. The title of his novel appeared on the screen.

SPARG FROM KRONK
Chapter One: Sparg Returns
Sparg stood on the hilltop and looked down on Kronk, the settlement of his birth. He grunted to his woman,

Barf, and she grunted back wordlessly, for the words had not yet been found.

They ran down the hill. Sparg's mother, Krun, watched her son and his woman come towards the fire. She grunted to Sparg's father, Lunt, and he came to the door of the hut. His eyes narrowed. He hated Sparg.

Krun threw more roots into the fire: she had not expected guests for dinner. It was typical of her son, she thought, to arrive unexpectedly and with a woman with a swollen belly. She hoped there would be enough roots to go round.

She was glad the words had not been found. She hated making small talk.

Sparg was here, in front of her. She sniffed his armpit, as was the custom when a Kronkite returned from a long journey. Barf hung back and watched the greeting ceremony. Her mouth salivated. The smell of the burning roots inflamed her hunger.

Because the words had not been found no news could be exchanged between mother and son.

Jake fell back from his computer terminal with a contented sigh. It was good, he thought, damned good. The time was right for another prehistoric novel without dialogue.

Tuesday January 21st

A letter from Bert Baxter. Almost illegible.

Dear Lad,

It seems a long time since I saw you. When are you coming to Leicester? I've got a few jobs that need doing. Sorry about the writing. I've got the shakes.

Yours,

Bertram Baxter

PS. Bring your toenail scissors.

Had a serious row with Bianca tonight. She accused me of:

a) Never wanting to go out
b) Excessive reading
c) Excessive writing
d) Contempt for Britain's industrial heritage
e) Farting in bed

Monday January 27th

At last reconciled, we went to the National Film Theatre tonight and saw a film about a Japanese woman who cuts her lover's penis off. During the rest of the film, I sat with my legs tightly crossed and at intervals looked nervously across at Bianca, who was staring up at the screen and smiling.

My hair is almost long enough for a pony tail. *The Face* tells me that pony tails are becoming passé. But it may be my last chance to try one. So I am going for it. Savage has been boasting that he has had his for five years.

Bianca has bought a secondhand electric typewriter and is typing *Lo!* She has already presented me with seventy-eight beautifully laid-out pages. It is amazing how much a novel is improved by being typed. I should have taken Mr John Tydeman's advice years ago.

Wednesday January 29th

UK heterosexual Aids cases rose by fifty per cent last year. I gave this information to Bianca as we walked to 'Savages' early this evening. She went very quiet.

I had to wait ages outside the bathroom tonight to clean my teeth. Eventually Norman came out and apologized for the new scorch marks on the frame of the mirror. He has been *told* not to practise in there.

When I got back to our room, I found Bianca reading a pamphlet written by the Terrence Higgins Trust.

I said flippantly, 'Who's Terrence Higgins when he's at home?'

'He's dead,' she said, softly. The pamphlet was about Aids.

Bianca broke down and confessed that in 1990 she had had an affair with a man called Brian Boxer, who in turn confessed to her that in 1979 he'd had an affair with a bisexual woman called Diane Tripp. I shall ring the Terrence Higgins Trust Helpline in the morning and ask for help.

Saturday February 1st

The first twenty-two chapters of *Lo! The Flat Hills of My Homeland* are now a pile of 197 pages of neat typescript. I keep picking it up and walking round the room with it in my arms. I can't afford to get it photocopied, not at ten pence a page. Who do I know in London who has access to a photocopier?

Flat 6
Brenda's Patisserie
Old Compton Street
London

Dear John,

I have taken your advice and revised *Lo! The Flat Hills of My Homeland*. I have also employed the services of a professional typist and you will be pleased to see that my manuscript now consists of twenty-two chapters in typewritten form. I consider that, when completed, *Lo! The Flat Hills of My Homeland* will be eminently suitable for being read aloud on the radio, possibly as part of your Classic Serials series.

As you can see, I have enclosed my MS and entrust it into your care. However, I still need to make several minor changes. Would it be too much trouble for you to photocopy

the hundred and ninety-seven pages and send a copy to me
at the above address?

   Thanking you in advance,

     Yours as ever,

       Adrian Mole

Tuesday February 4th

I walked to Broadcasting House this morning. As I
struggled to push the big metal doors open, a gaggle
of autograph hunters rushed towards me. I reached
inside my jacket for my felt tip, but before I could
extract it, I saw them surrounding Alan Freeman,
the aged DJ. I pushed through them and entered the
hallowed reception area of the British Broadcasting
Corporation, watched by the stern-looking security
staff. I walked up to the reception desk and joined the
short queue.

   In the space of four minutes, I saw famous people
galore: Delia Smith, Robert Robinson, Ian Hislop, Bob
Geldof, Annie Lennox, Roy Hattersley, etc., etc. Most
of them were being seen off the premises by young
women called Caroline.

   Eventually the blonde receptionist said, 'Can I help
you?' And I said, 'Yes. Could you please make sure
that Mr John Tydeman receives this parcel? It is most
urgent.'

   She scribbled something on the jiffy bag which
contained my letter and the manuscript of *Lo! The*

Flat Hills of My Homeland and threw it into a wire basket.

I thanked her, turned to go and bumped into Victor Meldrew, who plays the grumpy bloke in *One Foot in the Grave*! I apologized and he said, 'How kind.' He is much taller than he looks on television. When I got back to the room I told Bianca that I had been chatting to Victor Meldrew. I think she was quite impressed.

Wednesday February 5th

We both woke early this morning, but we didn't make love as usual. We had a shower and got dressed in silence. We went downstairs and had croissants and cappuccino in Brenda's Patisserie and listened to the gossip about the demise of the British film industry. Then, at 10.45 a.m., we paid our bill and walked to the clinic in Neal Street. (We forked out one pound, forty pence to the various beggars who met us on the way.)

We were counselled separately by a very empathetic woman called Judith. She pointed out that, should our tests prove positive, it wouldn't necessarily mean that we would develop full-blown Aids. After seeing Judith, we went for a drink in a pub in Carnaby Street to discuss our options:

a) Have the test and know the worst
b) Not have the test and suspect the worst

We decided to sleep on it.

Thursday February 6th

We have both decided to have the test and have pledged to care for each other until the day we die. Whatever the outcome.

Saturday February 8th

Mr Britten, the greengrocer who supplies 'Savages' with fruit and vegetables, came into the kitchen today and told us that he is going out of business next week. He said that Savage owes him seven hundred pounds in unpaid bills. I was outraged, but Mr Britten said defeatedly that Savage is only one of his many bad debtors. He said, 'If the Bank'd give me another two weeks I'd be all right, but the bastards won't.'

I made him a cup of tea and listened to him ranting on about interest charges and Norman Lamont. I think he felt slightly better by the time he left to make his next delivery.

I rang my mother to tell her about my conversation with Victor Meldrew and found that she has also been seeing a counsellor. A debt counsellor. I have been wondering for some time now how she has been paying her mortgage. Now I know. She hasn't. She has received a legal notice from the Building Society, informing her that the house where I spent my childhood is to be repossessed on March 16th. She begged me not to tell the other members of the family. She is hoping that something will turn up to avert disaster.

I didn't tell her that I have got one thousand, one hundred and eleven pounds in the Market Harborough Building Society. But I did say that Bianca and I would come to Leicester tomorrow. She sounded pathetically grateful.

Sunday February 9th

When we got to St Pancras Station, Bianca told me to look up.

'You are looking at one of the largest unsupported arch structures in the whole world,' she said. 'Isn't it beautiful?'

'Quite honestly, Bianca,' I said, 'all I can see is a dirty, scruffy roof covered in pigeon shit.'

'It was stupid of me to ask you to look at something further than your own nose,' she said, and stormed onto the train, leaving me to carry our overnight bags.

I'm always forgetting that Bianca is a qualified engineer. She doesn't look like one and since I've known her, she's only ever worked as a shop assistant and a waitress. She applies for at least two engineering jobs a week, but has yet to be called for an interview. She is considering calling herself 'Brian Dartington' on her cv.

The ticket inspector forgot to punch our three-monthly returns, so our journey to Leicester cost us nothing. But any feelings of happy triumph vanished as we got into the house. My mother was putting on a brave front, but I could tell she was inwardly distraught – at one point, she had one cigarette in her mouth, another in the ashtray and another burning on the edge of the kitchen window sill. I asked her how she'd got into such terrible debt.

She whispered, 'Martin needed the fees to finish his degree course. I borrowed a thousand pounds from a finance company, at an interest rate of twenty-four point seven per cent. Two weeks later, I lost my job with Group Five – somebody grassed on me and told them I was forty-eight.' I asked her to tell me the full extent of her indebtedness. She brought out unpaid bills of every description and colour. I urged her to tell Muffet the true nature of their financial situation, but she became almost hysterical and said, 'No, no, he *must* finish his engineering degree.'

I seem to be surrounded by engineers. Bianca informed my mother that she too was a qualified engineer.

I said jokingly, 'Yes, but she has not built so much as a Lego tower since she left university.'

To my amazement, Bianca took great exception to my harmless joke and left the room, looking tearful.

My mother said, 'You tactless sod!' and followed her into the garden.

I sat at the kitchen table, braced myself, and wrote three cheques: to Fat Eddie's Loan Co. (two hundred and seventy-one pounds); to the Co-op Dairy (thirty-six pounds, forty-nine pence); to Cherry's Newsagent (seventy-four pounds, eighty-one pence). I know it does not solve my mother's housing problem, but at least she can answer her front door now without being hounded by local creditors.

When Martin came back from Grandma's (where he is in the middle of replacing her two-pin sockets with three-pin ones), I introduced him to Bianca. Within seconds, they were bonded. They talked non-stop about St Pancras Station and unsupported arch structures. It is some time since I saw Bianca so animated. They sat next to each other at the dinner table and volunteered to wash and dry afterwards.

I helped Rosie with her English homework essay, 'A Day in the Life of a Dolphin'. I then went into the kitchen and found Bianca and Muffet droning on about the St Pancras Station Hotel and its architect, Sir George Gilbert Scott.

I interrupted them and informed Bianca that I was going to bed. She hardly looked up; just muttered, 'Okay, I'll be up soon.'

The spare bedroom was full of Rosie's hideous, fluorescent My Little Pony models.

Monday February 10th

I have no idea what time Bianca came up last night. She must have got into bed beside me without waking me up. All I know is that Muffet and my mother are not speaking and that I am utterly miserable.

11.30 *p.m.* Worked on *Chapter Twenty-Three: Conundrum.*

Jake sat in Alma's, the patisserie favoured by the intelligentsia, and scribbled on his A4 pad. Night and day, he worked on his novel. He was already on Chapter Four.

Chapter Four: Rocks

Sparg crept through the lush undergrowth. He knew they were there. He heard them before he saw them. They were grunting about their mutual interest in rocks.

Sparg parted a yukka plant and they were there in front of him: Moff and Barf, bathed in sunlight, tangled together. Their limbs were entwined in an intimate manner.

Sparg stifled a jealous grunt and crept back towards Kronk, the settlement of his birth.

Tuesday February 11th

We get our results tomorrow. I should be agonizing and reflecting on mortality, etc. But all I can think about is the way that Muffet looked at Bianca and the way that Bianca looked at Muffet when they said goodbye on Monday morning at Leicester station.

Wednesday February 12th

Judith told us that our tests are negative! We are not HIV positive! We are not going to die of Aids!

However, I feel that I may well die of a broken heart. Bianca has suggested another day trip to Leicester. She claims that she is tired of London. A feeble excuse. How could anyone be tired of London? I am with Dr Johnson on this one.

Thursday February 13th

A letter has arrived from the BBC.

Dear Adrian,

When my secretary handed me your letter and your manuscript of *Lo! The Flat Hills of My Homeland* yet again, I thought I must be hallucinating.

You have more cheek than a Samurai wrestler, more neck than a giraffe. The BBC does not run a free photocopying service. As to your laughable suggestion that your novel be read as one of our classic serials . . . The writers of such texts are usually dead, their work having outlived them. I doubt if your work will outlive you. I am returning the manuscript immediately. Owing to an administrative error, a photocopy *was* taken. I am sending this on to you, though with great reluctance. You really must not bother me again.

John Tydeman

Friday February 14th
St Valentine's Day

A disappointingly small card from Bianca. Mine to her was a thing of splendour. Large, padded, expensive, and in a box tied with a ribbon.

Savage is in a clinic for drug and alcohol abuse. Luigi went to see him on Sunday and said that Savage was playing ping-pong with a fifteen-year-old crack addict from Leeds.

Saturday February 15th

Bianca is going to Leicester for the day on Monday, to see my mother. I wish I could go with her, but I am now working a sixteen-hour day, seven days a week. Somebody has to keep my mother out of prison, and I am now the only person in our family who has a proper job.

My duties at 'Savages' now include the preparation of vegetables. It is tedious work, made more difficult by the obsessive attitude of Roberto, the chef. He insists on uniformity of vegetable length and width. I have to keep a tape measure in my apron pocket.

Sunday February 16th

It is now seven days and nights since Bianca and I made love. It is not only the sex I miss. It isn't the sex. It really isn't only the sex. I miss holding her and smelling her hair and stroking her skin. I wish that I could talk to her about how I feel. But I can't, I just can't. I really can't. I've tried, but I just can't. I held her hand in bed tonight, but it didn't count. She was asleep.

Monday February 17th

Before I went to work at 6.30 a.m., I wrote a note and left it propped against the bowl of hyacinths on the table.

Darling Bianca,
   Please talk to me about our relationship. I am unable to initiate a discussion. All I can say to you is that I love you. I know something is wrong between us, but I don't know how to address it.
   Love, for ever,
   Adrian

Bianca was very kind to me early this evening. She assured me that nothing has changed regarding her feelings towards me. But she was talking to me on the telephone from Leicester. She has arranged to stay another day, to help my mother.

When I got home from work at 11.30 p.m., I re-read the note, which was still on the table, and then tore it up and threw it down the lavatory. It took three full flushes before it disappeared completely.

Tuesday February 18th

I was very tired last night, but was unable to sleep, so I got out of bed, got dressed, and went for a walk. Soho never sleeps. It exists for people like me: the lonely, the lovesick, the outsiders. When I got home I read Dostoevsky's *The Humiliated and Insulted*.

Wednesday February 19th

The gods are not exactly smiling on our family. Mrs Bellingham has sacked my father and kicked him out of her bed. She was outraged to find out that my father had been selling her security lights for half price in low-life pubs. He is back living with Grandma. I only know this because Grandma rang me at work, complaining that my mother owes her fifty pounds from last December. Grandma needs the money because she is going to Egypt with Age Concern in June and needs to pay the deposit next week.

I pointed out to Grandma that she has got substantial savings in a high interest bank account. Couldn't she withdraw fifty pounds? Grandma pointed out that the bank requires a month's notice of withdrawal. She said, 'I'm not prepared to lose the interest.'

I casually asked Grandma if she had seen anything of Bianca. She casually answered that she had seen Bianca and Muffet on the top deck of a number twenty-nine bus, heading towards the town. She threw in a few details. They were laughing. Bianca was holding a bunch of freesias (her favourite flowers). And Muffet looked 'happier than I've ever seen him'. There was a twanging noise as she leaned back in her chair by the telephone and said, 'It doesn't take an Einstein to work that one out, does it, lad?'

Thanks, Grandma, Leicester's answer to Miss sodding Marple.

Thursday February 20th

I fear the worst. Bianca is still in Leicester. I received a brochure this morning from an organization called the Naxos Institute. They were offering me a holistic holiday on the Greek island of Naxos, complete with courses in creative writing, dream workshops, finding your voice and stress management. One photograph in the brochure showed happy, tanned holidaymakers scoffing green foodstuffs at long tables under blue skies. Close examination with a magnifying glass showed the foodstuffs to be made up of lettuce and courgettes with a bit of what looked like cheese thrown in. There were bottles of retsina on the tables, vases of flowers and rough-hewn loaves of bread.

Another photograph showed a beach and a pine forest and the bamboo hut accommodation spread over a hillside. It looked truly idyllic. I turned a page and saw that Angela Hacker, the novelist, playwright and television personality, was 'facilitating' the writing course for the first two weeks in April. I have not read her books or seen her plays, but I have seen her on the television programme *Through the Keyhole*. She has certainly got a gracious home, though I remember being struck at the time by the amazing amount of alcohol in evidence. There were bottles in every room. Loyd Grossman made a quip about it at the time, something about 'sauce for the goose'. The studio audience laughed itself stupid.

I closed the brochure with a sigh. Two weeks on Naxos talking about my novel with Angela Hacker would be paradise, but I can't possibly afford it. My Building Society reserves are running low. I'm down to my last thousand.

Saturday February 22nd

Bianca rang the restaurant at lunchtime and said that she would be catching the 7.30 a.m. train from Leicester tomorrow and would be arriving at St Pancras at around 9.00 a.m. Her voice sounded strange. I asked her if she'd got a sore throat. She replied that she'd been 'doing a lot of talking'. Every fibre of me longs for her, especially the bits around my loins.

Sunday February 23rd

I was on the platform when the train came in and saw Bianca jump onto the platform. I ran towards her, holding a bunch of daffodils I'd bought from a stall outside the Underground on Oxford Street. Then, to my surprise, I saw Martin Muffet step down from the train, carrying two large suitcases. He put them down on the platform and put his arm around Bianca's slim shoulders.

Bianca said, 'I'm sorry, Adrian.'

Muffet said, 'So am I.'

To be quite honest, I didn't know what to say.

I turned away, leaving the two engineers under the engineering miracle of St Pancras Station and made my way back to Old Compton Street on foot. I don't know what happened to the daffodils, but I hadn't got them when I arrived home.

Monday February 24th

Chapter Twenty-Four: Oblivion
Jake slipped the hose over the exhaust pipe and checked

that it was properly connected. Then he put the other end of the hose through the side window of the car. He took a long, last look at the glorious vista of the Lake District panorama spread beneath him. 'How glorious life is,' he said, aloud, to the wind. All around him the daffodils nodded their agreement. Jake took his portable electric razor from his toiletry bag and proceeded to shave. He had always been vain and he was particularly keen to look good as a corpse. His bristles flew into the wind and became as one with the earth. Jake splashed on Obsession, his favourite after-shave lotion. Then, his toilette completed, he climbed into the car and switched on the engine.

As the fumes filled the inside of the car, Jake ruminated on his life. He had visited four continents and bedded some of the world's most beautiful women. He had recovered the Ashes for England. He had climbed Everest backwards, and found the definitive source of the Nile. Nobody could say that his life had been without interest. But, without Regina, the girl he loved, he did not want to live. As Jake slipped into oblivion, the needle on the petrol gauge turned to 'E'. Which would run out first, Jake's oxygen supply, or Jake's petrol . . .?

Tuesday February 25th

Got the courage up to ring my mother. My father answered. He said that he has moved back to live with my mother 'on a temporary basis' until she has recovered from the immediate shock of the Bianca/

Muffet affair. Apparently, she is too ill to leave her bed and look after Rosie.

He asked how I had taken it.

I said, 'Oh me, I'm fine,' and then big, fat tears rolled down my cheeks and into the electronic workings of the telephone handset. My father kept saying, down the phone, 'There, there, lad. There, there, don't cry, lad,' in a tender voice that I don't remember him using before.

Roberto the chef came and stood at my side and wiped the tears away with his apron. Eventually, after promising to keep in touch, I said goodbye to my father. For years I have thought of him as a feckless fool, but I now see that I have misjudged him.

When I got back to the room, I found that Bianca had taken all her personal belongings, including the photograph of Isambard Kingdom Brunel.

Wednesday February 26th

I went to a place called Ed's Diner at lunchtime today and had a hot dog, fries, a Becks beer and a mug of filter coffee. I asked for a glass for my beer and then noticed that the other men of my age were swigging it from the bottle, so I pushed my glass away surreptitiously and did as they did. I sat at a high stool at the counter in front of a mini-jukebox. Each selection cost five pence. I selected only one record, but I played it three times.

I used to be able to recite the lyric of 'Stand by Me' off by heart. Bianca and I used to sing along with Ben E. King when we cooked Sunday breakfast together. Our percussion instruments included: a box of household matches, a spatula, and a tin of dried lentils.

In Ed's Diner I tried to sing the words under my breath but I couldn't remember a word.

At the end of the song I was in tears. Why couldn't she have stood by me?

A man sitting on the next stool asked if there was anything he could do. I tried to compose myself, but to my absolute horror I began to sob loudly and without restraint. There were tears; there was snot; there were undignified gulpings and heavings of the shoulders. The stranger put his arm around my shoulders and asked, 'Have you had a relationship gone wrong?'

I nodded, then managed to say, in between sobs, 'Finished.'

'Same here,' he said. Then 'My name's Alan.' Alan told me that he was 'devastated' because his partner, Christopher, had fallen for another man. I ordered two more beers and then I told Alan the whole story about Bianca and Martin Muffet. Alan confessed himself to be shocked and was thoughtful enough to enquire as to my mother's feelings. I told him that I'd phoned her last night and that she'd told me that her life was over.

Alan and I have arranged to meet for a drink at

8.00 p.m. tonight. Am I now, like Blanche Dubois, dependent on the kindness of strangers?

Midnight Alan didn't turn up. I sat in the 'Coach and Horses' for over an hour, waiting for him. Perhaps he met another stranger with a more original tragic story.

I miss her. I miss her. I miss her.

Thursday February 27th

Roberto stood over me this evening and made me eat a plate of tagliatelle with hare sauce. He said, 'A woman issa woman, but food issa food.'

Perhaps it has more meaning in the original Italian.

Jake handed the envelope containing the money to the sinister man.

'Quick and clean,' he said. 'They mustn't know what hit them.'

The man grunted and left the Soho drinking den. Jake looked around him, at the tawdry, painted girls, at the bestial faces of the late night drinkers. Was it only yesterday he was in the Lake District attempting suicide? As he rose to his feet, a young prostitute attempted to procure him. He pushed her away irritably, saying, 'Get lost, baby, I've known and lost the only woman I'll ever want.'

He strode out into the vibrant Soho night, his cowboy boots tapping strangely on the murky pavement. I must get them soled and heeled tomorrow, he thought. As he passed down Old Compton Street, he looked up at the window of the flat above Alma's Patisserie. The light was still burning but he knew that by now all human life had been extinguished. He was a murderer by proxy.

Tears poured inside his heart, but his face was as it always was, hard and unforgiving and without God's blessing.

Saturday February 29th

I have informed Mr Andropolosis, the landlord, that I have taken over the tenancy, and paid him a month's rent in advance, so the room is now mine. Thank God for the end of this month. It has surely been the worst since time began.

To complete our catalogue of family misery, Grandma was admitted to hospital during the early hours of this morning with abdominal pains. I rang the hospital this afternoon and was told by the ward sister that Grandma was 'comfortable'. If this is true, then she is the only member of the family who is – the rest of us are in total misery.

Sunday March 1st

I joined my mother, father and Rosie at Grandma's hospital bedside this afternoon. It was the first time I had seen Grandma without her teeth. I was shocked at how *old* she looked.

My mother has lost weight and her eyes looked sore, as though she has been weeping constantly since Muffet upped and left her. After visiting time was over and we were trooping down the ward, my mother said bitterly: 'They're in Hounslow, staying with his brother, Andrew.'

I said, 'I don't want to know, Mum.'

My father said, 'Let it drop, Pauline.'

Rosie said, 'I'm glad he's gone. I hope he never comes back.' She held her hand up and my father took it and steered her through the big double doors at the end of the ward. As we walked alongside the hospital tower blocks, the litter swirled around our feet and I had a premonition of doom.

I almost turned back to say a proper goodbye to Grandma, but I didn't want to keep the others hanging around in the potholed car park, so I didn't. Instead, we went home and had a Marks & Spencer's roast beef dinner each. Mine was quite nice, but it wasn't a patch on the real thing cooked by my grandma. As I was compressing the dirty tin foil trays into the kitchen pedal bin, the telephone rang. It was the hospital, telling us that 'Mrs Edna May Mole passed away at 5.15 p.m.'

I tried to remember where I was *exactly* at 5.15 p.m. I worked out that I was in a BP petrol station, helping my father to check the pressure in his car tyres.

I haven't shed a single tear for her yet. I'm dried up inside. My heart feels like a peach stone.

Monday March 2nd

It is a well-known fact that Grandma and my mother never got on, so nobody was prepared for the positively Mediterranean grief my mother is displaying over her mother-in-law's death: copious tears, breast-beating, etc. This morning she was lamenting, 'I owed her fifty quid' over and over again.

My father continues to astonish me with his maturity. He has dealt with all the death paperwork and haggled over the cost of the funeral with commendable efficiency.

Tuesday March 3rd

At 10.00 p.m. I rang 'Savages' to tell them that I am staying in Leicester for the funeral on Friday afternoon. Roberto said, 'I'm glad you ring, Adrian. Your flat has been called on by burglars.' He made it sound as though burglars had been invited to tea, brought flowers and left a visiting card. There's nothing I can do tonight. The police have employed the services of a locksmith. The new key is at 'Savages'. I feel strangely calm.

Wednesday March 4th

Train to Leicester 8.40 p.m.

They have taken everything, apart from my books, boxer shorts and an old pair of polyester trousers. How they got the bed down the stairs will probably always remain a mystery. The policeman I spoke to on the phone said, in answer to my question about the likelihood of their finding the culprits: 'You know what chance a snowball has in hell? Well, halve that. Then halve it again.' He asked if I had insurance.

I laughed scornfully and said, 'Of course not. This is Adrian Mole you're speaking to.'

I am now a man without possessions.

Thursday March 5th

I went into Grandma's home this morning. Everything was the same as ever. My GCE certificates were still there, framed on the wall. My dead grandad Albert's photograph was on the mantelpiece. The clock was still ticking. Upstairs, the linen lay folded in the cupboard and in the garden the bulbs pushed through the earth. The biscuit barrel was full of fig rolls and her second best slippers stood by her bed. Inside a kitchen cupboard, I found her Yorkshire pudding tin. She had used it for over forty years. Stupid to weep over a Yorkshire pudding tin, but I did. I then wiped it dry and replaced it in the cupboard, as she would have liked.

Friday March 6th
Grandma's Funeral

My mother and father, Rosie and I worked together as a team today and managed to give Grandma a good send-off. There was a respectable turnout in the church, which surprised me, because Grandma didn't encourage people to call on her. She preferred the company of Radio Four. She had been known to turn people away from her doorstep, should they be inconsiderate enough to call during the Afternoon Play.

The hymns were 'Amazing Grace' and 'Onward Christian Soldiers'. Bert Baxter sang out loudly, almost drowning the others in the congregation. For an atheist, he certainly enjoys singing in church. As I watched him, I couldn't help thinking wistfully that it should have been him who died instead of Grandma. The vicar said a lot of incredibly stupid things about Grandma being born into sin and dying in sin.

Anybody who knew Grandma knew that she was incapable of sin. She couldn't even tell a lie. When I asked her once if my spots were clearing up (I must have been about fifteen), she answered, 'No, you've still got a face like a ladybird's arse.' She occasionally used such mild profanities, but she was certainly not a sinner.

I don't like to think of her lying under the earth, alone and cold. Still, at least she was never burgled or mugged. She is safe from all that now.

The funeral tea was held at our house. My mother had been up most of the previous night, cleaning and polishing and trying to get the stains out of the lounge carpet.

My father replaced the missing light bulbs and mended the ballcock so that the lavatory flushed properly.

Tania Braithwaite came round to give her commiserations and kindly offered to defrost some vegetarian quiches she had in the freezer. She told us that Pandora had cancelled a lecture and was intending to come to the funeral tea and would be bringing six bottles of Marks & Spencer's champagne with her.

She said, 'Pandora believes in celebrating death. She sees it as a new adventure, as opposed to a rather boring ending.'

Bert Baxter had phoned to ask what time the service started, which reminded my mother that there was no beetroot in the house. So Rosie was given a personal safety alarm and sent round to the corner shop to buy a jar from Mr Patel's shop.

At midnight, I watched my parents spreading a white tablecloth over the dining-room table, which had had its leaves fully extended. As they flapped and adjusted the cloth, one at either end, I had a sudden sense of being a member of the family.

Rosie had arranged some daffodils and freesias nicely in a vase and was praised by everyone. Even the dog behaved itself. When we finally went to bed, the house looked perfect; everything was in its place and we Moles could hold our heads high. Grandma would have been proud of us.

After the funeral service, Rosie and I ran ahead of the other mourners to take the clingfilm off the sandwiches and sausage rolls.

Pandora was waiting outside the house in her car. We filled the bath with cold water and put the bottles of champagne into it to chill.

Pandora looked beautifully severe in a black tailored suit. However, I no longer felt in awe of her, so we were able to talk to each other as friends and equals. She complimented me on how well I was looking and she even praised my clothes. She fingered the lapel of my navy blue unstructured Next suit and said, 'Welcome to the nineties.'

The house soon filled up with mourners and I was kept busy circulating with glasses of champagne on a tray. At first, everyone stood around, not knowing what to say, nervous of enjoying themselves for fear of being thought disrespectful to the dead. Then Pandora broke the ice by proposing a toast to Grandma.

'To Edna Mole,' she said, lifting her glass of champagne high, 'a woman of the highest principles.'

Everyone clinked glasses and swigged back the champagne and it wasn't long before laughter broke out and I was fishing the bottles out of the bath.

My mother rummaged in the sideboard and brought out the photograph albums. I was astonished to see a photograph of my grandma at the age of twenty-four. She looked very dashing, dark-haired, with a lovely figure, and was laughing and pushing a bicycle up a hill. There was a man next to her wearing a flat cap. He had a big moustache and his eyes were crinkled against the sun. It was my grandad. Everybody remarked that I looked like him.

My father took the photograph out of the album and went into the garden and sat on Rosie's swing. After a while, I followed him out. He handed me the photograph and said, 'I'm an orphan, son.'

I put my hand on his shoulder, then went back inside to find that the funeral tea had turned into a party. People were laughing hysterically at the photographs in the album. Me at the seaside, falling off a donkey. Me in a secondhand cub's uniform three sizes too big. Me at six months, lying naked on a half moon-shaped rug in front of a gas fire. Me two days old with my grinning, young-looking parents in the maternity hospital. On the back was written, in my mother's handwriting, 'Our darling baby, two days old'.

There was a photograph I don't remember seeing before. It was my mother and father and my grandma and grandad. They were sitting in deckchairs, watching me, aged about three, playing in the sand. On the back was written: 'Yarmouth, Bank Holiday Monday'.

Rosie said, 'Why aren't I in the photo?'

Bert Baxter said, 'Cos you 'adn't been bleedin' born, that's why.'

At seven o'clock, Ivan Braithwaite offered to escort some of my grandma's elderly neighbours back to their pensioners' bungalows while they and he could still walk.

The rest of us carried on until eleven o'clock. Tania Braithwaite, who has been vegetarian for nine years, cracked and ate a sausage roll and then another.

My mother and father danced together to 'You've Lost That Loving Feeling'. You couldn't have slid a ruler between them.

Pandora and I watched them dancing. She said, 'So they're back together again, are they?'

'I hope so,' I said, looking at Rosie.

As I said before, it was a good send-off.

Monday March 9th

Old Compton Street
I am back in my room with only my books and boxer shorts for company. I have given the trousers away to a young man selling *The Big Issue*. I made a pillow out of my underwear and slept on the floor. I have often wondered what it would be like to be a celibate monk

in a bare cell. Now, thanks to burglary and desertion, I know.

I went into 'Savages' to help clean the kitchen. Savage himself was there, released from the alcohol abuse unit and looking fit and athletic and sipping on a glass of mineral water. He commiserated with me on my various losses and said that there was some old furniture in the attic above the restaurant that I could have.

'Just help yourself, kid,' he said.

I can't get used to this new, kind, philanthropic Savage. I keep thinking he must be Savage's long lost twin brother, recently returned from a missionary station in Amazonia.

My room is now furnished with rococo style banquettes and fag-stained *faux* marble tables. Stuff that was obviously thrown upstairs when Savage took over the restaurant. I now sleep on two banquettes pushed together. I have angels at my head and cherubs at my feet. Roberto gave me some cutlery and crockery and kitchen utensils. Most of my fellow workers brought something to work with them this morning, to donate to the Adrian Mole Disaster Fund. I cook on a ring fuelled by a gas canister and I read by a mock chandelier, both donated by Luigi.

Wednesday March 11th

I rang home this morning. My father is still there, living in sin with my mother. My mother told me that Bianca and Muffet are intending to set up an engineering partnership called 'Dartington and Muffet'.

I cannot bear the thought of Muffet's bony fingers touching Bianca's lovely pale skin.

I cannot bear it.

Thursday March 12th

Chapter Twenty-Five: Resurgence
Jake sat down at the *faux* marble table and began to write another chapter of his novel, *Sparg from Kronk*.

Chapter Five: Green Shoots
Sparg missed his woman, Barf. There was a part of him that would never be reconciled to her loss.

It was springtime. Green shoots showed through the earth. Sparg left his hut and went outside. He was glad to be outside, for the hut was damp and the damp was rising fast.

Sparg needed a woman, but the only woman in sight was Krun, his mother. Though her face was wrinkled, her thighs were inviting. But it was forbidden by Kronkian law to take your own mother, even if she agreed.

Sparg walked aimlessly up a small hill and then walked aimlessly down. He was bored. There was firewood to collect, but he was sick of collecting firewood. It did not challenge his intellect. He grunted in despair and wished it were possible to communicate with his fellow Kronkians. It was just his luck, he thought, to be born in prehistoric times.

If only there was *language*, grunted Sparg internally . . .

to be continued

Jake fell back. The intensity of the writing had left him drained and pale. He left his room and walked to Wilde's, his favourite restaurant, where he was greeted by Mario.

'Longa tima noa see, Mr Westmorland.'

'Hi, Mario. My usual table, please, and my usual bottle, well chilled, and I'll have my usual starter, usual main course and usual pudding.'

'And for your aperitif, Mr Westmorland?' purred Mario.

'The usual,' barked Jake.

I've got to finish *Lo! The Flat Hills of My Homeland* soon, but I can't do that until Jake has finished writing *Sparg from Kronk.* I wish he would hurry up.

Friday March 13th

More businesses are closing around us. Every day, the boards go up at shop and restaurant windows. Every night, I pray that 'Savages' stays financially viable. I need my job. I'm aware that I'm being exploited, but at least I have a reason to get up in the morning, unlike three and a half million of my fellow citizens.

Grandma left my father three thousand and ninety pounds in her will, so my mother is not going to have her house repossessed. This is truly joyous news. It means that I won't have to break into my Building Society savings. I couldn't have seen her thrown onto the street. At least, I don't think I could.

Saturday March 14th

I received the following message when I got to work this morning. It was written on the back of a paper napkin. 'Forgot G. Left 500.' Nobody knew what it meant or who had taken the message.

Monday March 16th

Received another brochure from the Naxos Institute. Why are they mailing me so assiduously? Who has put them on to me? I don't know any holistic types. I'm not even a vegetarian and I swear by paracetamol.

I went to the National Gallery today, but it brought back painful memories of B., so I went back to Soho and paid two pounds to watch a fat girl with spots remove her bra and knickers through a peephole. I *watched* her through a peephole. She didn't remove her underclothes through a peephole.

Query: Are there night classes in syntax?

Tuesday March 17th

I ran out of toilet paper last night and reached for the Naxos Institute brochure to help me out of my emergency, when something about Angela Hacker's face made me pause. It seemed to say, 'Come to me, Adrian.' Her face is nothing to write home about, in fact it's nothing to write *anywhere* about.

I put the brochure down and picked up the *Evening Standard* instead. It has far better absorbency qualities.

11.45 p.m. Can't sleep for St Patrick's Day revellers, so have idly filled in the booking form for the first two weeks in April at the Naxos Institute in Greece.

Thursday March 19th

Idly filled in a cheque made out to 'Naxos Institute', but I was only trying out a new pen. I couldn't possibly afford the time off work, or the money.

10.00 p.m. The full message was: 'Forgot to tell you Grandma has left you five hundred pounds, love, Dad.' Luigi, who had been away from the restaurant with food poisoning, returned today and congratulated me on 'Alla money ya got'. Naturally, I looked at him blankly. Confusion abounded for some minutes and then came the glorious realization, which we celebrated with a bottle of corked Frascati.

Saturday March 21st

The newly benign Savage has agreed to give me two weeks' leave (without pay). I posted my booking form this morning and this afternoon I bought some swimming trunks from a shop that was closing down in the Charing Cross Road. I can't wait to feel the warm Aegean sea on my body.

Worked on *Lo!* with Angela Hacker in mind.

Jake opened his manuscript book. The ivory handmade paper looked enticing. He took his Mont Blanc pen in his hand and began to write.

'Sorry, darling,' he said to the glorious example of English womanhood who sprawled opposite him, showing her knickers, 'but the Muse is upon me.'

Then he lowered his handsome head and was at once in Kronk, the home of his hero, Sparg.

Sparg grunted, recognizing the hated form of his father in the darkness. His father grunted back. Sparg threw a pebble from one hand to the other. Why hadn't something been invented to pass the hours of darkness before bed, he wondered. Something like a game such as cards, he wondered. He went back into his hut and pushed the animal skins listlessly around on his bed. He was cold at night without a woman. He determined that he would get up early the next morning and find one and bring her home to Kronk.

Thursday March 26th

I bought a short-sleeved shirt and a pair of Bermuda shorts from a stall in Berwick Street market. I have never worn shorts since reaching adulthood.

A new Adrian Mole is emerging from the ashes.

Savage turned up drunk and disorderly at the restaurant and proceeded to fire Luigi, Roberto and the whole of the kitchen staff apart from me. He said, 'You can stay, Adrian. You're a fucking loser, like me.'

He has promoted me to *Maître d'*, a position I do not want and cannot do.

Luigi and Roberto sat in the kitchen, smoking and talking in Italian. They didn't seem too concerned. Meanwhile, dressed in Luigi's suit, I was forced to fawn over customers, show them to their seats and pretend to be interested in their requirements. Savage sat at the bar, shouting out the biographical details of his customers as they came in. As one respectable-looking middle-aged couple entered, he yelled: 'Well, if it isn't Mr and Mrs Wellington. He's wearing a toupée and she's paid three thousand pounds for those perky looking titties.'

Instead of going straight back out, or thumping him on the side of his drunken head, Mr and Mrs Wellington grinned and allowed me to show them to table number six. Perhaps they are proud of their artificial attributes. As my recently dead grandma would say, 'There's nowt so strange as folk, especially London folk.'

Poor Grandma. She never went to London in her life.

For the past four days, I have been unable to write a word. The thought of Angela Hacker reading my manuscript has totally inhibited me. However, tonight I achieved a breakthrough.

He had writer's block. For over five hours he stared down at the mockingly empty page. His publisher was calling hourly. The printing presses were waiting, but still he could not finish his book. Jake looked out of the window, hoping for inspiration. The New York skyline stretched away into infinity . . .

'Infinity!' shouted Jake, excitedly, and he began to work on his novel, *Sparg from Kronk*.

Sparg had wandered far from Kronk and was standing on a high headland, looking in wonderment at a strange watery mass and a blue line ahead of him. Without knowing it (because there was no language), Sparg was marvelling over the sea and the far distant horizon. Sparg growled and began to descend the headland. He would walk to the far blue line, he thought. It would be something to do. Sparg thought this because there was as yet no swimming . . .

Received confirmation from Faxos Institute that I have a place on the Writers' Course. I am terrified.

Friday March 27th

Luigi has been reinstated and I am safely back in the kitchen, thank God. Roberto has been allowing me to watch him at work. For most of my life, I have been denied a proper food education. There was never anything to learn from my mother; she stopped cooking real food soon after reading *The Female Eunuch*. Though, ironically, the author of that seminal tome, Ms Germaine Greer, is a renowned cook and dinner party giver.

Thanks to Roberto's kindness, I can now cook pasta '*al dente*' and make a basic sponge cake and I've almost cracked making watercress soup. I now spring from my double banquettes in the morning, eager to get to work.

Plane tickets arrived today.

A new girl started work as a waitress at 'Savages' this evening. Her name is Jo Jo and she is from Nigeria. She is studying Art at St Martin's. She is taller than anybody else in the restaurant. Her hair is braided with hundreds of tiny beads. She rattles when she walks. Her mother is something big in the Nigerian tractor industry.

Saturday March 28th

Made a *tower* of profiteroles today. Roberto said: 'Congratulations, Adriana! The chocolate icing issa perfection.'

Jo Jo tasted the first one and pronounced it to be 'delectable'. Luigi happened to have his polaroid camera with him, so he photographed me and the tower and Jo Jo. I have pinned the photograph on my wall. I look quite handsome.

Sunday March 29th

I was still in bed at midday when there was a knock on the door. I never have visitors, so I was a little alarmed. I put my ear to the door, but all I could hear was a peculiar rattling noise. I eventually opened the door, but I kept the security chain on. I was delighted to see Jo Jo through the crack.

She smiled at me and said that she was going to the Tate Gallery.

'Do you want to come?' she asked.

I slipped the chain off and invited her in. She walked around the room and commented on how tidy it was.

She stopped at the table where my manuscript lay in its transparent folder and said, 'So this is your book.'

She touched it reverently. 'I would like to read it one day.'

'When it's finished,' I said.

I made her a cup of Nescafé and then excused myself and went into the bathroom to wash and change.

I looked at myself in the washbasin mirror. Something had happened to my face. I no longer looked like John Major.

Jo Jo likes walking, so we walked to the Tate. I was proud to be seen with such a stunning looking woman. I asked her about Nigeria and she spoke about her country with obvious love. She is a Yoruba and comes from Abeokuta.

She asked me about my family and I told her about the tangled web of relationships, the break-ups and the reconciliations.

She laughed and said, 'To work out the relationships in my family, you would need an extremely sophisticated computer.'

I had never been to the Tate, but Jo Jo knew it well. She guided me round and made me look at a few of her favourite paintings – all depicting people, I noticed. We looked at paintings by Paula Rego, Vanessa Bell and Matisse, and a piece of sculpture by Ghisha Koenig called 'The Machine Minders', and then she insisted that we leave before we got bored and our feet started to ache.

As we were going down the steps, Jo Jo asked if I would like to have tea at her flat in Battersea.

I said, 'I'd love to.' We crossed the road and stood at the bus stop, but then, on impulse, I flagged down a black cab and we rode to her flat in style.

She lives on the top floor of a mansion block. Every room is full of her paintings. Many of the paintings are nude self-portraits, in which she has depicted herself in many colours, including green, pink, purple, blue and yellow.

I asked her if she was making a statement about her colour. 'No,' she laughed. 'But I would get bored only using blacks and browns.'

We ate scones and drank Earl Grey tea and talked non-stop: about 'Savages'; Nigerian politics; cats; one of her art teachers, who is going mad; Cecil Parkinson; the price of paint brushes; Vivaldi; our star signs – she is Leo (but on the cusp of Cancer); and her girls' boarding school in Surrey, where she lived from the age of eleven until she got expelled at sixteen for climbing on the roof of the chapel in a protest against the lousy food.

Over a glass of cheap wine, we discussed trees; Matisse; Moscow; Russian politics; our favourite cakes; the use of umbrellas; cabbage; and the Royal Family. She is a republican, she said.

Over a final glass of wine and a plate of bread and cheese, I talked to her about my grandmother, my mother, Pandora, Sharon, Megan, Leonora, Cassandra and Bianca. 'You're carrying a lot of baggage,' Jo Jo said.

We parted at 10.30 p.m. with a friendly handshake. Before she closed the door, I asked how old she was. 'Twenty-four,' she said. 'Goodnight.'

Monday March 30th

I ran out of 'Savages' during my break time and bought Ambre Solaire (Factor 8), espadrilles, sleeveless tee shirts, three more pairs of shorts and sixteen thousand drachmas.

I worked on the book late into the night. I am nervous about Angela Hacker's opinion. Added more descriptive words to *Lo! The Flat Hills of My Homeland* and took out more descriptive words from *Sparg from Kronk*.

Tuesday March 31st

The staff arranged a small *bon voyage* party in the kitchen after the restaurant closed at lunchtime. I was very touched. Roberto cooked kebabs and arranged an authentic Greek salad in my honour. Jo Jo bought two bottles of retsina earlier in the day and we all clinked glasses and swore eternal friendship. Then Savage came in, complaining that Luigi had forgotten to add VAT to somebody's bill, so the party broke up. Jo Jo is good at packing, she said. She offered to come and help me.

I laid my clothes, toiletry bag and manuscript out on my bed before proceeding to pack, and then realized that the burglars had taken my suitcase.

Jo Jo ran to Berwick Street market and bought one of those man-made fibre striped bags, the type that refugees have on the television news. Once I was packed, I debated with Jo Jo on whether or not to take a warm coat with me. She said I ought to, but I decided not to. Instead, I slung a cotton sweater around my shoulders. Everybody has said that Greece is warm in April. My legs look very white at the moment in my shorts, but by the time I return, they will be gloriously tanned.

Spring

Spring

Hotel Adelphi
Athens
Thursday April 2nd
9.30 a.m.

Dear Jo Jo,

For the first time in my life, there is nobody to wish me a Happy Birthday. I am now twenty-five years old. Which is a millstone in anybody's life. Do I still qualify to be called a 'Young British Novelist'? I hope so.

Other participants in the Naxos Institute course are swirling around downstairs in the hotel lobby, chatting easily to each other. I fled back into the lift when I saw them, and went up to the roof terrace, but Angela Hacker was up there, smoking a cigarette and looking moodily at the Acropolis in the far distance. She is skinny and dresses in white clothes. She was weighed down by ethnic silver jewellery.

I don't know when the photograph of her in the brochure was taken, but in life she looks at least forty-eight. Obviously past it, sexually and artistically.

I didn't thank you properly for that afternoon in the Tate. I keep thinking about the pictures. I particularly liked those painted by that Portuguese woman, Paula something.

All best wishes,
Adrian

Ferry
Friday April 3rd

Dear Mum and Dad,

I am writing this on the first ferry, which is taking us to where we catch the second ferry to Naxos. Angela Hacker and most of the twelve members of the writers' group are already in the bar. The majority of them smoke. You would probably get along famously with them, Mum. The other, more holistic, holidaymakers are looking over the side of the ship, taking photographs or swapping aromatherapy recipes. I am keeping to myself. I don't want to lumber myself with a hastily-made 'friend' and spend the next fortnight getting rid of him or her. It has just started to rain. I will have to stop now and go inside.

Love from your son,
Adrian

Ferry
Friday April 3rd
4.00 p.m.

Dear Jo Jo,

There has been torrential rain for the whole of the three-hour crossing. I am wearing my cotton sweater, but am still cold. I now wish I'd followed your advice and brought a coat with me.

Angela Hacker has been falling down in the bar. The sea *is* choppy, but I think her lack of balance is due more to the copious amounts of retsina she is throwing down her neck. My fellow writers have been laughing non-stop since boarding the ferry. Some private joke, no doubt. I have not yet introduced myself to them.

Bamboo Hut Number Six
8.00 p.m.

The wind is whistling through the slats of my hut. Outside, the sky is grey and dotted with storm clouds. Supper was eaten in the open air, under a 'roof' of palm fronds. Not surprisingly, the ratatouille was cold.

I can hear Angela Hacker coughing from here, though her hut is at least two hundred yards further down the rocky hill.

There was a community meeting at eight o'clock, where the permanent staff and the facilitators introduced themselves and their work. The meeting was held in what they call here the 'Magic Ring', which is on the very top of the hill. The Magic Ring is a concrete base, surrounded by a low wall and covered in the usual palm frond and bamboo roof. There is nothing magical looking about it.

I was most concerned to hear Ms Hacker describe her course as 'Writing for Pleasure'. I get no pleasure from writing. Writing is a serious business, like painting.

There is a man here who wears his hair like yours. I saw him on the headland, looking out to sea. From a distance he looked like you. My heart did a backflip.

My hut is next to the hen-coop. A goat has just put its

head inside my hut and a donkey is braying somewhere in the pine woods. If Noah's Ark was washed up on the beach, I wouldn't be surprised.

Best wishes,
Adrian

Faxos
Sunday April 5th

Dear Pan,

You asked me to let you know how the Naxos course was, so I'll tell you about the first day.

The writers collected on the terrace at 11.15 a.m. I sat upwind, away from the cigarette smoke. At 11.30 a.m. Angela Hacker had still not appeared, so a man called Clive, who had seven boils on his neck, was sent to her hut. She eventually showed up at noon and apologized for having overslept. She then rambled on for an hour and fifteen minutes about 'Truth' and 'Narrative thrust' and 'developing an original voice'.

At 1.15 p.m. she sprang to her feet and said, 'Okay, that's it for the day. Write a poem including the word "Greece". Be prepared to read it aloud at 11.15 tomorrow morning.' She then headed for the bamboo bar, where she stayed for most of the day. When I'd written my poem, I went in for a cup of tea and heard her talking about your college in Oxford.

I asked her if she knew you and she said she had met you at Jack Cavendish's house a few times, 'before Jack left his third wife,' she said.

I said, 'It's a small world.'

'Try not to use clichés, darling,' she said.

She's a strange woman.

All the best from,

Adrian

Faxos

Monday April 6th

Dear Rosie,

I hope you like this postcard of the cheerful donkey. There is something about its daft expression that reminds me of the dog.

I have sent you a poem I was forced to write about Greece. It's time you started to take an interest in cultural matters. There is more to life than Nintendo games.

Love from your brother,

Adrian

Oh Greece, ancient cultured land
You wrap around my heart just like
An old elastic band.
Your hag-like women pensioners
Clad in clothes of black,
Are they unaware of all the services they lack?
Will they be content to watch
The donkey with its load?
Won't they want a vehicle to
Drive along the road?

Faxos
Tuesday April 7th

Dear Baz,

I am here on Naxos with Angela Hacker, whom I understand you know quite well. She and I hit it off immediately
and she has invited me to stay at her place in Gloucestershire
when we get back. I may be able to make the odd weekend,
but I am currently doing research in a restaurant kitchen
in Soho for my next book, *The Chopper*, so will not be able
to stay for a couple of weeks, as she would like.

The reason I am writing is to say that I hope there are
no hard feelings anymore over the Sharon Bott affair, because
we are likely to be moving in the same circles soon and I
would rather there were no acrimonious feelings between us.

Congratulations on finally getting to number one!

Cheers,

Your old friend,

Adrian Mole

Faxos
Wednesday April 8th

Dear John Tydeman,

As you cannot fail to see, if you have noticed the post-
mark, I am on the Greek island of Naxos. I am a member
of a writers' course being facilitated by Angela Hacker (she
sends you her love).

She asked us to write the first scene of a radio play, which
is something I have never attempted to do before.

I thought you might be interested to read what I have
written. I would be more than willing to finish it, if you
thought it had merit.

I shall be back in London at 3.00 p.m. on the 15th April, if you would like to talk to me face to face.

On second thoughts, the 16th would be more convenient for me. I shall probably need to rest after my journey.

Here is how the play opens:

The Cucumber Sandwich
A Play for Radio by Adrian Mole

A room in a wealthy house. A game of tennis can be heard through the french windows. Tea is poured. A spoon rattles in a cup.

LADY ELEANOR: A cucumber sandwich, Edwin?

EDWIN: Don't try to fob me off with your bourgeois ideas of gentility. I know the truth!

LADY ELEANOR (*gasps*): No! Surely not! You don't know the secret I have kept for forty years!

EDWIN (*contemptuously*): Yes, I do. The servant girl, Millie, told me.

A bell rings.

MILLIE: You rang, mum? Sorry to keep you, only I was 'elpin' cook with Master Edwin's twenty-first birthday cake.

LADY ELEANOR: You are dismissed, Millie. You have blabbed my secret.

MILLIE: What secret? Oh! The one about your being born a man?

To be continued

I do not wish to prejudice you in any way, but after I had finished reading this text, there was a stunned silence from my fellow writers. Angela's only comment was, 'You should have spun the secret out until the last scene of the play.'

Good advice, I think.

Anyway, I hope you enjoy *The Cucumber Sandwich*.

Yours,

With best wishes,

Adrian Mole

Faxos

Thursday April 9th

Dear Jo Jo,

The sun has shone for two days now and has turned Naxos into Paradise. The colours are breathtaking: the sea is peacock blue, the grass is peppermint green and the wild flowers are scattered on the hillside like living confetti.

Something has happened to my body. It feels looser, as though it has broken free and is floating.

I have been going to dream workshops at 7.00 a.m. The facilitator is a nice American woman dream therapist called Clara. I told her about a recurring dream I have that I am trying to pick up the last pea on my dinner plate by stabbing it with a fork. Try as I may, I cannot get the prongs of the fork to stab into the flesh of the pea.

For years I have woken up feeling frustrated and hungry after dreaming my pea dream.

Clara advised me to look at the dream from the *pea*'s

point of view. I did try hard to do this and, by discussing it with Clara later, I understood that I, Adrian Mole, was the pea and that the fork represented DEATH.

Clara said that my pea dream showed that I am afraid to die.

But who is *looking forward* to death? I don't know anybody who is cock-a-hoop at the prospect.

Clara explained that I am *morbidly* afraid of death.

How do you feel about death, Jo Jo?

I have made friends with the bloke with the beaded plaits like yours. His name is Sean Washington. His mother is Irish; his father is from St Kitts. He is here taking the stress management course, but he hangs out with the writers' group on the bar terrace.

We were both on vegetable chopping duties today and I was complimented by him and others on my expertise. I think I would like to be a chef. I may ask Savage if he'll give me a trial when I get back.

Angela Hacker has forbidden her writers' group to use clichés, but she will not be reading this letter, so I'll sign off by saying:

Wish you were here,

Adrian

Saturday April 11th

My first fax! It was addressed to 'Adrian Mole, Naxos Institute', and arrived at the travel agent's shop in the town. It was then conveyed to the Naxos Institute by greengrocer's van and delivered to me on the bar terrace by Julian, the handsome bald-headed administrator. It caused a sensation.

Dear Adrian,

Thank you for your letters. I wish I were there with you. It sounds idyllic.

I'm so glad that you feel at ease. When I first saw you in Savage's kitchen, I thought: that man is in *pain*. I wanted to touch you and comfort you there and then, but of course one does not do such a thing – not in England.

I think you have it in your power to become a happy man, providing you can let go of the past. Why not try to live in the present and leave all that baggage behind on Faxos when you return?

I couldn't wait to tell you that I have been offered a shared exhibition of 'Young Contemporaries' in September. Will you come to the opening? Please say you will.

Roberto is complaining that the man Savage has hired to take your place for a fortnight is massacring the vegetables and he now regrets letting you go on holiday.

Everybody at 'Savages' sends their best wishes. Roberto asks if you will bring a bottle of ouzo back for him.

I miss you.

I send you my best wishes as well,

    Jo Jo

Hut Number Six
Faxos Institute
Faxos
Sunday April 12th

Dear Jo Jo,

What fantastic news about the exhibition! Of course I will come to the opening. September seems a long way off, though. The spring is so glorious here. I've never seen such colours before.

At our meeting yesterday morning Angela Hacker asked the writers' group to write the first page of a novel.

I wanted to run up the hill to my hut immediately and present her with the whole manuscript of *Lo! The Flat Hills of My Homeland*, but I restrained myself. The book was only a few pages short of completion. Why spoil the ship for a ha'p'orth of tar? (Since being forbidden to use clichés, I find myself using them all the time.)

I worked all day and most of the night on *Lo!* And I think that now the book is finished. This is how it ends:

Jake got up from his computer terminal and paced around his study. He adjusted the painting of a stately African woman that he had recently bought in an exhibition.

He then stared moodily out of the window and watched a child dragging a stick along the ground.

Jake was desperate to finish *Sparg from Kronk*. He could hear the printer banging on his door, demanding the finished manuscript. His publisher had been admitted to hospital the night before with nervous strain, but the ending of his book continued to elude him.

The child outside the window stopped to scratch the stick into the dry earth of drought-hit London.

'Goddit!' shouted Jake, and he leaped into his state-of-the-art typing chair and began to write the end of his book.

Sparg wrestled with Krun, his father, for possession of the stick. He wondered why they were fighting over this particular stick. There were plenty of others lying around.

He looked at his father's old face, now disfigured by anger, and thought: why are we *doing* this? He let go of the stick and allowed his father to take it away.

Sparg sat on the baked earth and thought, if only there was *language*, we wouldn't have to be so damned *physical*.

He poked his finger into the dust. He drew it along. In a few minutes, he had made marks and symbols.

Before the sun had gone down, he had written the first page of his novel. He hoped it wouldn't rain in the night and obliterate his work.

Tomorrow, he would continue his work inside a cave, he thought. What should he call his novel? He grunted to himself and tried out several titles. Finally, he settled on one and hurried to the big cave to scratch it on the wall before he forgot:

A BOOK WITH NO LANGUAGE

Yes, that was it. And he picked up a stick and began to gnaw the end of it into a point.

Jake could hardly wait for the electronic printer to spew out the typewritten page.

'At last,' he jubilated, 'I have finished *Sparg from Kronk*!'

Please let me know what you think, Jo Jo. I really value your opinion.

I gave the completed manuscript to Angela Hacker this morning. She took it from me and groaned, 'Sodding hell. I only asked for one page!' Then she put it into the blue raffia bag that she carries everywhere with her and continued her conversation with Clara about a dream she'd had of being chased by a giant cockroach.

At 11.00 p.m., after spending the evening with my friends, singing on the bar terrace, I got back to my hut to find that the following note had been slipped under my door:

Adrian,

I've skipped through *Lo! The Flat Hills of My Homeland*. I won't waste words. It's typical juvenilia and has no merit at all. *Sparg from Kronk* has been done a million times, dearest boy. But *A Book With No Language* – Sparg's novel – is a truly brilliant concept.

I would like you to come and see me when we get back to London. I'd like to introduce you to my agent, Sir Gordon Giles. I think your originality will appeal to him.

Congratulations! You are a writer.

Angela Hacker

I may be a writer, Jo Jo, but I can't find the words to express my happiness.

My plane gets into Gatwick on Wednesday at 3.00 p.m.

Love from,
Adrian

Tuesday April 14th

Angela Hacker announced this morning that the writers' group's last meeting was to be held on 'Bare Bum Beach'. My penis shrivelled at the thought. I have never appeared in the nude in public before. 'Bare Bum Beach' is where the extrovert and confident desport themselves. I am neither of these things. However, after three glasses of retsina at lunchtime I found myself slithering over the rocks, heading for the nudist beach.

I was astounded by the ridiculous blue of the sea. The rocks shone pink as I stumbled towards the beach which was the colour of custard. It seemed the most natural thing in the world to shrug my shorts off and embrace the sand. For twelve long years I have worried about the size of my penis. Now, at last, by glancing at my fellow male writers I could see that I am made as other men. I easily fell within the 'normal' range.

At half past six in the evening I turned over and exposed myself to the sun. Nothing terrible happened.

There was no thunderbolt. Men and women did not run away, shrieking in horror at the sight of my full frontal nakedness.

I walked into the sea and swam towards the blood-red sunset. I allowed myself to float and to drift. It was almost dark when I swam back to the beach. I did not use my towel. I let the water dry on my body.

I walked back to the Institute in pale moonlight. I took a short cut through the woods. The floor was covered in pine needle debris, every footstep was a crackling aromatic delight.

I walked ankle deep through a glade of soft grass and wild flowers. Then I smelled honeysuckle and felt a tendril brush across my face. I reached the headland and stood for a moment, looking down at the Institute. The kitchen door was open. Out of it spilled bright light, laughter and the delicious smell of grilling meat.

Wednesday April 15th

10.00 p.m. I saw Jo Jo waiting beyond the barrier. I threw all my baggage down and ran towards her.

CELEBRATING 30 YEARS
OF ADRIAN MOLE

'One of literature's most endearing figures'
OBSERVER

In eight books, two TV series, a stage play and on radio, Adrian Mole has delighted millions of people young and old across the world over the last thirty years.

Whether you have grown up with Mole or have only recently become acquainted with his diaries, you will find on the following pages the full story about Adrian's literary birth as well as plenty of information about his creator Sue Townsend and her other works.

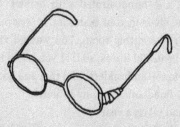

To find out even more about
Sue and Adrian don't forget to visit

www.suetownsend.co.uk

Turn the page and read on, starting with an
extract from Sue's latest Top 10 bestseller ...

Sue Townsend

Chapter 1

After they'd gone Eva slid the bolt across the door and disconnected the telephone. She liked having the house to herself. She went from room to room tidying, straightening and collecting the cups and plates that her husband and children had left on various surfaces. Somebody had left a soup spoon on the arm of her special chair – the one she had upholstered at night school. She immediately went to the kitchen and examined the contents of her Kleeneze cleaning products box.

'What would remove a Heinz tomato soup stain from embroidered silk damask?'

As she searched, she remonstrated with herself. 'It's your own fault. You should have kept the chair in your bedroom. It was pure vanity on your part to have it on display in the sitting room. You wanted visitors to notice the chair and to tell you how beautiful it was, so that you could tell them that it had taken two years to complete the embroidery, and that you had been inspired by Claude Monet's "Water-Lily Pond and Weeping Willow".'

The trees alone had taken a year.

There was a small pool of tomato soup on the kitchen floor that she hadn't noticed until she stepped in it and left orange footprints. The little non-stick saucepan containing half a can of tomato soup was still simmering on the hob. 'Too lazy to take a pan off the stove,' she thought. Then she remembered that the twins were Leeds University's problem now.

She caught her reflection in the smoky glass of the wall-mounted oven. She looked away quickly. If she had taken a while to look she would have seen a woman of fifty with a lovely, fine-boned face, pale inquisitive eyes and a Clara Bow mouth that always looked as though she were about to speak. Nobody – not even Brian, her husband – had seen her without lipstick. Eva thought that red lips complemented the black clothes she habitually wore. Sometimes she allowed herself a little grey.

Once, Brian had come home from work to find Eva in the garden, in her black wellingtons, having just pulled up a bunch of turnips. He'd said to her, 'For Christ's sake, Eva! You look like post-war Poland.'

Her face was currently fashionable. 'Vintage' according to the girl on the Chanel counter where she bought her lipstick (always remembering to throw the receipt away – her husband would not understand the outrageous expense).

She picked up the saucepan, walked from the kitchen into the sitting room and threw the soup all over her precious chair. She then went upstairs, into her bedroom and, without removing her clothes or her shoes, got into bed and stayed there for a year.

She didn't know it would be a year. She climbed into bed thinking she would leave it again after half an hour, but the comfort of the bed was exquisite, the white sheets were fresh and smelled of new snow. She turned on her side towards the open window and watched the sycamore in the garden shed its blazing leaves.

She had always loved September.

She woke when it was getting dark, and she heard her husband shouting outside. Her mobile rang. The display showed that it was her daughter, Brianne. She ignored it. She pulled the duvet over her head and sang the words of Johnny Cash's 'I Walk The Line'.

When she next poked her head out from under the duvet, she heard her next-door neighbour Julie's excited voice saying, 'It's not right, Brian.'

They were in the front garden.

Her husband said, 'I mean, I've been to Leeds and back, I need a shower.'

'Of course you do.'

Eva thought about this exchange. Why would driving to Leeds and back necessitate having a shower? Was the northern air full of grit? Or had he been sweating on the M1? Cursing the lorries? Screaming at tailgaters? Angrily denouncing whatever the weather was doing?

She switched on the bedside lamp.

This provoked another episode of shouting outside, and demands that she, 'Stop playing silly buggers and unbolt the door!'

She realised that, although she wanted to go

downstairs and let him in, she couldn't actually leave the bed. She felt as though she had fallen into a vat of warm quick-setting concrete, and that she was powerless to move. She felt an exquisite languor spread throughout her body, and thought, 'I would have to be mad to leave this bed.'

There was the sound of breaking glass. Soon after, she heard Brian on the stairs.

He shouted her name.

She didn't answer.

He opened the bedroom door. 'There you are,' he said.

' Yes, here I am.'

'Are you ill?'

'No.'

'Why are you in bed in your clothes and shoes? What are you playing at?'

'I don't know.'

'It's empty-nest syndrome. I heard it on *Woman's Hour*.'

When she didn't speak, he said, 'Well, are you going to get up?'

'No, I'm not.'

He asked, 'What about dinner?'

'No thanks, I'm not hungry.'

'I meant what about *my* dinner? Is there anything?'

She said, 'I don't know, look in the fridge.'

He stomped downstairs. She heard his footsteps on the laminate floor he'd laid so ineptly the year before. She knew by the squeak of the floorboards that he'd gone into the sitting room. Soon he was stomping back up the stairs.

'What the bloody hell has happened to your chair?' he asked.

'Somebody left a soup spoon on the arm.'

'There's soup all over the bloody thing.'

'I know. I did it myself.'

'What – threw the soup?'

Eva nodded.

' You're having a nervous breakdown, Eva. I'm ringing your mum.'

'No!'

He flinched at the ferocity in her voice.

She saw from the stricken look in his eyes that after twenty-five years of marriage his familiar domestic world had come to an end. He went downstairs. She heard him cursing at the disconnected phone then, after a moment, stabbing at the keys. As she picked up the bedroom extension her mother was laboriously giving her phone number down the line, '0116 2 444 333, Mrs Ruby Brown-Bird speaking.'

Brian said, 'Ruby, it's Brian. I need you to come over straight away.'

'No can do, Brian. I'm in the middle of having a perm. What's up?'

'It's Eva –' he lowered his voice '– I think she must be ill.'

'Send for an ambulance then,' said Ruby irritably.

'There's nothing wrong with her physically.'

'Well, that's all right then.'

'I'll come and pick you up and bring you back so you can see for yourself.'

'Brian, I can't. I'm hosting a perm party and I've got to have my own personal solution rinsed off in half an hour. If I don't, I shall look like Harpo Marx. 'Ere, talk to Michelle.'

After a few muffled noises a young woman came on the line.

'Hello . . . Brian, is it? I'm Michelle. Can I talk you through what would happen if Mrs Bird abandoned the perm at this stage? I *am* insured, but it would be extremely inconvenient for me if I had to appear in court. I'm booked up until New Year's Eve.'

The phone was handed back to Ruby. 'Brian, are you still there?'

'Ruby, she's in bed wearing her clothes and shoes.'

'I *did* warn you, Brian. We were in the church porch about to go in, and I turned round and said to you, "Our Eva's a dark horse. She doesn't say much, and you'll never know what she's thinking . . ." ' There was a long pause, then Ruby said, 'Phone your own mam.'

The phone was disconnected.

Eva was astounded that her mother had made a lastminute attempt to sabotage her wedding. She picked up her handbag from the side of the bed and rooted through the contents, looking for something to eat. She always kept food in her bag. It was a habit from when the twins were young and hungry, and would open their mouths like the beaks of fledgling birds. Eva found a squashed packet of crisps, a flattened Bounty bar and half a packet of Polos.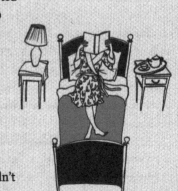

She heard Brian stabbing at the keys again.

Brian was always slightly apprehensive when he called his mother. His tongue couldn't form words properly. She had a way of making him feel guilty, whatever the subject of the conversation.

His mother answered promptly with a snappy, ' Yes?'

Brian said, 'Is that you, Mummy?'

Eva picked up the extension again, being careful to muffle the mouthpiece with her hand.

'Who else would it be? Nobody else phones this house. I'm on my own seven days a week.'

Brian said, 'But . . . er . . . you . . . er . . . don't like visitors.'

'No, I don't like visitors but it would be nice to have to turn them away. Anyway, what is it? I'm halfway through *Emmerdale*.'

Brian said, 'Sorry, Mummy. Do you want to ring me back when the adverts come on?'

'No,' she said. 'Let's get it over with, whatever it is.'

'It's Eva.'

'Ha! Why am I not surprised? Has she left you? The first time I clapped eyes on that girl I knew she'd break your heart.'

Brian wondered if his heart had ever been broken. He had always had difficulty in recognising an emotion. When he had brought his First Class Bachelor of Science degree home to show his mother, her current boyfriend had said, ' You must be very happy, Brian.'

Brian had nodded his head and forced a smile, but the truth was that he didn't feel any happier than he had felt the day before, when nothing remarkable had happened.

His mother had taken the embossed certificate, examined it carefully and said, 'You'll struggle to find an astronomy job. There are men with more superior qualifications than you've got who can't find work.'

Now Brian said, mournfully, 'Eva's gone to bed in her clothes and shoes.'

His mother said, 'I can't say I'm surprised, Brian. She's always brought attention to herself. Do you remember when we all went to the caravan that Easter in 1986? She took a suitcase full of her ridiculous beatnik clothes. You don't wear beatnik clothes at Wells-Next-The-Sea. Everybody was staring at her.'

Eva screamed from upstairs, ' You shouldn't have thrown my lovely black clothes into the sea!'

Brian hadn't heard his wife scream before.

Yvonne Beaver asked, 'What's that screaming?'

Brian lied. 'It's the television. Somebody's just won a lot of money on

Eggheads.'

His mother said, 'She looked very presentable in the holiday wear I bought her.'

As Eva listened, she remembered taking the hideous clothes out of the carrier bag. They had smelled as if they had been in a damp warehouse in the Far East for years, and the colours were lurid mauves, pinks and yellows. There had been a pair of what Eva thought looked like men's sandals and a beige, pensioner-style anorak. When she tried them on, she looked twenty years older.

Brian said to his mother, 'I don't know what to do, Mummy.'

Yvonne said, 'She's probably drunk. Leave her to sleep it off.'

Eva threw the phone across the room and screamed, 'They were men's sandals she bought me in Wells-Next-The-Sea! I saw men wearing them with white socks! You should have protected me from her, Brian! You should have said, "My wife would not be seen dead in these hideous sandals!" '

She had screamed so loudly that her throat hurt. She shouted downstairs and asked Brian to bring her a glass of water.

Brian said, 'Hang on, Mummy. Eva wants a glass of water.'

His mother hissed down the phone, 'Don't you dare fetch her that water, Brian! You'll be making a rod for your own back if you do. Tell her to get her own water!'

Brian didn't know what to do. While he dithered in the hallway his mother said, 'I could do without this trouble. My knee has been playing me up. I was on the verge of ringing my consultant and asking him to chop my leg off.'

He took the phone into the kitchen with him and ran the cold tap.

His mother asked, 'Is that water I can hear running?'

Brian lied again. 'Just topping up a vase of flowers.'

'Flowers! You're lucky you can afford flowers.'

'They're out of the garden, Mummy. Eva grew them from seed.'

' You're lucky to have the space for a garden.'

The phone went dead. His mother never said goodbye.

He went upstairs with the glass of cold water. When he handed it to Eva, she took a small sip, then put it on the crowded bedside table. Brian hovered at the end of

the bed. There was nobody to tell him what to do.

She almost felt sorry for him, but not enough to get out of bed. Instead, she said, 'Why don't you go downstairs and watch your programmes?'

Brian was a devotee of property programmes. His heroes were Kirstie and Phil. Unbeknown to Eva he had written to Kirstie, saying that she always looked nice, and was she married to Phil or was their partnership purely a business arrangement? He had received a reply three months later, saying 'Thank you for your interest' and signed ' Yours, Kirstie'. Enclosed was a photograph of Kirstie. She was wearing a red dress and showing an alarming amount of bosom. Brian kept the photograph inside an old Bible. He knew it would be safe there. Nobody ever opened it.

Later that night, a full bladder forced Eva out of bed. She changed from her day clothes into a pair of pyjamas that she had been keeping for emergency hospital admittance. This was on her mother's advice. Her mother believed that if your dressing gown, pyjamas and sponge bag were good quality, the nurses and doctors treated you better than the scruffs who came into hospital with their shoddy things in a Tesco's carrier bag.

Eva got back into bed and wondered what her children were doing on their first night at university. She imagined them sitting in a room together, weeping and homesick, as they had done when they first went to nursery school.

Chapter 2

Brianne was in the communal kitchen and lounge of the accommodation block. So far she had met a boy dressed like a girl, and a woman dressed like a man. They were both talking about clubs and musicians she'd never heard of.

Brianne had a short attention span and soon stopped listening, but she nodded her head and said 'Cool' when it seemed appropriate. She was a tall girl with broad shoulders, long legs and big feet. Her face was mostly hidden behind a long straggly black fringe which she pushed out of her eyes only when she actually wanted to see something.

A waiflike girl in a leopard-print maxi dress and tan Ugg boots came in with a bulging bag from Holland & Barrett which she stuffed into the fridge. Half her head had been shaved and a broken heart tattooed on to her scalp. The other half was a badly dyed lopsided green curtain.

Brianne said, 'Amazing hair. Did you do it yourself ?'

'I got my brother to help me,' the girl said. 'He's a poofter.'

The girl's sentences had a rising inflection as though she were permanently questioning the validity of her own statements.

Brianne asked, 'Are you Australian?'

The girl shouted, 'God! No!'

Brianne said, 'I'm Brianne.'

The girl said, 'I'm Poppy. Brianne? I haven't heard that before.'

'My dad's called Brian,' said Brianne tonelessly. 'Is it hard to walk in a maxi?'

'No', said Poppy. 'Try it on if you like. It might stretch to fit you.'

She pulled the maxi dress over her head and stood revealed in a wispy bra and knickers. They both looked as though they had been made from scarlet cobwebs. She seemed to have no inhibitions whatsoever. Brianne had many inhibitions. She hated everything about herself: face, neck, hair, shoulders, arms, hands, fingernails, belly, breasts, nipples, waist, hips, thighs, knees, calves, ankles, feet, toenails and voice.

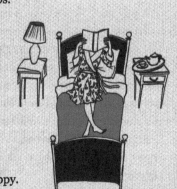

She said, 'I'll try it on in my room.'

' Your eyes are amazing,' said Poppy.

'Are they?'

'Are you wearing green contacts?' asked Poppy.

She stared into Brianne's face and pushed the fringe away.

'No.'

'They're an amazing green.'

'Are they?'

'Awesome.'

'I need to lose some weight.'

' Yeah, you do. I'm a weight loss expert. I'll teach you how to be sick after every meal.'

'I don't want to be bulimic.'

'It was good enough for Lily Allen.'

'I hate being sick.'

'Isn't it worth it to be thin? Remember the saying: "You can't be too rich or too thin." '

'Who said that?'

'I think it was Winnie Mandela.'

Poppy followed Brianne to her room, still in her underwear. They met Brian Junior in the corridor as he was locking the door to his room. He stared at Poppy and she stared back. He was the most beautiful man she had ever seen. She threw her arms above her head and affected a glamour girl pose, hoping that Brian Junior would admire her C cup breasts.

He said under his breath, but loud enough to be heard, 'Gross.'

Poppy said, 'Gross? It would be really useful to me if you would elaborate. I need to know which bits of me are particularly repellent.'

Brian Junior shifted uncomfortably.

Poppy walked up and down past him, did a twirl and rested one hand on a bony hip. She then looked at him expectantly but he did not speak. Instead, he unlocked the door to his room and went back inside.

Poppy said, 'He's a baby. A rude, mindblowingly awesome-looking baby.'

Brianne said, 'We're both seventeen. We took our A levels early.'

'I would have taken mine early but I had a personal tragedy . . .' Poppy paused, waiting for Brianne to ask about the nature of the tragedy. When Brianne remained silent, she said, 'I can't talk about it. I still managed to get four A*s. Oxbridge wanted me. I went for an interview, but quite honestly I couldn't live and study somewhere so old-fashioned.'

Brianne asked, 'Where was your interview – Oxford or Cambridge?'

Poppy said, 'Do you have auditory defects? I told you, I was interviewed in *Oxbridge*.'

'And you were offered a place to study at *Oxbridge* University?' Brianne checked, 'Remind me, where is Oxbridge?'

Poppy mumbled, 'It's in the middle of the country,' and went out.

Brianne and Brian Junior had been interviewed at Cambridge University, and both of them had been offered a place. The Beaver twins' small fame had gone before them. At Trinity College they were given what looked like an impossibly difficult maths problem to solve. Brian Junior went to a separate room with an invigilator. When they each put down their pencil after fifty-five minutes of frenzied workings-out on the A4 paper supplied, the chair of the interviewing panel read their workings as if they were a chapter of a racy novel. Brianne had meticulously, if unimaginatively, worked her way straight to the solution. Brian Junior had reached it by a more mysterious path. The panel declined to ask the twins about hobbies or pastimes. It was easy to tell that they did nothing outside of their chosen field.

After the twins had turned the offer down, Brianne explained that she and her brother would follow the famous professor of mathematics Lenya Nikitanova to Leeds.

'Ah, Leeds,' said the chairperson. 'It has a remarkable mathematical faculty, world class. We tried to tempt the lovely Nikitanova here by offering her disgracefully extravagant inducements, but she emailed that she preferred to teach the children of the workers – an expression I have not heard since Brezhnev was in office – and was taking up the post of lecturer at Leeds University! Typically quixotic of her!'

Now, in Sentinel Towers student residence, Brianne said, 'I'd sooner try the dress on in private. I'm shy about my body.'

Poppy said, 'No, I'm coming in with you. I can help you.'

Brianne felt suffocated by Poppy. She did not want to let her inside her room. She did not want her as a friend but, despite her feelings, she unlocked the door and let Poppy inside.

Brianne's suitcase was open on the narrow bed. Poppy immediately began to unpack and put Brianne's clothes and shoes away in the wardrobe. Brianne sat helplessly on the end of the bed, saying, 'No, Poppy. I can do it.' She thought that when Poppy had gone, she would arrange her clothes to her own satisfaction.

Poppy opened a jewellery box decorated in tiny pearlised shells and began to try on various pieces. She pulled out the silver bracelet with the three charms: a moon, a sun and a star.

The bracelet had been bought by Eva in late August to celebrate Brianne's five A*s at A level. Brian Junior had already lost the cufflinks his mother had given him to commemorate his six A*s.

'I'll borrow this,' Poppy said.

'No!' Brianne shouted. 'Not that! It's precious to me.'

She took it from Poppy and slipped it on to her own wrist.

Poppy said, 'Omigod, you're such a materialist. Chill out.'

Meanwhile, Brian Junior paced up and down in his shockingly tiny room. It took only three steps to move from the door to the window. He wondered why his mother had not rung as she had promised.

He had unpacked earlier and everything had been neatly put away. His pens and pencils were lined up in colour order, starting with yellow and finishing with black. It was important to Brian Junior that a red pen came exactly at the centre of the line.

Earlier that day, once the twins' belongings had been brought up from the car, their laptops were being charged, and the new Ikea kettles, toasters and lamps had been plugged in, Brian, Brianne and Brian Junior had sat in a line on Brianne's bed with nothing to say to each other.

Brian had said, 'So,' several times.

The twins were expecting him to go on to speak, but he had relapsed into silence.

Eventually, he cleared his throat and said, 'So, the day has come, eh? Daunting for me and Mum, and even more so for you two – standing on your own two feet, meeting new people.'

He stood up and faced them. 'Kids, make a bit of an effort to be friendly to the other students. Brianne, introduce yourself, try to smile. They won't be as clever as you and Brian Junior, but being clever isn't everything.'

Brian Junior said, in a flat tone, 'We're here to work, Dad. If we needed "friends" we'd be on Facebook.'

Brianne took her brother's hand and said, 'It might be good to have a friend, Bri. Y'know, like, somebody I could talk to about . . .' She hesitated.

Brian supplied, 'Clothes and boys and hairdos.'

Brianne thought, 'Ugh! Hairdos? No, I'd want to talk about the wonders of the world, the mysteries of the universe.'

Brian Junior said, 'We can make friends once we've obtained our doctorates.'

Brian laughed, 'Loosen up, BJ. Get drunk, get laid, hand an essay in late, for once. You're a student, steal a traffic cone!'

Brianne looked at her brother. She could no more imagine him roaring drunk with a traffic cone on his head than she could see him on that stupid programme *Strictly Come Dancing*, clad in lime-green Lycra, dancing the rumba.

Before Brian left, there were some badly executed hugs and backslaps. Noses were kissed instead of lips and cheeks. They trod on each other's toes in their haste to leave the cramped room and get to the lift. Once there, they waited an interminable time for the lift to travel up six floors. They could hear it wheezing and grinding its way towards them.

When the doors opened, Brian almost ran inside. He waved goodbye to the twins and they waved back. After a few seconds, Brian stabbed at the Ground Floor button, the doors closed and the twins did a high five.

Then the lift returned with Brian its captive.

The twins were horrified to see that their father was crying. They were about to step in when the doors crushed shut, and the lift jerked and groaned itself downstairs.

'Why is Dad *crying*?' asked Brian Junior.

Brianne said, 'I think it's because he's sad we've left home.'

Brian Junior was amazed. 'And is that a normal response?'

'I think so.'

'Mum didn't cry when we said goodbye.'

'No, Mum thinks tears should be reserved for nothing less than tragedy.'

They had waited by the lift for a few moments to see if it would return their father again. When it did not, they went to their rooms and tried, but failed, to contact their mother.

Sue Townsend

Sue Townsend was born in Leicester in 1946 and left school at 15 years of age. She married at 18, and by 23 was a single parent with three children. She worked in a variety of jobs including factory worker, shop assistant, and as a youth worker on adventure playgrounds. She wrote in secret for twenty years, eventually joining a writers' group at the Phoenix Theatre, Leicester, in her thirties.

At the age of 35, she won the Thames Television Playwright Award for her first play, *Womberang*, and started her writing career. Other plays followed including *The Great Celestial Cow* (1984), *Ten Tiny Fingers, Nine Tiny Toes* (1990), and most recently *You, me and Wii* (2010), but she has become most well-known for her series of books about Adrian Mole, which she originally began writing in 1975.

The first of these, *The Secret Diary of Adrian Mole aged 13¾* was published in 1982 and was followed by *The Growing Pains of Adrian Mole* (1984). These two books made her the best-selling novelist of the 1980s. They have been followed by several more in the same series including *Adrian Mole: The Wilderness Years* (1993); *Adrian Mole and the Weapons of Mass Destruction* (2004); and most recently *Adrian Mole: The Prostrate Years* (2009). The books have been adapted for radio, television and theatre; the first being broadcast on radio in 1982. Townsend also wrote the screenplays for television adaptations of the first and second books, and *Adrian Mole: The Cappuccino Years* (published 1993, BBC television adaptation 2001).

Several of her books have been adapted for the stage, including *The Secret Diary of Adrian Mole aged 13¾: the Play* (1985) and *The Queen and I: a Play with Songs* (1994), which was performed by the Out of Joint Touring Company at the Vaudeville Theatre and toured Australia. The latter is based on another of her books, in which the Royal Family become deposed and take up residence on a council estate in Leicester. Other books include *Rebuilding Coventry* (1988) and *Ghost Children* (1997).

She is an honorary MA of Leicester University, and in 2008 she was made a Distinguished Honorary Fellow, the highest award the University can give. She is an Honorary Doctor of Letters at Loughborough University, and a Fellow of the Royal Society of Literature. Her other awards include the James Joyce Award of the Literary and Historical Society of University College Dublin, and the Frink Award at the Women of the Year Awards. In 2009 she was given the Honorary Freedom of Leicester, where she still lives and works.

Sue Townsend was registered blind in 2001, and had a kidney transplant in 2009. She writes using a mixture of longhand and dictation.

Sue Townsend

Does the thirtieth anniversary of the first publication of the Secret Diary feel like a milestone or a millstone?

A milestone. He's certainly not a millstone. I think that authors who complain about the success of their most well-known characters are fools; although they mostly do this in private.

How did you spend your thirtieth birthday?

Nursing a month-old baby called Elizabeth; she was the last of my four children.

How has Adrian changed over the last 30 years?

In *The Prostrate Years* Mole has become more physically attractive, and is a much more sympathetic character.

Which is your favourite Adrian Mole book?

The Prostrate Years. I've had a lot of health problems and wanted to write about serious illness, yet still write in a comic form.

Do you have a favourite diary entry from the last thirty years?

Saturday April 3 1982 – The last line in the last entry of *The Secret Diary of Adrian Mole, aged 13¾*. Written after he had tried glue sniffing and accidentally stuck a model aeroplane to his nose: *'I rang Pandora, she is coming round after her viola lesson. Love is the only thing that keeps me sane...'*

I also like the sequence of entries in the same book made when Mole

as trying to paint his bedroom black to cover the Noddy wallpaper; only to be
repeatedly thwarted by the bell on Noddy's hat.

What has been Adrian's biggest mistake?

To ignore the many persons who have told him that his serial killer comedy,
'The White Van', and his memoir 'Lo, the Flat Hills of my Homeland',
are unpublishable. Mole does not suffer from a lack of self-belief in this
regard. Also at the Dept of the Environment when he misplaced a decimal
point, and erroneously stated that the projection of live newt births for
Newport Pagnall was 120,000.

And his greatest triumph?

He still believes his awful novels will be published one day.
That he is still a decent, kind person.

If Adrian Mole was a teenager today,
what would he be doing and writing about?

e would be exactly the same, but he wouldn't be using Twitter to memorialize
his life. He would keep a secret diary. Mole's privacy is still intact.
He would not use social networking.
There are still Mole types everywhere, watching the absurdities of
the world from the sidelines.

Are there any plot decisions that you made
that you subsequently regretted?

I should not have made Bert Baxter so old. I hated it when
I had to kill him off at the age of 105.

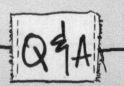

Sue Townsend

I regret Mole's marriage to Jo Jo, and the subsequent birth of William. It wa
tiresome (as it is in life) to have the child constantly there, or having to accou
for his whereabouts. It restricted Adrian's movements. He always had to be
at the nursery at 3.15 p.m. every weekday. I solved this for myself by sendin
William to live with his mother in Nigeria, and then forgot about him.

**Are any of the characters in the books, such as Adrian,
Pandora or Pauline, based on anyone in particular?**

All those characters have elements of the author within them.

**Before you put pen to paper, was there any point where Adrian
might have been a girl? If so, did she have a name?**

No, girls are more sociable, they talk to each other about
their emotional lives; boys don't.

I once wrote a column for the *London Evening Standard*, which took the for
of a diary written by a teenage girl called Christabel Fox. It didn't work for m
and after eighteen months it didn't work for the *Evening Standard* either.

What does the future hold for Adrian?

I don't know, but hopefully he will go onward, ever onward.

What limitations/opportunities are there to writing in diary form?

There are no limitations. The diary is one voice talking to you about peopl
places, events, high emotion, low spirits and the minutiae of everyday life.
Diaries have a simple structure. You just plod on, day by day, week by wee
month by month, until you've written a book.

What do you enjoy/dislike about the process of writing?

With each writing project I have a different type of nervous breakdown. I am convinced that I have chosen wrong words and placed them in the wrong order. Once published, I never read my own work.

There are sometimes a few exhilarating moments when the words come easily, when the tone and rhythm feel right.

It's great that writers don't have to leave the house and struggle through the rain to their place of work. They can lie in bed all day with a pen and notebook, which are the minimum requirements. Unfortunately I cannot allow myself to loll about in bed for longer than about six hours, as I am still brainwashed by the Calvinist work ethic.

Which authors have most influenced you as a writer?

In rough chronological order:
Richmal Crompton, Charlotte Brontë, Alfred E. Nuemann (*Mad* comic), Harriet Beecher Stowe, Mark Twain, Dickens, George Elliot, Oscar Wilde, Chekov, Dostoevsky, Tolstoy, Kingsley Amis, Evelyn Waugh, George Orwell, Stella Gibbons, Iris Murdoch, Flaubert, John Updike, Richard North.

Do you get much opportunity to meet or interact with your readers?

I have become a recluse lately as a result of ill health and late-onset shyness, but on rare outings I like to meet readers.

Is there any truth to the rumour put about by one A. Mole that you stole and profited from his life?

Yes. I ruthlessly exploited him. But he can't afford to sue me due to the new legislation on legal aid. Mole no longer qualifies. He should have taken me to court years ago.

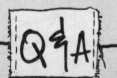

THE MOLE STORY

Adrian Mole is one of the most memorable and enduring comic creations of recent decades. Long before Bridget Jones we had the diaries of the neglected intellectual of Ashby de la Zouch: neurotic, acne ridden and hopelessly devoted to Pandora Braithwaite. Mole's is a particularly British story: that of continued, almost heroic, failure. Despite his best intentions he never quite gets what he wants. Like Basil Fawlty and, more recently, David Brent, much of the comedy in these books derives from self-delusion. It is the repetition of the same errors which invests these characters with a kind of tragic grandeur. We identify with them not because they are grotesque caricatures but because we know there is something of all of us within them.

Throughout the Mole books, Townsend has offered a caustic evaluation of contemporary Britain. There is an underlying seriousness to her work, a political consciousness, the desire to attack injustice and intolerance. Townsend is able to say in a couple of sentences what it would take many political journalists a thousand words to convey. Mole is an unknowingly subversive character and that is why he causes such delight. Laugh-out-loud funny, yet often painfully sad and poignant, the Mole books reveal Townsend's natural sense of comic timing and empathetic gifts.

Garan Holcombe, British Council Contemporary Writers

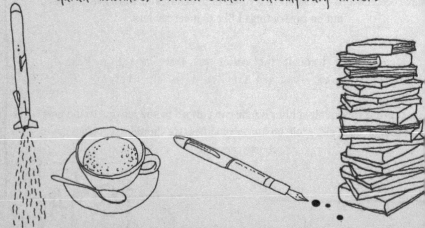

1946 - 1953

Sue Townsend is born in Leicester and
brought up in a semi-rural suburb, where
she lives in a prefabricated bungalow on an
unadopted mud road. Most of her free time is spent
playing in the surrounding fields and woods of a
country estate.

1953

At eight, she is frightened of her violent teacher, can't read, and
has had the same book on her desk for three years. While Townsend
is absent from school with mumps, her mother buys a stack of
Richmal Crompton's *Just William* books, and teaches her to read in
three weeks. It begins a life-long addiction to print. She reads three
books a day until local librarians accuse her of attention seeking.

1960

By fourteen she excels at English, writes for the school magazine
and has toured various churches and mental institutions as Jesus in the
Passion of Christ. Her book addiction is sated by second-hand orange
Penguin classics bought from market stalls. 'I would ponce about Leicester
with the spines of the books pointing to the public. A very indifferent
public.' After a school visit to Rome, Capri and Naples, returning to the
dour greyness of 1950s Leicester badly affects the young Townsend. After
this trauma, and heavily influenced by a recent reading of Dostoevsky: 'I
took to the black. White face, white lips, black eyes, black clothing. Juliette
Greco bohemian.'

Entering the only coffee bar in town, copy of *The Idiot* in hand, and asking
a man who looks intelligent how to pronounce Dostoevsky,
she is immediately accepted as a part of Leicester bohemian society.
There are few suitable careers in Leicester for a black-clad
aesthete with no qualifications. As school leaving day
approaches Townsend is urged by her Drama and
English teachers to transfer to the Grammar School
and take some exams; but the uniform would cost
her parents a month's wages, and she leaves school
a week before her fifteenth birthday.
She works in a shoe factory, sells encyclopaedias

door to door, and is sacked from the best and most pretentious dress shop in Leicestershire for reading Oscar Wilde in a changing cubicle. She works as a petrol attendant, with a paperback stuffed into the BP standard-issue duffle coat. She misses writing and carries on in secret

1964

At eighteen she marries a sheet metal-worker; the marriage doesn't last, and at twenty-three she is on her own with three young children and three jobs. Always tired and always worried, she writes semi-autobiographical prose and poetry when the children are asleep and hides it.

The only good job is at the youth club on her estate, where she works for eleven years, overhearing the conversations adults are not meant to hear. It leads to building and running an adventure playground on the tougher estate next-door. She writes pantomimes and plays for the children, receiving regular deputations of young men requesting knife fight scenes.

1975 Summer

'I was living in a council house at the time, on my own with three kids and three part-time jobs to keep us going. So Sunday was a total collapse; I was exhausted. My eldest son said, 'Why can't we go to safari parks like other families do?' The answer is that they have no money, no car and she feels sorry for the animals, but his martyred tone triggers the memory of her own harsh criticism of the adult world as a powerless child: 'That adolescent, self-pitying voice. Mole's voice. I just heard it. He descended with his family in the space of an afternoon.' She writes it down in diary form, completing the opening two and a half months in one burst, files it in a box and forgets it.

1978

She meets Colin Broadway, who will become her second husband. Three weeks after the birth of their daughter she admits to him that she writes secretly, and has done for twenty years. It fills a fridge-box stuffed into the under-stairs cupboard. He has heard of a writers' group at the Phoenix Theatre, and encourages her to join.

The Phoenix is Leicester's 300-seat 'second' theatre, with a writers group which uses actors to perform new plays. She attends two meetings without speaking. At the third, director Ian Giles asks her to bring some work that they can read and discuss. She has never written a play, but returns two weeks later with *Womberang*, a comedy set in a gynaecological waiting room. It has ten female parts, one male, and lasts thirty minutes. The structure is 'unorthodox', but as soon as the actors begin to read they are laughing out loud.

1979

Ian Giles puts *Womberang* forward for the 1979 Thames Television Playwright Award. John Mortimer is chair of the panel; he likes the play, reads it aloud and makes his fellow judges laugh. Townsend wins the prize, a £2,000 bursary to work for a year as writer in residence at the sponsoring theatre. She is terrified, and her training as a professional dramatist begins.

1980
July
Phoenix actor Nigel Bennett is auditioning for *Huckleberry Finn* and asks Townsend if she has anything he can use. She remembers the Mole diary and digs out the handwritten script. Bennett is the first to perform the Mole character, in a writers' group meeting. He types the script up and works on adapting it for a one-man show.

October
Townsend rewrites part of the original diary for a new local arts publication, edited by Leicester playwright David Campton, and put together on her kitchen table. Mole is published for the first time in the October 1980 edition of *the arts journal magazine*, under the title *Excerpts From the Secret Diary of Nigel Mole, aged 14 ¾*.

November
On a visit to Townsend's home, her theatrical agent Janet Fillingham sees a file of Mole material.

Fillingham thinks it would make a good radio script and sends a Nigel Mole monologue to Vanessa Whitburn at BBC Radio Birmingham. Ms Whitburn turns it down.

1981
February

A version of 'The Diary of Nigel Mole' is sent to the Assistant Head of Radio Drama for Radio 4, John Tydeman. It sit on his desk for a month, but 'When I finally read it, I thought it was marvellous.' He decides to produce it as a thirty-minute monologue.

March 10th

John Tydeman officially commissions 'The Diary of Nigel Mole' for Radio Four, and promises more episodes will be considered 'if it is as successful as it ought to be'.

April

There are concerns at the BBC that the character's name is too similar to the public schoolboy Nigel Molesworth, from the *Down with Skool!* books by Geoffrey Willans. Tydeman writes to Townsend that the character is established as Nigel Mole and will be broadcast under that title. He advises her that there 'is a lot of mileage in Mole' and that she should try to get a diary published.

September

Janet Fillingham sends the radio script to Geoffrey Strachan at Methuen, who is responsible for the Monty Python books and Simon Bond's hugely successful *101 Uses of a Dead Cat*. He is, in the words of Fillingham's colleague Giles Gordon, later Townsend's agent – 'the greatest publisher of the humour book'.

November/December

Geoffrey Strachan is keen on the script and the writer. 'I met Sue soon after and was immediately impressed. She was very funny and had a tremendous sense of what she was doing.' He requests a treatment for the book that he can sell to the Methuen board, but is unhappy with the similarity to 'Nigel Molesworth' and asks for a name change. Townsend sends him

a typescript treatment using 'Malcolm Mole'. A contract is signed with Methuen.

'Malcolm' reminds Townsend of blocked sinuses and she looks for an alternative. A handwritten sheet shows her working through some unlikely variations; wisely putting a cross next to the name of her second son, who would have been very unhappy with 'Daniel Mole'. She is looking for something 'upper working class', unthreatening, with a soft, feminine quality. After the low point of 'Darius' and 'Marius', 'Adrian' appears twice at the right-hand side of the page.

Townsend is not convinced and writes to Strachan, asking him to reconsider. 'Are you absolutely dead set against "Nigel Mole"? I am suffering severe withdrawal symptoms. I have lived closely with Nigel for a couple of years and Adrian can't take his place. I've tried to accommodate him but failed.' Strachan's long experience as a publisher tells him that the two characters would always be confused, and he is not persuaded. It is a bad moment for university lecturer Adrian Mole, who in an interview in a Sunday broadsheet, claimed that his life has been ruined by sniggering students.

1982
January 2nd

The Diary of Nigel Mole, aged 13¾ is broadcast on Radio Four's Thirty Minute Theatre, read by Nicholas Barnes. *The Times* calls it 'a delightful original', and within days five publishers have contacted John Tydeman.

April/May

The book is sent to Strachan in instalments. He commissions Caroline Holden to provide the illustrations. A number of people at Methuen are in favour of printing 3,000 copies, but Strachan thinks the book is 'a bit special' and decides on a first edition of 7,500, at the accessible price of £4.95.

Townsend asks Strachan if her name can be removed from the cover, arguing that 'It was supposed to be written by a 13¾-year-old boy. It seemed stupid to have my name on it. But he said gravely it was a wonderful thing to write a book, and that I should take the credit.' She has an advance of £1,500 and is worried about covering it.

'I thought Methuen were mad to print 7,500. I thought it would be remaindered by Christmas'.

June
The Methuen sales team are selling the book before it even exists. Often the booksellers have heard the radio production and are enthusing about the character to the reps.

July 30th
In the first mention of an Adrian Mole book in print media, Leo Cooper in *Publishing News* praises 'The funniest book I have read for ages...I welcome a genuine new talent.'

September
Pre-publicity is limited, with very few author interviews. There are serializations in the *Evening Standard* and *Woman's Realm*, and Radio Four puts out seven 15-minute episodes to a hugely positive response. Tom Sharpe reads an advance copy and is reduced to tears of laughter. The most successful comic novelist of the time gives a rave review for the jacket.

October 7th
The Secret Diary of Adrian Mole, aged 13¾ is published by Methuen. The initial run sells out before publication. The book is reprinted and continues to sell quickly through word of mouth; helped by a Jilly Cooper review which calls it 'touching and screamingly funny', and comparing it to *Catcher in the Rye*. Strachan commissions a sequel.

October 31st

The book enters the *Sunday Times* bestseller charts at number six. Townsend idly scans the book charts as usual and is amazed, delighted and relieved.

November

The *Secret Diary* tops the best-seller list.
It will remain in the charts for twenty weeks.
Thames buy the TV rights for ITV.

1983

By the end of January hardback sales are over 60,000.

October 27th

The paperback edition of the *Secret Diary* is published. The book
reaches the widest possible audience and sales explode. According to
David Ross, marketing director of Methuen, 'it started with the parent
generation and filtered downwards. The paperback put Adrian Mole
into the school playground.' Adrian Mole is one of the rare popular
classics that was originally written for adults and eventually appealed
to every generation.

November 7th

The paperback hits number one in the *Sunday Times* bestseller charts, with
275,000 copies in print. More than two years later it is still at number two,
kept from the top spot by its sequel.

1984

At the end of March sales have exceeded 600,000. Strachan estimates it is
selling 10,000 copies per week. Townsend has spent the winter and spring
working on the sequel, and by April Methuen have the complete manuscript
of *The Growing Pains of Adrian Mole*.

August 2nd

The Growing Pains of Adrian Mole is published. On publication day
100,000 hardback copies are in print, supplied in a 56-copy
string-vest display box.

September

250,000 hardback copies of *Growing Pains* have been sold.
Sue Townsend has the number one book in both hardback and
paperback charts. After the Frankfurt book fair Paul Marsh has
sold translation rights to every country in Western Europe.

November

The paperback edition of the *Secret Diary* has sold more than one million copies.

Adrian Mole: The Play, premiered at the Phoenix Theatre in Leicester, begins a run of two years in the West End.

1985

In January hardback sales of *Growing Pains* stand at 450,000.

1st August

The paperback of *The Growing Pains of Adrian Mole* is published, enters the bestseller chart at number one, and stays there for over a year.

September

The Secret Diary of Adrian Mole is premiered on ITV, written by Townsend and Trevor Waite, starring Gian Sammarco as Adrian Mole, Julie Walters as Pauline and Beryl Reid as Grandma Mole. Sammarco has been chosen from 6,000 applicants. *Mole* runs for two series, with Lulu taking over as Pauline Mole for season two, *The Growing Pains of Adrian Mole*, written by Patrick Barlow. The theme song by Ian Dury, 'Profoundly in Love with Pandora', reaches 45 in the singles charts.

November

The paperback editions of the Mole books remain at the top of the bestseller chart two years after the original paperback publication of the *Secret Diary*. Total paperback sales are approaching four million.

1986

The two original Mole books are published in the US by Grove, as a one volume edition, *The Adrian Mole Diaries*. The reviews are characterize as 'simply extraordinary' by the publisher. The great American comedienne Phyllis Diller is an early fan: 'A wonderfully touching, hilarious book. It goes beyond *Catcher in the Rye*. You must read it. Trust me!' *Newsweek* pronounces that 'Adrian Mole, superstar, has become one of the biggest successes in the history of British publishing'. The *New York Times* raves: 'Part Woody Allen, part a kindred

spirit to Philip Roth's early novellas...as sad and devastating as it is laugh-out-loud funny!

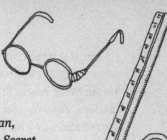

1990

In an end-of-the-decade survey in the *Guardian*, headlined 'Mole triumphant over Archer', *The Secret Diary of Adrian Mole* is the top paperback of the eighties, with three million copies sold, beating *Kane and Abel* by Jeffrey Archer into second place. Jackie Collins and Barbara Taylor Bradford trail behind. *The Growing Pains of Adrian Mole* is the top hardback. Total Mole sales in English alone total six million and Sue Townsend is the best-selling author of the eighties in terms of individual books. Later, through a third party, Archer lets it be known that he would like to speak to her. Townsend has little to discuss with the ex-Deputy Chairman of the Conservative Party, and a meeting doesn't take place.

1993
August 31st
Adrian Mole: The Wilderness Years is published with a 'New Adult Adrian Mole!' sticker on the front. Mole begins the book wearing a blazer and ends it swimming naked in the Aegean.

1999
Following consolidation within the publishing industry and the loss of key staff at Methuen, Townsend moves to Penguin, who acquire the rights to her future books and the Adrian Mole backlist.

Michael Joseph publish *Adrian Mole: The Cappuccino Years*. It is a number one bestseller and remains in the top three for four months.

2000
Penguin publish the paperback edition of *Adrian Mole: The Cappuccino Years*. The original audio-book is read by Nigel Planer, a later issue by Paul Daintry.

2001

Adrian Mole: the Cappuccino Years is produced as a six-part series for BBC1, written by Townsend, with Stephen Mangan as Adrian Mole, Alison Steadman as Pauline Mole, Helen Baxendale as Pandora, Zoe Wanamaker as Tania Braithewaite, Alun Armstrong as George Mole, and Keith Allen as Peter Savage.

Mole fan Steven Mangan also reads the audio book re-recording of *The Secret Diary of Adrian Mole*.

2004

Adrian Mole and The Weapons of Mass Destruction is published to wide acclaim, spends three months in the top ten, and is one of *The Village Voice*'s books of the year.

2007

Adrian Mole and The Weapons of Mass Destruction is re-released in the classic Penguin three-pane orange cover as one of the 'Celebrations' series.

2009
Autumn

As Townsend's health suffers she is drawn to the subject of serious illness, and gives Adrian prostate 'trouble'. He is maddened by the mispronunciation of prostate to 'prostrate' by his family and friends. *Adrian Mole – The Prostrate Years* is published by Michael Joseph in early November.

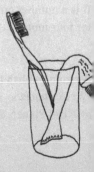

Sue Townsend's papers, including the original Adrian Mole manuscripts, are held in the Special Collections archives at the University of Leicester, where she is a Distinguished Honorary Fellow, the highest award the University can give. She is an Honorary Doctor of Letters at Loughborough University and a Fellow of the Royal Society of Literature. Her awards include the Frink Award at the Women of the Year Awards, and a James Joyce Award of the Literary and Historical Society of University College Dublin. In 2009 she was given the Honorary Freedom of Leicester.

ADRIAN'S CV

Name: Adrian Albert Mole

DOB: 2nd April 1967

Place of Birth: Leicester, England

Address: 1 The Old Pigsty
                      The Piggeries
                      Bottom Field
                      Lower Lane
                      Mangold Parva
                      Leicestershire

Height: 5 feet seven inches

Weight: 10 Stones eight pounds in 1989

Marital Status: Married but only just

Next of kin: Mr and Mrs George Mole
                      2 The Old Pigsty
                      The Piggeries etc. etc. an alarming proximity

Key Skills:
— Novelist (unpublished: see enclosed literary CV for explanation)
— Poet (ditto)
— Playwright (unperformed)
— Fluent in Antiquarian Book Phraseology
— Offal Cheffing
— Parenting
— Proficient in cycling (major village-town commute)

Current Employment:
— Senior Bookseller and Assistant Manager, Carlton-Hayes'
  Second-hand and Antiquarian Books; High Street, Leicester
  takings last week: £132.69

Employment History and Reasons for Leaving:

— Catering Manager - Eddie's Tea Bar

Two months frying burgers and changing the Calor-gas cylinder in an A46 lay-by. I couldn't forget Eddie's warning words on my first day: 'You'll never shake off the stink of the fat, lad. It makes it hard to get a woman outside the trade.'

— Turkey Operative (Seasonal) — Mr Nobby Brown, Poulterer

plucking recently deceased birds with six cackling women in an ill-lit shed

— Presenter of *Offaly Good!* (Pie Crust Productions)
  Millennium Channel, Wednesdays, 10.30 a.m
  (Co-presenter Dev Singh)
  I realised that cooking offal and/or television presenting
  was not my forte.

It was the review from A.A. Gill in *The Times*:
'Offally Good! is offally bad. A wooden presenter, Adrian Mole, stumbles and bumbles his way through twenty minutes of Cross-roads-quality TV. We watch with horrible fascination as he makes sheep's head broth. After twenty minutes Mole produces a pot of grey liquid, on the surface of which floats a layer of scum.'

And the G2 section of the *Guardian*:
'Dev's dazzling wit and uproarious physical comedy is in glorious contrast to the dour televisual presence of Adrian Mole, a pedant from Middle England.'

Employment History continued:

— Head Chef (Offal) at Hoi Polloi, Dean Street, London

I was reviewed in the national press: A.A. Gill in the *Sunday Times*. The memory still hurts:

'The sausage on my plate could have been a turd: it looked like a turd, it tasted like a turd, it smelled like a turd, it had the texture of a turd. In fact, thinking about it, it probably was a turd.'

— Assistant Chef at Savages, Dean Street, London

washer upper, vegetable chopper

— Security consultant — Bell Safe, Evington, Leicester

Three weeks selling alarms door to door for the alluring Bellinda Bellingham. A low point in my life. My sales patter started: 'Don't you think your family deserves more protection from the dark forces of evil that are at large in our community?'

— Civil Service Scientific Officer Grade One
  Department of the Environment - Wildlife, Oxford

— Newt Development Officer,
  with later responsibility for Badgers and Natterjack toads

sacked due to bogus biology A level certificate

— Library Assistant — Leicester Central Lending Library

I left after a dispute over Jane Austen with Miss Froggatt, the head librarian. I still maintain that her work is romantic fiction and does not belong in the literary stacks

— Paper delivery boy — Mr Cherry's Newsagent

Resigned after Mr Cherry attempted to pervert me with free copies of Big 'n' Bouncy

Voluntary Work:

— Writing/Directing/Producing/Training
   actor-dogs for the Mangold Parva Community Play

— Chairman of the Leicestershire and Rutland Writers' Group

Two members remaining

— I am perpetually surrounded by needy pensioners

Education:

inadequate due to parental indifference
and lack of Anglepoise lamp

Recreations:

— Writing

— Reading

— Purchasing Stationary

— Letter Writing

— Contemplating Nature

Depressingly, I am tempted to add bickering with wife, eating crab
paste sandwiches and satisfying mild addiction to both Starburst
(formerly Opal Fruits) and hardcore Nurofen. Is this the summation
of my life so far?

References:

Mr. Hugh Carlton-Hayes, Antiquarian Bookseller

Dr. Pandora Braithwaite MP (with whom I once shared a flat in Oxford)

ADRIAN'S LITERARY CV

I am attempting to write my literary CV. I feel the need to reassess
my writing career and the inexplicably negative critical response to my
work. What to include from the vast body of material I have accumulated
over the years? This is my hesitant first draft; it lacks a certain
Je ne sais quoi that only I can do.

LITERARY CURRICULUM VITAE (BREVIS)

Adrian A. Mole

Published Work:

— *Offally Good! – The Book!* (Stoat Books, 1991)
  Cookbook based on the cult Millennium Channel offal cookery show

Ghost-written in five days by Pauline Mole for 50% of all
royalties and residuals. This explains chapter ten, 'The Future
For Men Is Bleak', and the general over-emphasis on gender
politics. My three-month struggle with the text tragically led to
only one recipe - for pig's trotters. My foreword - a learned
treatise on primitive man's experiments with the offal cut out
of woolly mammoths etc. - which started so brilliantly, sadly came
to nothing.

  Reviewed in the *Sunday Times* Book Section - 'Briefly' column:
  '100 ways with offal – a hoot.'

I bought six copies of the *Sunday Times*. My mother rang later
to ask if I'd seen 'her' review

LITERARY CURRICULUM VITAE (BREVIS)

Unpublished Work: everything else

Novels

— *Lo! The Flat Hills of My Homeland*
  Later to be titled: *Birdwatching*
  A Lawrentian treatment of late twentieth-century man and his
  dilemma, as Jake Westmoreland returns to the town of his birth after
  experiencing The World

— *Sparg from Kronk*
  Or *Krog of Gork*
  Originally a novel by Jake Westmoreland, hero of *Lo!*
  The novel without language within Jake Westmoreland's novels was
  praised as 'a brilliant concept', by the renowned novelist and celebrity
  Angela Hacker. Faxos – April 1992

Query: was Angela Hacker just being kind? She was drunk on Amstel
most of the time. Is a novel without language within the hero's
unfinished Stone Age novel without dialogue within my novel about
the dilemma of 20th century man worthy of the adjective 'brilliant'?
I wish I knew.

— *Sty*
  The intellectual progress of a discontented pig

My diary from Wednesday, April 12 1999 shows some early difficulties:

I embarked on a new novel, *Sty*, today. Progress was slow. I only
managed to write 104 words, including the title and my name.

LITERARY CURRICULUM VITAE (BREVIS)

Sty, by Adrian Mole

The pig grunted in its sty. It was deeply sad. Somehow it felt different from the other pigs with which it shared a home.

'Look at them,' thought the pig. 'They are oblivious to the fact that they are merely part of the food chain.' The pig had felt discontented since it had glimpsed Alain de Botton's TV programme, *Philosophy: A Guide to Life*, through a gap in the pig farmer's curtain. The wisdom of Socrates, Epicurus and Montaigne had brought home to the pig that it was completely uneducated and knew nothing of the world beyond the sty.

Notes on new novel:
1. Should the pig have a name?
2. Should the pig's thoughts be in quotes?
3. Has the story got legs? Or is the main protagonist (the pig) too restricting a character, i.e., being (a) unable to communicate with the other pigs and (b) never leaving the sty?

Epic Poetry

— *The Restless Tadpole*
  A tadpole's journey from the early days of frogspawnhood to the dying moments of old frogdom

Prospectus for Monograph (Non-fiction)

— *Celebrity and Madness*
  (A work in progress)
  Charts the rise of celebritocracy and the subsequent demise of democracy in Britain today
  I present part of the original preface:

LITERARY CURRICULUM VITAE (BREVIS)

I have been working on a book called *Celebrity and Madness*, for some weeks. On many an occasion I have stayed up until almost midnight; honing the sentences, adding the adjectives and creating new verbs. (I distinctly remember, while watching the Olympics with my mother, asking her 'Has Britain medalled yet?')

But, I digress. *Celebrity and Madness* is a well-researched work – many copies of the *News of the World*, *Hello* and *Heat* magazines were read. Scores of letters were written, though it must be said that few celebrities had the courtesy to reply. I listened to countless anecdotes told by my dearest friend, the recently disgraced Dr. Pandora Braithwaite M.P., former junior minister in the Department of the Environment, whose own book, *Out of the Box* was published last year, and condemned by *Playboy*, who said, 'leaves a bad taste in the mouth'.

The book contains many examples of celebrities and their madness:

> David Beckham has locked the keys inside his car on 91 different occasions!
> Prince Charles tried to teach his favourite dog, Toby, to recite the Lord's Prayer!
> Liz Hurley keeps a succession of lucky spiders in a customized, Gucci, matchbox!
> Sven Goran-Eriksson has a photograph of a long-dead pet reindeer on his bedside table!

Professor Laurie Taylor, the eminent sociologist, was sent a rough first draft and returned a compliment slip acknowledging receipt

Situation Comedy

— *The White Van*
   A serial killer comedy, hopefully starring Russell Brand as the serial killer and Kerry Katona as his wife.

(The performers have yet to be approached).

LITERARY CURRICULUM VITAE (BREVIS)

Plays

— Plague!

Writer/Dramaturg of a community play involving the total population
of Mangold Parva (144 Souls plus intelligent animals), loosely based on
the fact that the village was a centre for the Black Death. The animals are
required to take part.

A typical stage direction would be: 'The dogs bow their heads in unison
and the chicken goes to centre stage and lays an egg'. This coup de
theatre may require the help of an animal trainer.
Difficult, but I think we can pull it off.

Agent : Brick Eagleburger at Brick Eagleburger Associates
brickeagleburger@yanklit.com

Tuesday, November 21, 2000:
Brick Eagleburger has sent my epic poem, The Restless Tadpole,
to a certain Geoffrey Perkins at BBC TV Centre. I asked Brick
which department Mr Perkins worked in. Brick said, 'The guy's head
of fuckin' comedy.' I angrily pointed out that The Restless Tadpole
is an entirely serious dramatic work written in the tradition of the
Icelandic sagas. Brick said, 'Listen up, Adrian, I flicked through the
fuckin' manuscript Tadpole and I godda tell ya I almost peed my fuckin'
pants, it's so funny.' Brick carried on, 'My favourite scene is when
the tadpole is lying in Marilyn Monroe's garden pond and it overhears
Arthur Miller talking crap about Tolstoy.'

I have always known that Brick Eagleburger is a Philistine, however,
he is now totally misrepresenting me and my work.

This is where Mr Eagleburger and myself parted company for a while.

ADRIAN'S FAMILY TREE

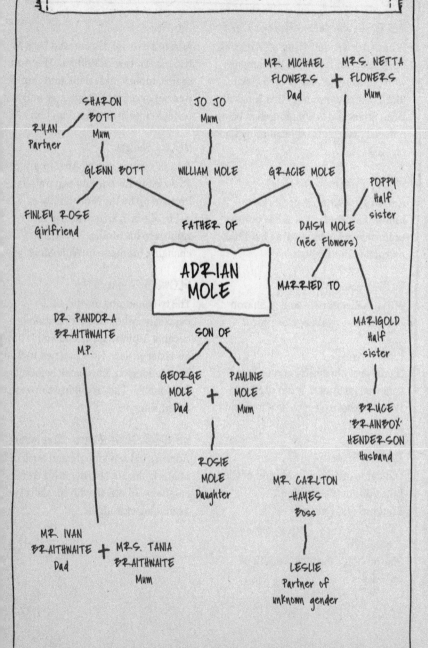

ADRIAN'S FAMILY TREE

MOLE, Daisy (née Flowers):
Wife of Adrian, half-sister of Marigold.
Dark, ravishing ex-PR to the famous
who claims to be 'author of my own
life'. Loathes the countryside, longs for
Dean Street and is not amused at being
reduced to flogging off her Jimmy Choos
on eBay.

MOLE, Gracie:
Adrian's daughter. A precocious
mini-Stalinist who hates her nursery
uniform, preferring to drag her little
mermaid tail to school.

BOTT, Glenn:
Adrian's illegitimate son by Sharon
Bott, in the Royal Logistics corp.

Finley Rose:
Glenn's very beautiful and well-
balanced girlfriend. A fan of *Silent
Witness*, she aspires to be a forensic
pathologist.

BOTT, Sharon:
Old flame of Adrian's. Mother of Glenn
Bott. Also mother of Kent,
Bradford and Caister.

Ryan:
Sharon Bott's partner, a youth of
27 years.

Jo Jo:
Adrian's ex-wife. Has moved back to
Nigeria. Mother of William. Has beaut
brains, money and talent, and frankly
was out of Adrian's league, as well as
being four inches taller than him.

MOLE, William:
Adrian's young son by African princes
Jo Jo. After his parents' separation,
brought up by the Mole family in
Ashby-de-la-Zouch. Unsurprisingly
returns to his mother in Nigeria,
changing his name to Wole Mole.

FLOWERS, Marigold:
Thirty-something on-the-shelf
depressive who once accidentally
became Adrian's girlfriend and is now
his sister-in-law. Now married to Brai
box Henderson, über-geek before it wa
fashionable. They regularly converse i
fluent Klingon.

HENDERSON, Bruce 'Brainbox':
Adrian's old schoolmate and husband
of Marigold. He also owns his own
company, Idiotech, who specialize in
'technology for idiots'.

LOWERS, Michael:
ather of Marigold and Daisy,
roprietor of Country Organics. Keen
ember of the Madrigal Society.

LOWERS, Netta:
ife of Michael and mother of
arigold and Daisy, another Madrigal.

LOWERS, Poppy:
ster of Marigold with extraordinarily
ng hair.

OLE, George:
drian's father. Although his many
isodes of hospitalization, depression,
employment and erectile dysfunction
ve taken their toll, he is still chain
noking and has had an ashtray welded
to the arm of his wheelchair. Despite
eir various tribulations, he still loves
uline Mole.

OLE, Pauline:
drian's perennially unfulfilled mother.
ving in a semi-detached converted
gsty with the stroke-ridden George
ole is not how she expected things
turn out. Still possessing a certain
wdry glamour, she is determined
have one last sexual fling before
e dies.

MOLE, Rosie:
Adrian's much younger sister.
Has adopted the 'rebel' persona,
and is currently failing at Leeds
University alongside her latest
inelegantly wasted boyfriend.
The doubts about her paternity are
finally settled live on *The Jeremy Kyle
Show*.

BRAITHWAITE, Ivan:
Father of Pandora. Supposedly
freelance dairy management consultant
and freethinker.

BRAITHWAITE, Dr. Pandora:
Adrian Mole's beautiful, treacle-haired
first girlfriend and lifelong obsession.
Now a Junior Minister in the Foreign
Office. Willing to confide in Adrian as
a trusted friend, but her autobiography
Out of the Box has two entries under
'Mole, Adrian', and 112 under 'Lovers'.

BRAITHWAITE, Tania:
Mother of Pandora. Teaches Women's
Studies at De Montford university.

CARLTON-HAYES, Mr:
Adrian's employer.

Leslie:
Mr Carlton-Hayes' partner of
unknown gender.

THE ADRIAN MOLE DIARIES

The Secret Diary of Adrian Mole Aged 13 ¾ & The Growing Pains of Adrian Mole

(January 1981 – June 1983)

BAXTER, Bert

Belligerent and filthy 89-year-old communist who has sworn not to die until capitalism is destroyed; eventually becoming the oldest man in Leicester. Lives on beetroot sandwiches, Vesta curry and brown ale, and speaks fluent Hindi. After joining 'Good Samaritans' in a misguided attempt to avoid maths, Adrian becomes his toe-nail cutter, bottle washer and friend for the next sixteen years.

BRAITHWAITE, Pandora

Adrian Mole's beautiful, treacle-haired first girlfriend and lifelong obsession. In youth, a pony riding swot whose motto is 'get to Oxford or die'; she soon leaves Adrian and 'the wretched provinces' far behind. Academic stardom smoothes her way to Parliament, the edge of power and a love affair with the TV cameras. A political Helen of Troy, her ambitious path to become Labour's first woman Prime Minister is littered with strategic conquests. Although willing to confide in Adrian as a trusted friend, her autobiography *Out of the Box* has two entries under 'Mole, Adrian', and 112 under 'lovers'.

BRAITHWAITE, Ivan

Father of Pandora. In 1981 a self-satisfied, bourgeois-left dairy accountant. After transforming into a freelance information consultant he suffers several episodes of technology induced mania and Choice Overload Syndrome. Involved in the great Mole family partner swap. A sartorial disaster area.

BRAITHWAITE, Tania

Mother of Pandora. A pretentious well-groomed bohemian who later lost her dress sense after a mild stroke. Also involved in the great Mole family partner swap. A fanatical devotee of Japanese gardening, she can often be seen raking the gravel.

Dog, The

The Mole dog, never given a proper name by family tradition. Follows Adrian to school, stands in front of the television and is always expensively at the vet's.

ELLIOT, Courtney

Erudite ex-academic postman with a red-spotted bow tie and ruffled shirt.

ill help with exam-coaching and lend
iver when the giro fails to arrive.

ENT, Barry

Irian's nemesis and tormenter. School
lly and local yob leader. Taught to
ad in prison, he performs as 'Baz the
inhead poet' and fashions a career
a poet and novelist, delighting the
elligentsia with political rants in
exaggerated Leicester accent. His
odern classic, 'Dork's Diary' featuring
den Vole' is still selling strongly.
Irian is constantly surprised by the
tent of his hatred for Kent, which is
diminished after twenty years.

MON, Rick

cially conscious leader of the 'Off
e Streets' youth club, where he
courages Adrian to be an individual
d throw off his petit-bourgeois
ackles. Has since moved out of a
iat and bought a new semi on the
dger's Copse Barrett estate.

CAS, Mr (Creep Lucas)

xt-door neighbour to the Mole
nily. A smarmy, self-assured
urance salesman. Embarks on
oomed affair with Pauline Mole
ich ends badly in a Sheffield bed-sit.
lieves himself to be Rosie Mole's
her.

LUCAS, Mrs

Estranged wife of Mr Lucas
who left him for another woman.

MANCINI, Hamish

Adrian's American 'holiday friend'
who becomes an unwanted pen pal
and guest. Overenthusiastic and under
analysis; his psychiatrist in New York
is doing great things with his libido.

MOLE, George

Adrian's father. His many episodes
of hospitalization, depression,
unemployment and erectile
dysfunction have taken their toll.
A cynical persona hides a self-pitying,
sentimental streak; will admit to crying
over *Jonathan Livingston Seagull*,
the only 'literature' he has ever read.
Has made several attempts to join the
middle-classes by pronouncing his
aitches, but is sabotaged by his liking
for HP sauce on toast and a lack-lustre
employment history. In later life
dresses to give the impression that
he was once in the music business,
but will always look like a retired
storage heater salesman. Despite
their many tribulations he still
loves Pauline Mole, but yearns for
pre-feminist times when she wore
high heels in the house and women
were not allowed to captain warships.

THE ADRIAN MOLE DIARIES

MOLE, Albert (Granddad Mole)

George Mole's father, Adrian's long-dead grandfather, whose memory is revered by May Mole. Shaved daily in the trenches at Ypres even though rats ate his soap. A rich source of inspiration for Adrian's various therapists.

MOLE, May (Grandma Mole)

George Mole's mother; Adrian's fearsome grandmother. The only real authority figure in the Mole family, the provider of proper Sunday dinners, constant electricity and unwanted religion. An enemy of Bert Baxter, whom she regards as a disruptive influence on Evergreen's coach trips.

MOLE, Pauline (née Sugden)

Adrian's mother is a mass of contradictions; an ardent feminist in the early eighties, she nevertheless still tends to define herself by the men in her life. She has a tawdry glamour and would not pick the milk up from the doorstep without first applying her lipstick. Pauline knows that she has not reached her full potential: 'I haven't got a single letter after my name and only Mrs in front.' She craves drama and excitement, which could explain why she has been married five times, (three to the same man, George Mole), and is very fond of litigation. Stumbling over a cracked paving slab, in Pauline's world, is a marvellous opportunity to make money and appear as a dramatic witness in the Small Claims court. As George Mole's health deteriorates, Pauline finds that she is not a natural nurse; the virtues of patience and constancy are foreign to her, as are the domestic arts — she was a pioneering and enthusiastic user of boil-in-the-bag convenience meals.

She has balsamic vinegar and HP sauce on the table, Barbara Taylor Bradford and Raymond Carver on her bookshelves and records *The Jeremy Kyle Show* and *Newsnight* on Sky Plus. She is determined to have one last sexual fling before she dies.

MOLE, Rosie

Adrian's much younger sister. Since the day he witnessed her birth she has been a worry to him. At three she was 'Rosemary' and followed him 'like a little shadow'; by fourteen a foul-mouthed vamp who regarded him with loathing. Although reconciled with Adrian, she has been known to spend Christmas day in Hull with a crack addicted boyfriend rather than endure the Mole family celebrations. There have always been doubts about her paternity.

MOLE, Susan

Adrian's aunt. A prison officer at Holloway, smokes Panama cigars and partner to the glamorous and sexy Gloria

ETHERINGTON, Nigel
drian's life-long best friend, a cynical
server of his suffering over the years.
gel's abundant consumer goods
e a constant reminder to the young
rian of his relative poverty and
rental neglect. A seeker, Nigel flirts
th various sexualities, religions and
bcultures, finally escaping to London
r 'music and sex' after being removed
m NatWest counters for wearing
ddhist robes. Well connected in
e Soho 'pink mafia', he is registered
nd in 2002 and returns to Leicester
bittered and unemployed.

eenie
rt Baxter's new wife, described by
rian as 'one of those loud types of
l lady that dyes her hair and tries to
k young'. Their romance scandalizes
e residents of the Alderman Cooper
nshine Home.

CRUTON, Mr (Pop-eyed Scruton)
anic Headmaster of Neil Armstrong
mprehensive School who terrifies
pils and staff alike. His fanatical
lief in dress standards is indirectly
sponsible for Adrian's Pandora
aithwaite fixation, via the 'red socks'
otest movement. A devout admirer of
rs Thatcher.

SINGH FAMILY
The Mole family's new next-
door neighbours, temporary carers
for Bert Baxter.

SLATER, Doreen (Stick Insect)
George Mole's anorexic lover, a single
mother with 'no bust and no bum'.
Mother of Adrian's half-brother Brett.

TYDEMAN, John
Kindly Assistant Head of Radio Drama
for the BBC. The accidental recipient
of Adrian's handwritten manuscripts,
ensuring torment and large return
postage bills for many years. Later
Head of Radio Drama.

SABRE
Bert Baxter's irritable, vicious Alsatian.
Fellow Alsatians cower as he passes
by. Needs a four-mile daily walk or he
chews the sink for entertainment.

SUGDEN, Mr & Mrs
Adrian's maternal grandparents.
Norfolk potato farmers incapable of
enjoying themselves unless something
is being harvested or slaughtered. They
have never understood why Pauline
Mole abandoned the black fields for
the bright lights of Leicester, but see it
as their duty to spend every Christmas
disapproving of her 'wanton' lifestyle.

PRINCIPAL CHARACTERS

THE ADRIAN MOLE DIARIES

True Confessions of Adrian Albert Mole, including Adrian Mole and the Small Amphibians

(October 1985 – January 1991)

BOTT, Sharon
Adrian's second girlfriend and the mother of his son, Glenn. 'A provincial dullard working in a laundry', in the harsh assessment of the 18-year-old Adrian. Since their disastrous first date at fourteen she has dramatically expanded and is now reminiscent of 'Moby Dick with a perm'. Adrian thinks their relationship was always doomed due to the class divide: he upper-working/lower-middle, she lower-working/underclass. A warm-hearted but ineffectual mother who lives in mild squalor.

BROWN, Mr
Adrian's boss in the Newt Section at the Department of the Environment in Oxford. A wildlife fanatic dressed by Man at C&A who claims to have not taken a day off in twenty-two years. Has spent Christmas Day classifying seaweed at Dungeness.

MUFFETT, Martin
Wilbur Smith-loving engineering student who holds Adrian and all intellectuals in contempt. A lodger in the Mole household who becomes Pauline Mole's second husband, ageing ten years in the process.

LIVINGSTONE, Rocky (Big Boy)
Pandora's live-in lover in Oxford. A 16-stone bodybuilder with a chain of gyms, he is happily unaware of the existence of the things Adrian worries about and 'lives in a world of sight and sound only'.

TWYSLETON-FYFE, Julian
Pandora's horse-faced gay husband. Amiably studying Chinese at Oxford, but doesn't intend to sit his finals. A minor aristocrat who strives for eccentricity and fails to achieve it.

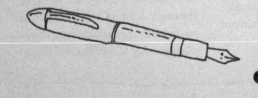

Adrian Mole: The Wilderness Years
(January 1991 – April 1992)

ELLINGHAM, Belinda
George Mole's glacial new partner/
employer, the managing director of a
burglar alarm company with
questionable sales tactics. A frightening
blonde.

CAVENDISH, Jack (Bluebeard)
Pandora's lover. An aged professor of
linguistics at Oxford. A three-times
divorced, rumpled, womanizing
alcoholic with ten children, many in
therapy or rehab.

PARTINGTON, Bianca
A hydraulic-engineering graduate
working at a newsagent's in Oxford.
Quietly pretty, she is attracted to an
oblivious Adrian, eventually drawing
him to London despite his reservations
over her profligate use of exclamation
marks and love of Guns 'n' Roses. She
gets him out of grey slip-on loafers and
into Next and the 1990s.

De WITT, Leonora
Beautiful Gestalt psychotherapist,
with long flowing 'midnight river'
hair and no shortage of clients suffering
from transference. Adrian is quite
willing to pay her £30 and beat
a chair with a stick. A boxing fan.

HACKER, Angela
Celebrity novelist and drinker,
teaches Adrian 'Writing for
Pleasure' at the Faxos Institute,
Faxos. She 'facilitates Adrian's
epiphany' and encourages him to
swim naked in the Aegean.

HEDGE, Mrs
Adrian's mournful literary landlady.
Slovenly.

MOLE, Jo Jo
African Princess. Heiress to her mother's
Nigerian lorry tyre conglomerate. Tall,
beautiful, dreadlocked, marries Adrian
out of a mixture of pity and love.
A talented artist and mother of
William Mole. Out of Adrian's
league in every way possible,
the marriage can only be seen
as a folie à deux.

PRINCIPAL CHARACTERS

THE ADRIAN MOLE DIARIES

PALMER, Christian
Adrian's live-in landlord/boss. An undercover popular-culture academic with three precocious children and a babysitting problem. Wears his hair in 'late-period Elvis' style, and laughs like a barking dog.

PALMER, Cassandra
Shaven-headed wife of Christian; absent directing a film on mutilation in LA, where she learns to function on the cutting edge of politically correct.

Her return is not joyfully celebrated by the Palmer household.

SAVAGE, Peter
Adrian's boss; a rotund celebrity alcoholic with a Bob Hoskins accent. Owner of Savage's and it's later perfection, Hoi Polloi, and winner of the 'Rudest Restauranteur of 1990' award. His arbitrary banning orders exclude most of the population of central London from his premises.

Adrian Mole: The Cappuccino Years
(April 1997 – May 1998)

BANKS, Les
A very unlucky builder contracted to work on the roof of Rampart Terrace.

BOTT-MOLE, Glenn
Adrian's long unidentified illegitimate son, by Sharon Bott. Semi-literate and a stranger to correct grammar, but with an optimistic and loving nature. Easily satisfied; the happiest time of his life was when Leicester City first won the Worthington Cup. Adrian cannot wait to get him out of gangsta clothes and into Junior Next.

FLOOD, Eleanor
Glenn's neurotic home-tutor, head of remedial studies at the Keith Joseph

Academy. Adrian's stalker, obsessed with phoenix symbolism and wears only black.

Justine
Adrian's Soho confidante, with all the latest gossip. An exotic dancer at Large Alan's with the dress sense expected of a woman who regularly embraces a python for cash.

KENT, Edna
Mother of Barry Kent. Toilet cleaner; later secretary to Pandora Braithwaite courtesy of an access course and two degrees. One of which is in family law, where she has a good head start.

…gi
…e very Italian Maître d' of Hoi Polloi.
…as been in the business twenty-seven
…ars, and is a 'personal friend' of Sophia
…ren and Tommy Steele.

…lcolm
…shwasher at Hoi Polloi. Illiterate, but
…lieves Tony Blair's new regime will
…ach him all he needs to know.

…LE, William
…drian's young son by Jo Jo. Obsessed
…th Teletubbies and 'motoring oaf'
…remy Clarkson; living with the Mole
…mily in Ashby-de-la-Zouch after his
…rents' separation. Spends most of
…s days sitting inside a cardboard box.
…ter moves to Nigeria, changing his
…me to Wole Mole.

…NTEFIORI, Zippo
…oppy-fringed producer of Adrian's
…ytime cookery show, *Offally Good!*
…ever seen without his black Armani
…ercoat, but doesn't sweat. There
… rumoured to be a waiting list for
…tential girlfriends.

…OG, New
…eplacement for the original Dog.
…drian is secretly less fond of it,
…lieving it to lack character.

SINGH, Dev
Eye-rolling, double-
entendre-loving Sikh
co-presenter of *Offally Good!*
A manufactured cult figure for students
and the real star of the show, he is
secretly scared by his own performance.

SAVAGE, Kim
Peter Savage's estranged wife, a former
society florist from the East End with no
intention of taking elocution lessons.

STOAT, Arthur
Head of Stoat Books, editor of *Offally
Good! – The Book*. His record for
turning a book around is three weeks,
with *Diana at My Fingertips* by her
personal manicurist. Adrian Mole
presents more of a challenge.

TAIT, Archie
Ancient, ascetic revolutionary socialist,
with one leg and one lung. Gravely ill
and lives alone with his cat, Andrew.
Adrian is compelled by conscience to
help him, despite wondering if he will
ever be free of pensioners with their
'liver-spotted hands circling my neck'.

PRINCIPAL CHARACTERS

THE ADRIAN MOLE DIARIES

Adrian Mole and The Weapons of Mass Destruction

(October 2002 – July 2004)

ANIMAL

Monstrously strong builder helping
George and Pauline Mole to renovate
The Piggeries. Communicates with
Pauline in grunts and listens to the
anecdotes George has told thirty times
before. When asked his real name
answers 'Animal'.

BLUNT, Ken

Long-serving member of the
Leicestershire and Rutland Creative
Writing Group, specializing in rabidly
anti-American polemic. Not a natural
diplomat, but a friend to Adrian.

BOND, Johnny

Travel agent at Latesun Ltd who
steadfastly refuses to refund a £57.10
deposit for Adrian's cancelled holiday.
The ability or otherwise of Saddam
Hussein to deliver Weapons of Mass
Destruction to Cyprus within 45
minutes is central to his case.

CARLTON-HAYES, Hugh

Adrian's elderly employer; one
of the last of the provincial
antiquarian booksellers. The
person that Adrian most admires,
despite knowing nothing about his
private life. A refined and gentle

man, but not averse to a punch-up; he
is a life-long enemy of Michael Flowers
after they came to blows over Tolkein's
prose style in the car park of the Central
Lending Library.

FLOWERS, Daisy

Half-sister of Marigold. Darkly
fascinating London-based PR to the
famous who claims to be 'the author
of my own life'. Adrian is strangely
attracted to her hedonism and complete
disinterest in Dostoevsky; frightened
by her passionate opposition to the
Iraq war. Immaculate, but not as
individualistic as she would like to
believe, having recently undergone a full
Nigella Lawson re-model. She lives in
expensive disorder, with a growing pile
of high-ticket designer goods flagged as
potential returns.

FLOWERS, Marigold

A thirty-something on-the-shelf
depressive who works at Country
Organics and accidentally becomes
Adrian's girlfriend. Builds miniature
dolls' houses; performs Mary in a
peripatetic Nativity with the Leicester
Mummers, and is even less fun than
this sounds. Fatally for Adrian, she has
beautifully soft skin and fragile wrists.

'manipulative, hysterical
'pochondriac', according to
aisy Flowers.

LOWERS, Michael
ather of Marigold; the scratchy-
-eatered proprietor of Country
-rganics and counter-tenor in the
adrigal Society. An English 'back to
ature' fascist with plans for Adrian
-ole, he is both repulsive and oddly
-rsuasive. Has a severe aversion to
-exico and Mexicans.

LOWERS, Netta
-other of Marigold, uncommitted
-fe of Michael. Incredibly pink, she
-sembles a very pretty pig. Shows more
-fection for her compost heap than her
-mily.

LOWERS, Poppy
-ster of Marigold. Scientologist maths
-acher whose distinguishing feature
-d main reason for living is her
-traordinarily long hair. Not keen on
-r family's medievalism; she prefers
-e Romans, for their civilizing influence
-d 'amazing hair products'.

DRDINGBRIDGE, Gladys
-derly member and regular host of the
-icestershire and Rutland Creative
-riting Group. Her literary output
-nsists entirely of sub-Pam Ayres cat

poems; one of which, 'Naughty
Paws', achieves the difficult
task of rhyming 'Whiskas' with
'discus'.

Geilgud
Evil leader of a disruptive flock of
swans at Rat Wharf, named after
his resemblance to the classical
English actor. Adrian believes Geilgud
holds a personal grudge, claiming to see
'a sneer on his beak' during his attacks.

Graham
Nigel Hetherington's guide dog. The
only living thing he has ever truly
loved and a better friend to him than
Adrian ever was. A creature with eerie
intelligence.

Leslie
Mr Carlton-Hayes' partner, of whom
Adrian knows absolutely nothing, except
that she/he is reportedly not as keen on
books as Mr Carlton-Hayes.

HENDERSON, Bruce ('Brainbox')
Adrian's old school 'friend', winner of
'geek of the year' at Neil Armstrong
Comprehensive. Owns his own
consultancy firm, Idiotech, supplier of
non-threatening technology solutions to
computerphobes. Has plenty of money
and needs somebody to spend it on.

THE ADRIAN MOLE DIARIES

HOPKINS, Bernard
Very temporary assistant at Carlton-Hayes' Books. A hopelessly drunk ex-bookseller and one of the most politically incorrect men in Leicester; his standard term of address is 'cocker.' Disdains all 'bint' authors and anything written after Nabakov, although 'Salman' is supposedly a personal friend.

MILKSOP, Gary
Over-sensitive, tetchy member of the Leicestershire and Rutland Writing Group. The author of an epic experimental novel that has been worked on for fifteen years. The masterpiece spends two thousand words on Gary's first memory of eating a Hobnob and is unfinished.

Ivan
Tastelessly named replacement for the NEW DOG, which died on Christmas Day 2001, or was 'killed' by Adrian, according to his parents.

PARVEZ, Mohammed
Adrian's friend and financial adviser. A realist who lives within his means, choosing to work from a bedroom office with Postman Pat wallpaper. His concerned but pragmatic advice is generally ignored. Enjoys the drama of cutting up his clients' charge cards.

STAINFORTH, Robbie
Glenn Mole's best friend, a shy 18-year old fellow soldier in the Royal Logistic Corps. According to Glenn, he knows 'a lot about everything'. Adrian sends him 'improving books' by BFPO and privately wishes Glenn was more like Robbie.

WONG, Wayne
Adrian's old school friend; the cynical owner of the best Chinese restaurant in town, the Imperial Dragon (Wong's), the only place Adrian really feels at home. A ten per cent discount and a good table near the fish tank are usually available. Not a fan of Marigold Flowers, whom he thinks resembles one of his 500-quid-per-throw carp.

Adrian Mole: The Prostrate Years
(June 2007 – May 2008)

DOCTOR PEARCE
An English lecturer with John Lennon glasses and 'overlarge breasts'. She enthusiastically pursues the possibility of an affair with Adrian, to his dismay. Overrun by her four children.

DR WOLFOWICZ
Adrian's Polish GP. A mournful giant who looks more like 'a Gdansk steelworker' than a doctor. Yearns for his wife and home.

FAIRFAX-LYCETT, Hugo
Heir of Fairfax Hall. A ravaged but handsome aristocrat and self-confessed establishment figure, who is building a safari park in his grounds. Employer of Daisy Mole, who is sourcing his giraffes.

LEWIS-MASTERS, Dorothea
Elderly upper-class world traveller and former camel-accessory importer. Frequently quotes the wisdom of the North African 'men of the desert'. She lives in a large Georgian house, stuffed full of animal skins and heads.

MOLE, Gracie
Adrian and Daisy's four-year-old daughter, who is already displaying 'alarmingly Stalinist tendencies'. Usually to be found wearing her little mermaid costume and being carried, as 'Fish can't walk.'

Sally
A 'small but sturdy', homely radiotherapist. Adrian is fascinated by her disastrous relationship with wolf-conservationist boyfriend, Anthony.

THE MOLE BOOKS

FRIDAY JANUARY 2ND

I felt rotten today. It's my mother's fault for singing 'My Way' at two o'clock in the morning at the top of the stairs. Just my luck to have a mother like her. There is a chance my parents could be alcoholic. Next year I could be in a children's home.

Meet Adrian Mole, a hapless teenager providing an unabashed, pimples-and-all glimpse into adolescent life.

'Townsend has held a mirror up to the nation and made us happy to laugh at what we see in it'
Sunday Telegraph

SUNDAY JULY 18TH

My father announced at breakfast that he is going to have a vasectomy. I pushed my sausages away untouched.

In this second instalment of teenager Adrian Mole's diaries, the Mole family is in crisis and the country is beating the drum of war. While his parents have reconciled after both embarked on disastrous affairs, Adrian is shocked to learn of his mother's pregnancy.

'The funniest, most bitter-sweet book you're likely to read this year'
Daily Mirror

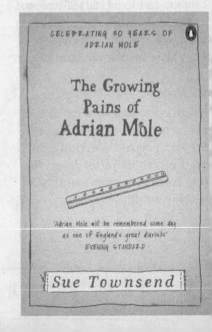

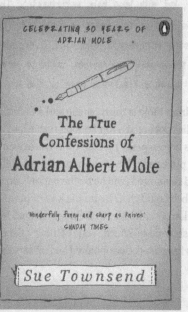

MONDAY JUNE 13TH

I had a good, proper look at myself in the mirror tonight. I've always wanted to look clever, but at the age of twenty years and three months I have to admit that I look like a person who has never even *heard* of Jung or Updike.

Adrian Mole is an adult. At least that's what it says on his passport. But living at home, clinging to his threadbare cuddly rabbit 'Pinky', working as a paper pusher for the DoE and pining for the love of his life, Pandora, has proved to him that adulthood isn't quite what he expected. Still, without the slings and arrows of modern life what else would an intellectual poet have to write about . . .

'Essential reading for Mole followers' *Times Educational Supplement*

THURSDAY JANUARY 3RD

I have the most terrible problems with my sex life. It all boils down to the fact that I have no sex life. At least not with another person

Finally given the heave-ho by Pandora, Adrian Mole finds himself in the unenviable situation of living with the love-of-his-life as she goes about shacking up with other men. Worse, as he slides down the employment ladder, from deskbound civil servant in Oxford to part-time washer-upper in Soho, he finds that critical reception for his epic novel, *Lo! The Flat Hills of My Homeland*, is not quite as he might have hoped.

'A very, very funny book' *Sunday Times*

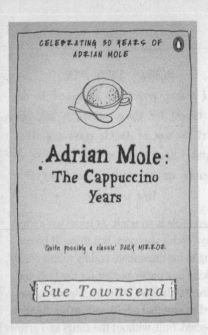

Adrian Mole:
The Cappuccino Years

'Quite possibly a classic' DAILY MIRROR

Sue Townsend

WEDNESDAY AUGUST 13TH

Here I am again – in my old bedroom. Olde
wiser, but with less hair, unfortunately. Th
atmosphere in this house is very bad. Th
dog looks permanently exhausted. Every tim
the phone rings my mother snatches it u
as though a kidnapper were on the line.

Adrian Mole is thirty, single and a father.
His cooking at a top London restaurant
has been equally mocked ('the sausage on
my plate could have been a turd' – AA Gill)
and celebrated (will he be the nation's first
celebrity offal chef?). And the love of his life
Pandora Braithwaite, is the newly elected M
for Ashby-de-la-Zouch – one of 'Blair's Babe
He is frustrated, disappointed and undersexe

'Three cheers for Mole's chaotic, non-achieving, dysfunctional family. We need him
Evening Standard

MONDAY JANUARY 3, 2000

So how do I greet the New Millennium?
In despair. I'm a single parent, I live with
my mother . . . I have a bald spot the size
of a jaffa cake on the back of my head . . .
I can't go on like this, drifting into early
middle-age. I need a Life Plan . . .

The 'same age as Jesus when he died',
Adrian Mole has become a martyr: a single
father bringing up two young boys in an
uncaring world. With the ever-unattainable
Pandora pursuing her ambition to become
Labour's first female PM, his over-achieving
half-brother Brett sponging off him, and
literary success ever-elusive, Adrian tries to
make ends meet and find a purpose.

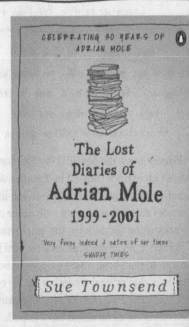

The Lost Diaries of
Adrian Mole
1999-2001

'Very funny indeed A satire of our times'
SUNDAY TIMES

Sue Townsend

'One of the great comic creations of our time.' *Scotsman*

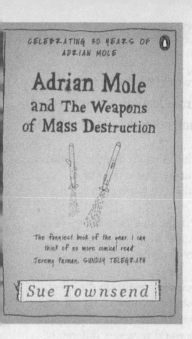

Adrian Mole
and The Weapons of Mass Destruction

'The funniest book of the year. I can think of no more comical read'
Jeremy Paxman, SUNDAY TELEGRAPH

Sue Townsend

WEDNESDAY APRIL 2ND

My birthday.

I am thirty-five today. I am officially middle-aged. It is all downhill from now. A pathetic slide towards gum disease, wheelchair ramps and death.

Adrian Mole is middle-aged but still scribbling. Working as a bookseller and living in Leicester's Rat Wharf; finding time to write letters of advice to Tim Henman and Tony Blair; locked in mortal combat with a vicious swan called Gielgud; measuring his expanding bald spot; and trying to win-over the voluptuous Daisy . . .

'Completely hilarious, laugh-out-loud, a joy' *Daily Mirror*

SUNDAY 1ST JULY
NO SMOKING DAY

A momentous day! Smoking in a public place or place of work is forbidden in England. Though if you're a lunatic, a prisoner, an MP or a member of the Royal Family you are exempt.

Adrian Mole is thirty-nine and a quarter. He lives in the country in a semi-detached converted pigsty with his wife Daisy and their daughter. His parents George and Pauline live in the adjoining pigsty. But all is not well.

The secondhand bookshop in which Adrian works is threatened with closure. The spark has fizzled out of his marriage. His mother is threatening to write her autobiography (*A Girl Called Shit*). And Adrian's nightly trips to the lavatory have become alarmingly frequent . . .

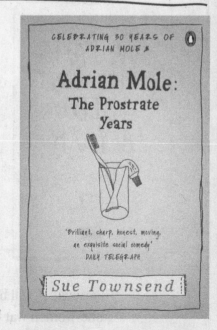

Adrian Mole:
The Prostrate Years

'Brilliant, sharp, honest, moving, an exquisite social comedy'
DAILY TELEGRAPH

Sue Townsend

'Unflinchingly funny' *Sunday Times*

'Laugh-out-loud . . . a teeming world of characters whose foibles and misunderstandings provide glorious amusement. Something deeper and darker than comedy' *Sunday Times*

The day her twins leave home, Eva climbs into bed and stays there. For seventeen years she's wanted to yell at the world, 'Stop! I want to get off!' Finally, this is her chance.

Her husband Brian, an astronomer having an unsatisfactory affair, is upset. Who will cook his dinner? Eva, he complains, is attention seeking. But word of Eva's defiance spreads.

Legions of fans, believing she is protesting, gather in the street, while her new friend Alexander the white-van man brings tea, toast and an unexpected sympathy. And from this odd but comforting place Eva begins to see both herself and the world very, very differently. . .

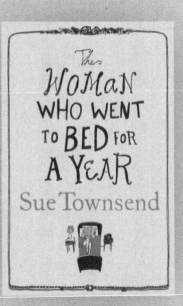

'She fills the pages with turmoil, anger, passion, love and big helpings of wit. It's full of colour and glows with life'
Independent

'Touching and hilarious. Bursting with witty social commentary as well as humour'
Women's Weekly

'A funny, poignant look at modern family life'
Daily Express

'Touching and ridiculously funny . . . just genius'
Closer

'Hilarious . . . will have you cheering Eva's one-woman war on everything' *Now*

THE MONARCHY HAS BEEN DISMANTLED

When a republican party wins the General Election, their first act in power is to strip the Royal Family of their assets and titles and send them to live on a housing estate in the Midlands.

Exchanging Buckingham Palace for a two-bedroomed semi in Hell Close (as the locals dub it), caviar for boiled eggs, servants for a social worker named Trish, the Queen and her family learn what it means to be poor among the great unwashed. But is their breeding sufficient to allow them to rise above their changed circumstance or deep down are they really just like everyone else?

'Kept me rolling about until the last page' *Daily Mail*

'There are two things that you should know about me immediately: the first is that I am beautiful, the second is that yesterday I killed a man. Both things were accidents ...'

When Midlands housewife Coventry Dakin kills her neighbour in a wild bid to prevent him from strangling his wife, she goes on the run. Finding herself alone and friendless in London she tries to lose herself in the city's maze of streets.

There, she meets a bewildering cast of eccentric characters. From Professor Willoughby D'Eresby and his perpetually naked wife Letitia to Dodo, a care-in the-community inhabitant of Cardboard City, all of whom contrive to change Coventry in ways she could never have foreseen ...

'Splendidly witty ... the social observations sharp and imaginative' *Sunday Express*

What if being Royal was a crime?

The UK has come over all republican. The Royal Family has been exiled to an Exclusion Zone with the other villains and spongers. And to cap it all, the Queen has threatened to abdicate.

Yet Prince Charles is more interested in root vegetables than reigning . . . unless his wife Camilla can be Queen in a newly restored monarchy. But when a scoundrel who claims to be the couple's secret lovechild offers to take the crown off their hands, the stage is set for a right Royal showdown.

'Wickedly satirical, mad, ferociously farcical, subversive. Great stuff'
Daily Mail

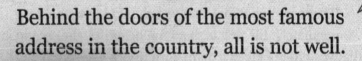

Behind the doors of the most famous address in the country, all is not well.

Edward Clare was voted into Number Ten after a landslide election victory. But a few years later and it is all going wrong. The love of the people is gone. The nation is turning against him.

Panicking, Prime Minister Clare enlists the help of Jack Sprat, the policeman on the door of No 10, and sets out to discover what the country really thinks of him. In disguise, they venture into the great unknown: the mean streets of Great Britain . . .

'A delight. Genuinely funny . . . compassion shines through the unashamedly ironic social commentary' *Guardian*

He just wanted a decent book to read ...

Not too much to ask, is it? It was in 1935 when Allen Lane, Managing Director of Bodley Head Publishers, stood on a platform at Exeter railway station looking for something good to read on his journey back to London. His choice was limited to popular magazines and poor-quality paperbacks – the same choice faced every day by the vast majority of readers, few of whom could afford hardbacks. Lane's disappointment and subsequent anger at the range of books generally available led him to found a company – and change the world.

'We believed in the existence in this country of a vast reading public for intelligent books at a low price, and staked everything on it'
Sir Allen Lane, 1902–1970, founder of Penguin Books

The quality paperback had arrived – and not just in bookshops. Lane was adamant that his Penguins should appear in chain stores and tobacconists, and should cost no more than a packet of cigarettes.

Reading habits (and cigarette prices) have changed since 1935, but Penguin still believes in publishing the best books for everybody to enjoy. We still believe that good design costs no more than bad design, and we still believe that quality books published passionately and responsibly make the world a better place.

So wherever you see the little bird – whether it's on a piece of prize-winning literary fiction or a celebrity autobiography, political tour de force or historical masterpiece, a serial-killer thriller, reference book, world classic or a piece of pure escapism – you can bet that it represents the very best that the genre has to offer.

Whatever you like to read – trust Penguin.